The Dark Nest

Lindsay Woodward

Copyright © 2021 Lindsay Woodward

All rights reserved.

ISBN: 978-1-9995855-7-0

For John & Eileen

ONE

It was chaos. Even with a toddler playing or screaming, the sheer size of Beth and Simon's mansion meant that it was always possible to find peace and quiet somewhere. But on that Sunday afternoon in early May, the whole place was like Piccadilly Circus.

'The bar is going in the garden,' Simon Bird instructed. He pointed through the patio doors towards the acre of land at the back of the house. The two men who were carrying boxes nodded, displaying the normal obedience that Simon always commanded of people, such was his natural intimidating essence.

'The balloon lady's arrived,' Beth, his wife said, as she joined Simon in the kitchen. 'She wants to know where to put things.'

'Has she not got the plan? I emailed her over the plan,' Simon replied.

'Can't we just tell her?'

'I have told her. In a very detailed plan.'

'You sent her what pretty much looked like a blueprint of our house with to-scale diagrams of party decorations in select locations,' Beth said.

'Precisely. She has everything she needs.'

'She's a party planner, not an architect. I think she's a bit confused.'

Simon took a breath. 'Okay. I'll go and explain. Can you make sure the pop-up bar is put on the other side of the garden to the bouncy castle.'

'With the food marquee in the middle. I know. I studied the plans. That's how much I love you.'

'Why are you giving me that look?' Simon asked.

'What look?' Beth replied, unable to resist a little grin.

'I know you think this is over the top.'

'It's our daughter's second birthday. This event is bigger than our wedding. She won't remember it.'

'She might do. She's very special. Besides, it's a good excuse to get family and friends together.'

'Well, family and work colleagues.'

Simon looked into Beth's eyes. 'She's our daughter. We have the space and money to throw an epic party. Why would we not?'

'Epic doesn't cover it. I think the only thing missing is a magician.'

Simon and Beth both laughed at this.

'We so should have hired a magician,' Beth said. 'And then we could have messed with him using our actual magic powers. A bit of entertainment for the adults!'

Simon grinned. 'That's terrible. You have a wicked mind.'

Beth was still smirking. She'd needed that giggle to ease the stress of the organising.

She felt the power within her with delight. She still found it incredible that she had actual magic powers. Powers that were shared only in the small community of the Malancy: a secret group that very few people knew about.

'Maybe next year,' Beth said.

'I think there are some animals outside,' a man said, as he struggled past with a pile of boxes.

'Oh good, that will be the petting zoo. Can you deal

with them?' Simon said to Beth.

She nodded. 'Yes. The zoo is going near the face painting station. Right?'

'Near, but not too close. I'll go deal with the balloons.'

'Hi both,' Jim, one of their closest friends said as he joined them in the kitchen. He was carrying a large present. 'I've never seen this house so busy.'

'Hi Jim,' Beth said, kissing him on the cheek. Simon just nodded, keeping his usual distance from people.

'Can I help with anything?' Jim asked.

'Oh yes, go and see Scarlett, will you?' Beth replied. 'She's with Carly. I think in the living room? It's her birthday and so far we've barely been able to give her any attention.'

'Can I give Scarlett her present now?' Jim asked.

'No. Present opening is at three o'clock,' Simon answered.

'She's had presents from us,' Beth quickly added. 'We're not that cruel. It's just guest's presents at three o'clock.'

'There's a table for presents in the marquee,' Simon said. 'Sorry, I'll have to leave you to it. Where is this balloon lady?'

'By the front door.'

Simon nodded and shot off.

'I should let you get on,' Jim said to Beth.

'Sorry for making Carly work at the weekend,' Beth said.

'You need your nanny today. It's fine. She loves looking after Scarlett.'

'But I know you need your time with her as well. We already monopolise her most of the week.'

'It's fine. Stop worrying. If it wasn't for you hiring her, I never would have met her. Now go and sort things out.'

'Okay. I have rabbits to deal with. Don't ask.'

Beth darted off to the driveway where she met the petting zoo people.

An hour later and most things were in place, and there was still a good half hour to go before the party was due to start. As always, Simon had organised things perfectly.

Beth was playing with Scarlett and some of her new toys in the living room, enjoying the little time she knew she'd actually get with her daughter that day. Scarlett was a happy child who could often be heard giggling somewhere in the house. She wanted for nothing, having parents who were millionaires, but Simon and Beth's own sense of discipline and order meant she was also not spoilt rotten.

Carly had left them a short while before, apparently needing to urgently speak to Simon about some concerns she had with the set-up. Beth had wisely chosen to steer well clear of that conversation. Carly was a strong willed woman, but Beth knew no one stood a chance against Simon.

The doorbell chimed for what must be the hundredth time that day. Knowing everyone else was in the garden, Beth assumed it would fall down to her to answer it. She picked up Scarlett, who was busy playing with her new little animal set, and immediately Scarlett starting whining with annoyance.

'Let's go see who's at the door!' Beth sang in a cheery voice, trying to distract her daughter. 'Maybe it's another surprise for Letty! Who knows what else Daddy has in store!'

Beth headed out of the large, artfully decorated living room, through to the enormous light reception area and, bouncing Scarlett gently in her arms, she opened the door.

'Hello. You must be Beth. And this must be Scarlett.' Beth stared at the two tall, skinny people in front of her, who were perhaps both in their late fifties. She didn't recognise either of them.

'Yes we are. Can we help you?' Beth replied.

'We heard it was a special girl's birthday today,' the woman said with a smile that weirdly didn't meet her eyes.

'Yes. Two years old today.'

'We've brought you a present.' The lady presented a beautifully wrapped box.

'Thank you,' Beth said as she desperately tried to work out who these people could be. She felt reluctant to ask in case she absolutely should know them. 'We weren't expecting you,' she added.

The woman forced that smile again. 'Of course not. We're friends with Paul. We knew Simon when he was just a boy. He used to come round and play with our son. We just had to pop by and wish his daughter a happy birthday.'

'Oh. Right. Well, thank you for coming.'

'We won't stay for long. Perhaps we could just go straight through to the garden and put our gift with the other presents?'

Beth was growing increasingly uncomfortable. Something about this woman and that sinister smile made her skin prickle. 'How do you know where the presents are being kept?'

The woman laughed. 'We've known Simon a long time. He's nothing if not predictable.'

The chill Beth felt was heightened. Simon was anything but predictable.

'I'll just go and get Simon,' Beth said.

'No. Don't bother him. I'm sure it's chaos inside with all the party set-up. We'll drop the present off and then catch up with him later.'

'I should get Simon now.'

'No!' the woman said, grabbing Beth's arm.

A car pulled through the gates at the end of the driveway – gates that were normally locked tightly shut but had been pinned open just for the festivities. Beth instantly recognised the BMW and she was relieved to know she had some sort of back-up.

'It's Great Uncle Paul and Aunty Jane,' she said to Scarlett, trying to keep the situation light. Paul, Simon's only remaining family, was a high spirited man, about the same age as the couple on the doorstep.

'Happy birthday!' Paul said, grinning from ear to ear as he got out of the car and approached the doorway. He was yet to look at the couple in front of Beth. 'We have a boot full of presents for our special birthday girl!'

'Hi Paul,' Beth said. 'I believe these are friends of yours. Do you know them?'

Paul glanced at the two people that he was now standing next to. He went instantly pale.

'What are you doing here?' he asked.

'Who are they?' Beth pushed.

Jane, Paul's wife, joined them. She was always far more formal than her jovial husband. 'Is everything all right?'

'Get Simon now,' Paul said to her.

'We don't need to bother Simon. He'll have a lot on his plate today,' the mystery woman insisted.

'Jane, please,' Paul said.

'He's in the garden,' Beth told her.

Jane scurried into the house.

'Who are these people?' Beth asked Paul. 'They said they were friends of yours. That Simon had played with their son growing up.'

'I suppose that's true,' Paul said. He turned to them. 'What are you doing here?'

'We heard it was Scarlett's birthday,' the man said, for the first time opening his mouth. He seemed shaky and unsure, as if he wanted to be anywhere but at that front door.

'From who?' Paul demanded to know.

The woman made that smile again. 'Simon is one of the wealthiest and most powerful people in the world. It's not hard to find out it's his daughter's birthday.'

'I thought you said someone told you,' Beth challenged.

'She meant find out as in people gossip,' the man explained. 'You have half the businesses in Buckinghamshire supplying catering, decorations and entertainment. How could we not hear about this?'

'We thought after everything that has happened, it

would only be right to offer a gesture on this special day,' the woman added.

'What's going on?' Simon said, coming to the door. As soon as he stood next to Beth, she could feel him tense up. 'What are you doing here?'

'Who are they?' Beth said, virtually shouting now with the impatience of the fact that she still didn't know. This rise in tension instantly made Scarlett cry. It was all far from a pleasant experience, and not at all what Beth wanted for this special occasion.

'I'll take Letty,' Jane said from behind them.

'Thank you,' Beth said, handing Scarlett over. Knowing Jane wasn't exactly the maternal type, she added, 'All her toys are out in the living room. Just set her down next to them. She was playing with the farm animals.'

'Okay. Let's go and have a look at your new toys!' Jane took Scarlett away and Beth focused back on the still unidentified couple.

'Can someone now tell me who these people are?' Beth demanded.

Paul turned to Simon and for a moment no one spoke. Then Simon uttered, 'Damien's parents. This is Mr and Mrs Rock.'

Beth shivered as ice spiked through her.

'What do you want?' Simon asked.

'We used to be friends,' Mrs Rock replied.

'We know it's not your fault, what happened with Damien,' Paul said. 'But I don't think today is the right time to be talking about this. Do you?'

'We won't stay for long. We'll just drop our present off, have a quick drink with you, and then we'll leave. We want to make amends.'

'As Paul said, we don't blame you,' Simon confirmed. 'But today is not the day for this.'

'Please can we just have five minutes of your time?' Mrs Rock said, now virtually pleading.

'Not today.'

'Damien is doing so well. He's been ever so good. Prison's changed him.'

'He's served just two years of a twenty year sentence,' Simon stated. 'I think he has a long way to go before he's rehabilitated.'

'Or he's been rightfully punished for all the horrific things he did,' Beth added. 'He made our lives a misery.'

'I know he did. But he really has changed,' Mrs Rock said. 'Perhaps you could just go and visit him?'

'Are you joking?' Beth snapped, her anger rising.

'Like any criminal,' Simon said, far more calmly, 'he has to serve his punishment.'

'He's in a Malant prison,' Paul added. 'It's not like a normal prison. He's being well looked after.'

'We could have him put in a normal prison,' Simon stated. 'After all, he's no longer got any powers. I could arrange that if you'd prefer.'

'No, please,' Mrs Rock said. 'I just want us all to be friends again. We used to all get along so well.'

'Until your son abused the power he had,' Beth said. 'In every possible sense. Not just his magic, but his position in Bird Consultants. Simon gave him a fantastic job, but he still wanted more. He almost ruined us.'

'We know. And we're very sorry,' Mr Rock said. 'But don't punish us for our son's mistakes. Let's have a drink and try to renew our friendship.'

'I agree that we should discuss this more,' Paul said. 'But not today. You need to leave.'

'Can't we just come into the garden for a short while?' Mrs Rock said.

'Why are you so desperate to come into the garden?' Beth asked.

'Because it seems so unfriendly on the doorstep.'

'What's going on?' Carly asked, appearing in the reception area behind them. Despite her cute appearance, Beth knew that Carly could be quite feisty. It was her mix of kindness and steadfastness that had made Beth and

Simon hire her.

'Nothing,' Simon replied. 'These people were about to leave.'

'We just want a quick drink with you,' Mrs Rock tried again.

'Why don't you go and find Letty,' Carly said. 'Let me see these people out.'

'Yes, that's a good idea,' Beth said. 'Come on, Simon.'

'We'll talk soon,' Paul said to Mr and Mrs Rock.

Beth took Simon's hand. She turned and headed straight into the living room, not looking back.

The second the door was shut, she hugged Simon tightly, burying her head into his chest.

'Are you okay?' he asked her as he kissed her head.

'Who were those people?' Jane said from the floor where she was playing with Scarlett's horses.

'Hello, Letty,' Paul said, joining them.

'Perhaps you could take her out to see the real animals,' Simon said. 'The girl of the day should have the first chance at stroking them all!'

'Good idea. Come on, Letty,' Paul said, picking Scarlett up. He was so natural with her, almost a grandfather figure rather than an uncle. 'Do you want to see some real animals?'

Jane followed Paul out and the room soon fell silent.

'I'm sorry that just happened,' Simon said.

Beth looked up at him. 'It's not your fault.'

'You're shaking,' he said, hugging his wife tightly.

'I just need a minute. That's a name I thought I'd left behind a long time ago. It's amazing how quickly all that horror comes back to you.'

'I know. But he's locked away now. He won't be seeing the light of day any time soon. Just relax.'

'I know. I know.'

Simon curled Beth's dark brown hair behind her ears and studied her face. 'We can't let him ruin this party.'

Beth looked into his deep chocolate eyes. From the

first moment she'd seen them, she hadn't been able to resist those eyes. 'You're right. We haven't done all this planning to let that family ruin it all.'

'*We* did all this planning, did we?' Simon gibed.

'Behind every great man...' Beth giggled.

'You are the greatest woman I know,' Simon replied, kissing her.

'Right, let's go and celebrate the first two years of our little girl being on this planet.'

'Two years old. You know, when I was two that's when I first started to show powers. I wonder if she'll be the same.'

Beth shook her head. 'Life is never boring as a Malant, is it?'

'Oh no. But would you swap it?'

'Not in a million years.'

TWO

The next morning, Beth was drinking a cup of tea at the breakfast bar in the large, modern kitchen, whilst checking her emails on her laptop.

She heard the front door open. 'Hello,' a voice called. It was Carly.

'In the kitchen,' Beth called back.

'Sorry I'm late,' Carly said, rushing in to join Beth. 'It won't become a habit, I promise.'

'It's fine.'

'But I've made you late for work now.'

'It doesn't matter. Perks of being the boss.'

'My car wouldn't start.'

'You explained. It's fine. You should get Jim to have a look at it for you. He's great with mechanics.'

'I don't like to bother him. He's so busy.'

'He loves you. He'd jump at the chance to help you out.'

'Yeah. Maybe he could pop over later. Anyway, how are you?'

'I'm fine, thanks. For a Monday.'

'Where's Simon?'

'He's upstairs. He said he was working, but I know he's

playing with Scarlett.'

'He's like a big kid, that one.'

Beth smirked. 'Tell me about it.'

'Morning Carly,' Simon said, appearing through the doorway with Scarlett in his arms. Following a little bit of encouragement, Scarlett waved politely at Beth and Carly and mumbled something that resembled hello.

'I've been teaching her about earthquakes,' he said.

Beth rolled her eyes.

'Did you feel that tremor last night?' Carly asked.

'How could you miss it?' Beth replied.

'I can't remember the last time we had one of those,' Carly said. 'I suppose maybe we were due something like that.'

'We could always ask our two year old who no doubt knows all about the Richter scale now.' Beth smirked at Simon.

'Actually, in a sense, yes she does,' Simon replied smugly. 'We've been falling about, acting out what it's like to be in different forces of earthquake.'

'You mean you've been falling about and she's been laughing at you,' Beth stated with a grin.

'Perhaps. But either way, it was both a hilarious and informative game.'

'The best kind,' Beth replied. 'I'll have to join you later. But for now, we'd better get going.' Beth closed her laptop, put it in her bag and popped her mug into the dishwasher, whilst Simon handed Scarlett carefully over to Carly.

'You have a good day,' he said to his daughter who was still happily giggling. 'And watch out for earthquakes.'

'You'll scare her,' Beth said. 'It was just a small tremor. Nothing to worry about.'

'I'll be here to look after her,' Carly said. 'We're going to have a good day, aren't we?'

'Come on, we really have to go,' Beth said.

'Okay, I'll just grab my jacket,' Simon said. 'See you in

the car.'

Beth walked over to Scarlett and kissed her on the cheek. 'Goodbye gorgeous girl. We'll see you later. Have fun with Aunty Carly.'

'Bye bye,' Scarlett replied, waving again, that huge smile still dominating her face.

'We shouldn't be late tonight,' Beth said to Carly.

'Have a good day,' Carly replied.

Beth made her way to the front door, grabbing the car keys from the hook just next to it before she exited the house.

The Bird couple owned six cars between them. Three were kept in the garages and the other three on the drive. Four were Simon's and two were Beth's, but there was only ever one choice when they commuted to the office together. It was and always had been Simon's Aston Martin. His Vantage was the newest of his collection and his pride and joy. He might adore Beth, but even she wasn't allowed to as much as touch the steering wheel.

She settled into the passenger seat and waited for Simon to join her.

He soon appeared, laptop bag in hand. He got in the driver's seat and turned the engine on as he waited for the large gates to slowly open.

'I don't know about you, but I'm shattered after yesterday,' Beth said.

'I know. Perhaps we shouldn't have stayed up with the Champagne after Scarlett had gone to bed.'

Beth giggled. 'I hate to say it, but that was my favourite part of the day.'

Simon squeezed her knee with a lascivious smile. 'It certainly was a very good end to the day.'

Beth stroked his hand before he moved away to change gear.

'Have you got a lot on today?' he asked her.

'Yes. Tons. And I've got my monthly team meeting at eleven that I'm nowhere near ready for. How has it suddenly got so busy?'

'I know what you mean. That new Sales Director is causing me a lot of issues. I have to meet with another client this afternoon that he's upset.'

'Has he been promising the world again?' Beth asked.

'More like all the planets in the solar system.'

'What is he thinking?'

'It should have been quite a simple contract. The client has got into business with quite a dodgy supplier, but there could have been a million ways to resolve it. However, in all his wisdom, he recommended that we change the way the supplier thinks to make them good people. Apparently that's the Bird Consultants way.'

'Doing the impossible you mean? He's a Malant. He should know better.'

'Oh, he knows. He just thinks you can say anything to win the client, and then let the contracts team and spell-makers worry about how to make it actually happen. Every time he messes up, I have to go in and deal with it. We're going to have to get rid of him. This will be his final warning. I can't actually believe I'm about to say this, but at times like this I miss Damien.'

'Don't say that.'

'He was an evil son of a bitch, but he was good at his job. He made all his clients happy, and he was great with his team. Just a shame he got so greedy.'

'So we need to find someone who is as good as Damien, but who's actually a decent person as well.'

'Know of anyone?'

'Doesn't Paul? He knows everyone,' Beth asked.

'He knows loads of great sales people, but not Malant ones. We need the directors to be Malants. We can hide the true nature of the business to most of the staff, but not the directors. If only the Malant population was bigger. There are so few talented sales people in our secret little community.'

'We'll find someone. Bird Consultants is one of the few

truly Malant businesses. That's a big pull if you're a Malant. Maybe we'd be better finding a younger person with tons of potential?'

'You mean drop them in at the deep end and hope they'll swim?'

'That's what you did with me.'

'Not exactly.'

'Something good will happen. It always does. Life always has a way of working out. Just you see.'

'I love how you're always so optimistic.'

'Have I ever been wrong?'

Simon smirked. 'No dear. Of course not.'

'No I haven't!' Beth laughed and hit him playfully on the arm.

'Ow, not when I'm driving. If I steer wrong and hurt my Aston Martin, there will be hell to pay.'

Beth laughed again. 'Ooh, that sounds like a dare!'

The couple joyfully taunted each other, making each other laugh, for the rest of the twenty five minute journey. Before they knew it, Simon was pulling in to his dedicated parking space at the back of the Bird Consultants building.

They got out of the car and headed around to the front of the ten-storey block. The glass was glimmering against the Spring morning sunlight, and the bright red Bird Consultants logo seemed to sparkle, as if it were eager to begin another working day.

They made their way into the large, cold reception, and Beth's stiletto heels clicked against the stone floor. How she loved that sound.

'Morning Margaret,' Beth said, greeting the receptionist. Simon just looked forward, ignoring everyone. He always preferred to keep a distance between himself and the staff.

'Morning, Mrs Bird,' Margaret replied.

The lift was waiting and they stepped right in, pressing for the tenth floor.

'When's the next board meeting?' Beth asked. 'Is it this

week?'

'Yes, Thursday. Something else I've got to prep for. And don't forget we're at Malancy HQ tomorrow for the quarterly meeting as well.'

'Didn't we just have one of those a few weeks ago?'

'Feels like it doesn't it,' Simon nodded.

'I'm not ready for either meeting.'

'You've got loads of time. A whole twenty-four hours.'

'Are you sure with all our power that we can't magic a few extra hours in the day?'

Simon laughed. 'Believe me, if we could, I'd have done it a long time ago.'

The lift doors opened and they headed out, across the soft carpeted floor and through some glass doors embossed with the company logo. This led to the Executive Floor where the seven other directors of the company were already busy working away.

They walked over to the end office that Simon and Beth shared – her desk at one end and his at the other.

'Cup of tea?' Beth asked as she placed her bag on her desk. Tea was always her first priority of the day.

'Yes please,' Simon replied, taking out his laptop.

She picked up her phone to ask one of her team to bring them up a cuppa, when she stopped. The kitchen was one floor down, right next to where her admin team sat, and Beth regularly liked to pop down to check on them. As good as it was that all the directors sat together, Beth often felt isolated from the rest of the company, especially the people she worked directly with day to day.

'Actually, I'm going to pop down myself,' she said.

Simon nodded. He understood. She'd never explained her frequent trips to the kitchen, but he'd always seemed to just know what she was doing.

Beth made her way back to the lifts and down to the ninth floor. Stepping out, she passed the entrance to the kitchen and glanced through the glass doors that led to the main office, only to find that most of the desks across the floor were empty.

There seemed to be a gathering in the corner by the window. It looked like quite the hub of activity. She spied Gayle, Michelle and Warren joining the crowd that was fascinated by something. Only Diane, one of the longer serving members of Beth's team, stood back.

Diane was a nosey busy-body who loved to stir up trouble. She was excellent at her job but often caused issues with other members of staff. Beth knew she didn't do it deliberately (well, not always). She just had this natural way of interfering and upsetting people. It had caused Beth no end of difficulties through the years.

Beth studied the group closer. Were they looking out the window at something? Whatever it was, Beth knew that if Diane wasn't there at the front, then it really couldn't be that interesting.

She left them to it and quickly made two cups of tea in the unusually quiet kitchen. Then she made her way back to her office, passing Simon his tea before getting comfortable at her own desk.

For about fifteen minutes they enjoyed perfect silence and they both got stuck into their work. Then there was a knock at the door.

'Come in,' Simon ordered in his familiar stern tone.

'Sorry to bother you,' Eric, the Contracts Director said, poking his head through the doorway. 'There seems to be a bit of a disturbance downstairs. You might want to take a look.'

'You mean on the ninth floor?' Beth said. 'Yes, I saw that. What is everyone doing?'

'It's not just the ninth floor,' Eric replied, cautiously. He actually looked worried. 'It's every floor.'

'What's going on?' Simon asked.

'I think you need to see it.'

'Just tell us,' Simon demanded impatiently.

'I don't really know how to say this.'

'What is it?' Beth asked. She began to feel quite

nervous about what he was going to say.

'It's just that... Everyone's got powers.'

'What do you mean everyone's got powers?' Simon asked.

'Just that. All the non-Malants across the company seem to be... casting spells. It seems everyone is... magic.'

THREE

Simon and Beth immediately shot to their feet. They glanced at each other with confusion, before both darting to the lift.

Simon knew it had to be a mistake. Non-Malants could not have powers. It was simply impossible. You were born as a Malant. It was something passed down through generations. It wasn't a gift you could just learn or something you could gain through practice.

He and Beth got out on the ninth floor and headed through the glass doors. As soon as they entered, a file flew across the room and all the staff gasped with a mixture of horror and delight.

'My turn next!' a young girl shouted. Simon was so distanced from his employees, he barely knew who anyone was. He even struggled with Beth's team, not that he openly admitted that to her face. It just wasn't his concern who made up each department. He had more pressing matters to deal with.

'What is going on?' Simon asked as he walked towards the crowd that had gathered near the window. Beth was closely following behind. As soon as they approached the group, Simon could see that everyone was gathered around a plant. There was too much excitement for Simon's presence to be noticed, though.

'What is going on?' he repeated, far more strikingly, and this time his intimidating voice brought immediate silence. Every member of staff glared at him with fear.

'What is going on?' he asked a third time, ready to explode with impatience.

'The plant...' a young man started, before his voice trailed away.

'What about the plant?'

'When anyone touches the plant, they can send items flying around the room,' Gayle, one of the few people Simon did know, stated from the back of the group. 'We're not sure what's going on. It seems anyone can make it happen.'

'Show me,' Simon demanded. He knew for a fact that Gayle wasn't a Malant, but as one of Beth's closest friends she had learnt all about the Malancy. She had also been sworn to secrecy.

It was only the senior management team who knew about the true nature of the business and how it used the power of the Malancy to magic away problems for businesses – at a very hefty price. Most employees were led to believe that Bird Consultants was merely a general business consultancy. Staff were given vague details about everything and paid very well not to ask questions.

'I haven't done it yet,' Gayle replied. 'I'm not sure I know how to.'

'Who just sent that file across the room?' Simon asked, determined to see with his own eyes just what was happening.

After a moment's hesitation, a small voice squeaked. 'Me.' It was the youngest of Beth's staff, but Simon couldn't recall her name.

'Tell Gayle what you did,' Simon asked.

'Please, Michelle,' Beth added.

Michelle stepped forward. 'It was Liz who did it first.'

'I was just cleaning the leaves. They looked a bit dusty,' the voice of a middle aged woman said. 'The next thing I knew that pen pot flew in the air.' Liz pointed to a pot of pens on the nearest desk.

'It hasn't worked for everyone straight away,' Gayle explained.

'We worked out that Liz was pissed off with... something,' Michelle added, casting Liz a small glance. 'So we all started trying to do it while thinking about something that made us mad. It's like the plant is feeding off our anger.'

'Please try,' Simon said to Gayle, now very sure that this was Malant related. The magic worked when a person tapped into their emotion.

Gayle stepped forward. She touched one of the leaves of the plant and closed her eyes. After a few seconds, the pot of pens and a stapler on the same desk shot across the room, smacking against a chair near the door.

'Wow,' Gayle said. She threw Beth a look. Simon had always been in awe of how the pair could not say a word to one another yet completely understand what each other meant. He'd ask Beth later to translate.

He pushed through the crowd to reach the plant. Everyone willingly stepped back, away from their boss.

He placed his hand over the top of the small plant to sense its energy. It was no more magic than any other element. All Malants casted spells by drawing power from natural elements, be it a stone, plant, water or soil. The only exceptions were Simon and Beth who possessed the innate ability to create magic autonomously, and this unique gift was the reason that they were now in charge of the Malancy government.

Simon concentrated on the plant. He could tell that power could be drawn from it as per any natural element, but it didn't contain anything special that a non-Malant could utilise in another way.

There was only one other explanation that Simon could

think of.

'What's happening?' Beth asked.

'It's just an illusion. A practical joke,' Simon stated. 'Everyone back to work. I don't want to see another person near that plant. Do you understand?'

Mumbles of yes spread through the office and everyone quickly headed back to their desks.

Simon signalled for Beth to follow him and they headed up to the Executive Floor.

'What's going on?' Beth asked as they stood in the lift.

'They were using that plant to activate magic just as any Malant would.'

'But how can that be the case? Not one person on that floor is a Malant.'

'I have no idea.'

'It must have been something in the plant.'

'No. It definitely wasn't. I sensed the power in it. Trust me, the plant was just augmenting what everyone else was feeling.'

'But that's impossible.'

The lift doors opened and Simon made his way to the middle of the floor. He addressed all seven of the directors that sat there.

'For reasons that I can't yet explain, it would appear that everyone has developed magical abilities. I've just witnessed a non-Malant sending inanimate objects flying through the air. Obviously, we need to stop this happening. Beth and I are going to head to Malancy HQ now to find out what's going on. I want every single element that is found anywhere within this building to be removed. I mean everything.'

'What about water? We can't turn off the taps,' Eric said.

Simon thought for a second. 'Don't worry about that. Beth and I will deal with that. I want you each to visit your departments, remove any natural element and explain to your team that this is some elaborate joke. Whether your staff know about the Malancy or not, we cannot have non-Malants believing they have power. This is far too dangerous. Do I make myself clear?'

All the directors nodded in agreement and they each headed on their way to deal with their respective teams.

'What are we going to do?' Beth asked as she followed Simon into their office.

'Pack your stuff up...' Simon's mobile rang, cutting him off. He saw it was Jane calling, the joint head of the Malancy government. Whereas Simon and Beth, as the most powerful Malants alive, were ultimately in charge, they'd put Jane and Jim in place to manage the day to day operations. Simon and Beth then only had to deal with larger issues and oversee things from afar. Although for the three years that they'd been in power, they had yet to see anything that warranted their attention. Until now.

'Please don't tell me you're calling due to issues with non-Malants showing magical abilities,' Simon said the second he answered the call.

'You know then,' Jane replied.

'Any idea what's going on?'

'Not a clue. We've got Ralph working on it. I've never seen anything like this. I didn't even know this was possible.'

'I'd say it wasn't, except for the fact that I've witnessed it with my own eyes. We're on our way.'

'Just to let you know, Jim isn't here.'

'Where is he?'

'He called in sick this morning, and I can't get hold of him now. He did sound in a bad way. I'll keep trying. No matter what the ailment, I'm sure he'll want to know about this.'

'Yes, please keep trying. Have you told Paul?'

'Not yet.'

'I'll call him on the way. We need all the minds we can get working on this.'

'Agreed. See you shortly.'

Simon hung up.

'Jane?' Beth asked.

'It's not just here. God knows how big a problem this is.'

'Well, I'm ready to go.' Beth was standing by her desk, bag in hand. Simon quickly pulled together his things, grabbed his suit jacket from the back of his chair and they made their way out of the office.

Simon quickly locked the door behind them, as he always did, and they paced over to the lifts.

'What are we doing about the water?' Beth asked.

'We're going to have to drain the power from the whole system.'

'Drain the water or just the power?'

'No, just the power. Do you know how to do that?'

'No,' Beth replied.

Simon had learnt about his powers from a very young age and had had years of practising over Beth. She still wasn't quite aware of just how powerful she was. Simon normally loved showing her new and wonderful aspects of their abilities, but today it had to be all business.

'We'll do the kitchen on the ninth floor first,' Simon said. 'We'll have to do it one room at a time. I don't want to wipe the whole place of power. Malants still have their rights. I just want to make it empty enough so that someone who doesn't know what they're doing won't accidentally be able to set something off. Agreed?'

'Totally. We have to respect our Malant people. This isn't going to be fair on them.'

Simon couldn't stop his smile. Beth was one of the loveliest people he'd ever met. She spent her whole time constantly worrying about being fair and treating people with respect. She made a truly worthy leader. Sometimes he couldn't believe how lucky he was that she was his partner in life.

They reached the ninth floor kitchen. There were a couple of staff members huddled around the urn.

'Please leave,' Simon said, interrupting them in their mid-coffee-making flow.

'We've had some complaints about issues with the water,' Beth added. Simon had never felt relaxed with the good cop, bad cop routine that seemed to play out whenever he was with Beth at the office. He wouldn't change Beth for the world, and he adored her kind, caring nature, but he hadn't made up his mind yet whether her additions to his demands undermined him or not. It was something he'd have to discuss with her. On another occasion. 'Please could you give us a minute to explore the problem?' Beth finished with her warm smile.

The two people nodded. They put their mugs down and left the kitchen.

'Why would the CEO and a director of the company be checking out so-called water issues?' Simon asked. He couldn't possibly be angry with Beth, but sometimes her need to explain everything rendered the most ridiculous tales. The "just do as you're told - you don't need to know the reasons why because I'm in charge and I'm telling you" approach made them look far less stupid.

'Because there's been some sort of practical joke across the company,' Beth justified. 'They'll think it relates to the water. Maybe poison? If we're checking it out then it has to be important.'

'So now we're poisoning the staff?' Simon said with a drop of humour.

'I said nothing of the sort,' Beth replied. 'But at least now they're out the way. They'll fill in the blanks themselves.'

'I love the way your mind works. Okay, let's get to it.'

Simon turned around, clicked his fingers and the door to the kitchen locked shut. They couldn't take the risk of any further interruptions. Then he turned back to face the room and hesitated. 'I have no idea how a water system works. I don't know what pipe is what. I've never needed to know before.'

'Can't we just touch the tap?' Beth asked.

'Every tap in the building? That could take forever. No, we'll have to draw out the power across the whole room.'

'Can we put it back again afterwards?'

'Yes. Easily. It'll be time consuming but worth it. Don't worry, it won't affect us. We have the power built into us.'

'I wasn't worrying.'

'I didn't know if you used your power to make tea or something.'

'Why on earth would I use my power to make tea? Can I use my power to make tea? I've never even thought about that!'

'You really don't use your ability much at all, do you?' For a brief moment Simon got lost in the thought of how one of the most powerful people to ever have lived was so set against exploiting that power in any way. He knew he was exactly the same, though. Although with him it had always been because of a fear of how far his magic could go. His lack of using it was more for control than anything. He surmised that Beth's lack of use probably related more to her deep sense of morality. What an interesting pair they made.

'Right, let's get on with this,' Simon said, focusing on the task in hand. He took a step back so he was pressed against the door, and he signalled for Beth to stand beside him. 'All you need to do is stick out your hand and suck the power up. Tap into every element in the room and absorb it into yourself. Do you want to give it a go?'

Beth nodded. She stood tall and held out her hand. She closed her eyes to concentrate and Simon felt the room slowly empty of power. Something only he and Beth would ever be able to accomplish.

'Wow, what a rush!' Beth said, as she finished the spell.

'Can you feel it's gone?'

'I can feel it coursing through me, so I know the room has been cleared of it. It's quite a sensation.'

'It won't last long. Which is good, because we've got

three more kitchens and five toilets each to do. You do the ladies, I'll do the gents. The only ones we can leave out are those on the top floor. Only the directors use those and they're Malants anyway.'

'Agreed,' Beth nodded. 'How about I do the kitchen on the ground floor and you do the others?'

'Sounds good. I'll see you in reception.'

'And don't shout at people if they're in the way. Be kind.'

'I'll tell them I'm here to do the plumbing,' Simon said with a smirk. 'I'm sure they'll understand.'

'There's no need for sarcasm.' Beth kissed Simon on the cheek before heading off to her first set of toilets.

Simon took a deep breath. He hadn't said anything to Beth, but clearing the building of power was only a temporary fix to the staff in his office. Speaking to Jane had indicated that this problem could be massive. They couldn't neutralise all elements of their power, but how could they let the Malancy become widespread? It was a gift to be treasured. And it was something that could so easily be abused.

If the whole world suddenly had the power to cast spells, this could become very messy indeed. Frighteningly so.

FOUR

Beth waited in reception for Simon to appear. She'd just finished in the final kitchen and her body felt alive. The power was sparking across her, and her skin looked faintly swollen with a tinge of orange light. It was a most uncomfortable sensation. She'd always been aware of her magic, but it was normally a refreshing and energising strength that she enjoyed. However, the overwhelming charge of having absorbed so much extra power was now prickling at her and she couldn't stand still.

She could sense Margaret watching her from the reception desk, but she knew that Margaret would be too afraid to ask her if anything was the matter. Ever since Beth had married Simon and she'd been promoted to director, the staff had mostly stopped being friendly with her. The only friend she had at work was Gayle. Beth didn't really mind. She could understand why people were cautious around her, and she knew it was mainly because they feared Simon rather than it being about Beth. But sometimes she missed having a good gossip.

The lift doors opened and Simon appeared.

'All done?' he asked her.

She couldn't see much of his skin because he was

dressed fully in a suit, but a quick glance at his hands revealed the small orange tinge he had too. It was so faint, someone probably wouldn't notice it if they weren't looking for it, but it made Beth feel better that he had the same affliction. Even more so that he didn't look remotely worried. Not that Simon ever outwardly showed his emotion.

'Yes. You too?' Beth said.

'Yes. Let's go.'

'We've got a meeting to go to now, Margaret,' Beth said.

'Shall I forward calls to your mobiles?' Margaret asked, very politely.

'No, just take messages if you would. We've got a big day ahead.'

'Very well. See you soon.'

Beth and Simon headed back to his car.

'I feel so weird,' Beth said, the second the doors were shut. 'Please tell me you feel it too.'

'Yes, don't worry,' Simon assured her. 'It stings a little, doesn't it. It will soon pass, though.'

'How soon is soon?'

Simon thought through his answer. 'Considering the fact that we've absorbed quite a lot of power, I'd say maybe half an hour.'

'Oh God. Are you going to be all right to drive?'

'Yes, of course. Do you feel that bad?'

'Like I'm so charged up I want to punch the wall.'

'Oh, Beth, I'm sorry. I suppose you're really not used to it. Take a few deep breaths.'

Beth did as Simon suggested as he pulled the car away.

They made their way through Heaningford, towards Central London and on to London Bridge, where the Malancy Headquarters could be found.

'I'd better call Paul,' Simon said.

Most people would fiddle with the in-car Bluetooth at this point, but Simon just took a moment of silent contemplation and a ringing sound could be heard. Beth loved that trick, of phoning someone with just her mind.

After being single for two years and having struggled financially juggling multiple jobs, she'd moved to London to start a new life. It was then that she met, fell in love with and married her millionaire boss who changed her life completely. One part of that change was that she'd gained two luxury cars with all of the state-of-the-art gadgets to boot. It was only then that she learned she could overpower them all with just her mind. That about summed up life to Beth.

'Mate, how's it going?' Paul said through the in-car speaker.

'Not good. Where are you?' Simon answered.

'On the golf course. Well I was. We're at the nineteenth now. Just having a coffee mind. There are some shit players out today. We couldn't carry on. What's the matter?'

'I don't even know where to start. You won't believe this, but it looks like non-Malants have started to develop powers. Things were flying around the office with not a Malant in sight. We're on our way to HQ now. Can you meet us there?'

There was silence on the other end.

'Paul?' Simon nudged.

'That would explain it then.'

'Explain what?'

'There were golf balls flying all over the place. Three hit me from God knows where. I just thought there were amateurs across the course. All that grass, it must have been sending things wild. How the hell can this be happening?'

'No idea. I would have said it was impossible. Jane's already got Ralph on the case. We need as many heads together as we can. We have to stop this from escalating.'

'I'm on my way, mate. I'll be about an hour.'

'See you soon.'

Simon hung up.

'I didn't know semi-retired also meant full time golfer,' Beth said with a small grin, enjoying a distraction from the worrying. 'He's addicted.'

'He's earned the right. He's worked hard for a long time, but he's still there when we need him. Both at the office and as a consultant for the Malancy.'

'I'm not knocking him. I think the world of Paul, you know I do. I actually admire him. It's like he's got it all sorted. The owner of an international, hugely successful company, about a hundred million in the bank, and absolute flexibility on how he wants to spend his day. Add to that a dedicated nephew who he can trust implicitly to run things day to day, and life certainly is good for Paul Bird.'

'He deserves it though, doesn't he.'

'Oh yes. Best man I've ever met. You aside. And my dad and brother, of course.'

'Of course.'

'I dread to think what would have happened after your parents died if he'd not been there for you. You were so young.'

'I don't even want to think about that.'

'How come you never play golf with him? I mean apart from the fact that you have very little time. You could go on a Sunday or something, though. I bet he'd love that.'

'Oh no he wouldn't. He took me once when I was about nineteen. I couldn't hit the ball at all for about ten minutes... and then... I just found my way.'

Beth giggled. 'You mean you just magically found your way to getting eighteen holes in one?'

'It wasn't eighteen. I didn't want to be that obvious.'

'I bet he was so mad!'

'It was really boring. I'm more of a rugby man. I prefer the fast paced action.'

Beth laughed. 'I've never played golf in my life. We should so go together and do it our way. I bet that would be so much fun. And certainly fast paced.'

Simon laughed along with Beth. 'I love that idea. As soon as we clear all this madness up, we're having an afternoon on the golf course.'

'Afternoon, twenty minutes... Let's see how fast we can magic our way around it.'

'And let's not tell Paul.'

'There you go. You said earlier that I don't use my ability much. This is a brilliant way of having some fun with it.'

'Yes,' Simon said, the smile dropping from his lips.

'What is it?'

'You just got me thinking. It should be fun for Malants, and it's their birthright to use it. But it could get very dangerous if the whole world really does start to develop magical abilities.'

'You mean because they'll be using magic they don't understand?'

'Maybe. Or maybe it will be worse if the general public does learn to use it properly and then they decide to abuse it. The Malancy government works extremely well at the minute as there are so few people we have to manage. But how could we take charge of millions of people? We haven't seen an incident of dark magic in over three years. Not since Damien set out to destroy us through his jealousy. And even if someone did try, we could easily control it with just a few thousand Malants to oversee. But how could we maintain law and order... well it would be billions of people across the world. The buck ultimately stops with us. This could change the human race as we know it forever and there could be nothing we could do about it.'

'That can't happen,' Beth stated. 'It simply can't. No matter what, no one is more powerful than us. And they're never going to be. We're a unique pair, you and me, and we need to work together to ensure that we nip this strange occurrence in the bud as fast as humanly possible.

And then we stop anyone who may be involved in bringing about this bizarre turn of events before they cause any more damage.'

'You think a person is behind this?'

'Someone is always behind bad things like this. When totally inexplicable things happen for no apparent reason, someone like Damien is always to blame.'

'Except this time Damien is locked up in prison with all of his powers removed. He can't possibly be involved.'

'He also can't be the only one who'd ever try to mess with us.'

'You mean mess with me,' Simon stated.

'With us. We're equally powerful.'

'But you're well liked. Everyone loves Mrs Bird. I'm the one who people have always feared. And people do strange things with fear, as we well know.'

'Look, let's not jump to conclusions. There could be a million reasons as to why this has happened. When we first met, you said to me that being a Malant was like a rollercoaster ride. Things have been plain sailing for a while. It was only a matter of time before we were sent off in all directions again. We just need to focus on working together and finding a solution as quickly as possible, before any of this gets out of hand.'

'You're right. My gorgeous, wise Bethany Bird. Best wife a man could wish for.'

'You are very lucky, yes.'

They both chuckled as the end of London Bridge came into sight. Thankfully, the traffic had been relatively light. Simon drove over the bridge, to the south of the River Thames, and then they turned right into a side street. At about halfway along, next to a building that was barely noticeable if a person didn't know it was there, stood a large iron gate. As the car approached it, it slowly opened, automatically sensing the presence of the Bird couple. They drove through to a small car park, and Simon stopped the car in the dedicated space always made available for the two people who were overall in charge of the Malancy government.

They got out of the car and quickly made their way through the large doors at the back of the building. They entered a corridor that was brightly lit, the green of the carpet almost reflecting off the stark white walls. They got straight in a lift and headed up to the sixth floor.

As soon as the lift doors opened, they turned left and made their way straight to Jane's extremely large and impeccably tidy office. Jane was always perfectly presented, with smart clothes and never a hair out of place, and everything that she touched was the same.

'You're here! Fantastic,' Jane said as they entered through the doorway. 'Paul's called. He's on his way too.'

'Any word from Jim?' Simon asked.

'Still getting his voicemail.'

'He seemed so well yesterday,' Beth said. 'And Carly said nothing this morning. Maybe we could pop round later if we still haven't heard anything. This is most unlike him.'

'Yes,' Simon agreed. 'This isn't like Jim at all. And, you're right, he was in very good spirits yesterday. Let's see how the day pans out, then we'll make a plan later.'

'Take a seat,' Jane said, pointing to the table towards the back of her office. 'Tea?'

'Yes please,' Beth said and Simon nodded.

Jane picked up her phone and requested for tea to be brought up.

'How is Ralph progressing?' Simon asked as Jane joined them at the table.

After Beth and Simon, Ralph was the next most powerful Malant and a true asset to the government. It wasn't that he possessed any extra special powers, though, like Beth and Simon did. Ralph was just highly skilled. He was more like a scholar who had learnt his craft through extensive studying and had developed a deeper understanding of the Malancy than anyone else.

'He's not updated me yet,' Jane replied. 'We had a call from a couple of Malants who had noticed their non-Malant friends being able to exercise powers in ways they shouldn't have been able to. Then you must have seen the news.'

'No,' Beth said, with growing concern.

'It's all over the world; spreading quite quickly. As soon as one person appeared to have this ability, others have given it a go and have too managed to somehow perform magic.'

'Just like at the office,' Beth said.

'The media is stating that natural elements seem to have become possessed with some sort of energy, or something like that. They all think it's the elements that are generating the power. Thankfully, they don't understand what's really happening, and our Malant people are being tight lipped. For now.'

'What power has been experienced so far? Anything dangerous?' Simon asked.

'From what I can gather, it's merely moving items around. Where we all begin. That's why the press believe it to be related to a strange kinetic energy. Some scientist was being interviewed stating some nonsense relating to that. Without the guidance of a Malant, I can't see anyone quickly realising the true extent of the power. After all, it's very simple to move a pen around the room. It's far more difficult to cast other spells. That comes with teaching, and as long as our Malant people remain silent, that teaching will never happen.'

'Do you think they will remain silent?' Beth asked.

'I'd say we all have a lot to lose if we start to become vocal about our secret group. But the nature of people is that someone always strays. Do you want me to send out a communication to all Malants in some way? We've never had to do anything like that before, but it might be best to exercise our authority right now.'

'No, I don't think we need to do that just yet,' Simon

said. 'What do you think?' he asked, turning to Beth.

'I agree with Simon. Let's get some more facts together first. For all we know this could all disappear by tonight and be like a twenty-four hour bug thing. Let's wait to hear from Ralph and then take it from there.'

'Whatever you think is best,' Jane said. 'I don't know if it's worth us starting to look through some of the Malancy books to see if we can find any sound reason as to why this has happened? With five hundred years of history, there might be something in the past that indicates how this could be possible.'

'We need to do something productive,' Simon said.

Jane's phone rang and Beth felt her heart stop. She had finally calmed down from the magic pulsating through her body, now she was edgy with the nerves of what they were going to find out next. This was getting bigger by the second.

'Jane Bird,' Jane said. She was the newest member of the Bird family – but only just. She and Paul had got married just a few months after Beth and Simon had tied the knot, while Beth was carrying Scarlett. That certainly had been an eventful year.

'What?' Jane said, with fear in her voice. Beth watched as the colour drained from Jane's face. Beth had rarely seen Jane look so worried. Like Paul, she normally took everything in her stride. 'Thank you. They're here now. I'll let them know. I'll be in touch.'

'Ralph?' Simon asked. Beth could sense him tense up. She could tell he was as nervous as she was, although anyone else wouldn't have noticed. As usual, there was no emotion in his expression.

'No,' Jane said, almost breathless with agitation.

'What is it?' Beth asked.

'That was Ivor. The prison director.'

Beth felt dizzy as she waited for Jane to continue. She desperately feared that she knew exactly what was coming next. Everything began neatly slotting into place.

'Damien,' Simon said, reading Beth's mind, his voice cold and to the point.

'They can't find him anywhere,' Jane stated. 'They can't explain it. He's vanished from prison. Somehow Damien has escaped.'

FIVE

'Hi gang,' Paul said as he stepped into the office. His familiar smile dropped the second he spotted the desperate concern on everyone's faces. 'What's wrong?'

'Damien's escaped from prison,' Beth said.

'This is no coincidence,' Simon stated. 'On the day that Damien finds a way out of prison, the whole world develops powers. I don't know what he's done, but he's involved somewhere. He has to be. And I would guess dark magic is involved somewhere too.'

'I'm going to go down to see Ralph,' Jane said. 'He needs to know about this.'

Simon stood up, so fast he almost knocked his chair over behind him. A terrifying idea had punched him in the stomach. It was rare that he ever feared anything, but suddenly he felt weak with it.

'We have to get home,' he told Beth. 'We have to get to Scarlett.'

'What are you saying?' Beth asked, the fear in her voice almost palpable. 'Damien wouldn't do anything to Scarlett. Surely not.'

'If Damien's escaped from prison then I can't see him going anywhere near your house,' Paul reasoned. 'It's like escaping from Belmarsh only to run straight into Scotland Yard. He'll be far away from here now. He might be evil, but he's not stupid.'

'Isn't Carly looking after her?' Jane noted. 'If there was anything to worry about, she would have called.'

'My phone's on silent,' Beth said with alarm, quickly picking up her bag and rummaging through it. She pulled out her mobile. 'I've got three missed calls. Oh my God!'

Simon stopped breathing as he waited for Beth to find out who the calls were from.

She sighed and he almost collapsed. 'It's okay. They're from Gayle.'

'I'm sure she realises you have bigger things on your plate right now,' Simon said, almost trembling. He'd never felt so scared in his life.

'We were supposed to have a team meeting this morning. I bet she just wants to know where I am.'

'Well she'll have to wait.'

'I know. I'll call her back later.' Beth threw her phone back into her bag. 'Let's get home. I think we'll both feel better if we're with Scarlett and we know for sure she's safe.'

'Let's teleport,' Simon said, barely able to control the jittery sensation that rattled through him.

'Teleport?' Jane asked with surprise.

'Si, even with your immense power, it'll still knock you for six,' Paul said.

'I don't care. We'll be at home. We can recover there. Beth, we have to get back to her. We can come back for the car later.'

'I agree. We need to know our daughter's safe.'

'I'm sure she's absolutely fine,' Paul said in a calming voice. 'Damien wouldn't dare go near here.'

'He's miraculously escaped from prison,' Simon argued back. 'Anything's possible when it comes to Damien. We have to know our daughter is safe.'

'All right.'

'We'll let you know.'

'You just go get your daughter and we'll keep working on things here,' Paul said, squeezing his nephew's shoulder.

Simon reached out his hand and Beth held it tightly. A small red glow fizzled between them as their combined power surged.

'You imagine it, I'll do the spell,' he whispered to her.

'Like last time,' she whispered back.

'We always work best together.'

Simon watched Beth close her eyes and he knew she'd be picturing their home. He could sense the incredible energy that the two of them produced when they touched. He tapped into his insurmountable fear of losing his daughter and he concentrated it all like a ball in his chest.

He squeezed Beth's hand as the small red glow suddenly flamed brightly and a crimson wave soaked up both of their bodies. He felt the images in her mind connect to the spell, and he closed his eyes to focus his attention on the power.

As the magic reached its peak, he knew it had worked.

'We're here,' he gasped, opening his eyes. Like a flash, they were back in their living room. Both of them crashed down onto a settee as they fought for breath. It was a very tiring spell. It was virtually impossible for any other Malant to render the colossal power that such a spell took, but to Simon and Beth it merely winded them for a short while.

After a few seconds, Simon tried to find his feet. He was still quite wobbly and out of breath, but they hadn't got time to rest.

'Carly,' he shouted, although his usual force just wasn't available.

Beth followed him slowly, also panting. 'Carly?' she called.

There was no response.

'The garden!' Beth suggested. It was, after all, another beautiful day. They both staggered through to the kitchen, but as they glanced across the acre of land at the back of the house, not a soul could be seen.

'I'll check upstairs, you cover down here,' Beth said, as she dragged herself towards the front of the house to reach the staircase.

'Carly? Scarlett?' Simon called. He checked the play room, the study, the dining room, the utility room, the living room a second time just in case; he even went out to check the drive and three garages, but Carly and Scarlett were nowhere to be seen.

'Any luck?' Beth asked as she appeared on the grand staircase that arched across the reception area, still panting.

'No. You?'

'No. There's no one here. I've just tried to call her but it went straight to voicemail. I suppose there could be a reasonable explanation. They could have gone to the park, gone shopping.'

'Of course, Carly's car isn't here!' Simon said, a moment of relief springing through him.

'She didn't bring her car today,' Beth said. 'That's why she was late. It's broken down. She had to get a taxi here.'

'Then where could she be?' Simon asked, now quite panicked. 'Everything they could possibly need is in this house.'

'Let's give ourselves a moment to think logically,' Beth said, taking a seat on the stairs.

'Yes. You're right. I'm sure there's a really logical explanation. It's just really worrying that Damien is out of prison and we have no clue where our daughter is.'

'Location spell!' Beth said. 'Let's do a location spell.'

Simon took a deep breath. 'Great idea, except I don't think I can. I'm still weak from teleporting. It could be an hour or so before we're back to full strength.'

'Okay. Let's go and sit down for a few minutes and conserve some energy.'

'We don't have time to wait. You know, I bet we could augment the power.'

'You mean use an element like a normal Malant?'

'Yes. I have a selection of stones in the back garden that I've used on the odd occasion. It's worth a try.'

Beth was already on her way. Simon followed her out towards the solitary tree that stood towards the back of the garden. At the bottom of it there were dozens of stones scattered around. Simon's personal element collection, just in case he ever needed them.

'Let's both do it,' Beth said. 'You search for Carly, I'll search for Scarlett.'

'Good idea.'

Simon rummaged through the stones carefully, trying to find ones big enough to give the right boost to their power. He knew he had the perfect stone somewhere. It was his favourite stone for spell-casting. He'd found it at the beach about ten years ago and something about its flawlessly smooth and round shape made it very effective. His panicked state wasn't making it easy to look, though, and after a few moments he decided to just grab any two stones that would suffice. There just wasn't the time to look properly.

He passed a stone to Beth and took another similar one in his own hands.

'I'll stand over there,' Beth said, pointing nearer the house. 'You distract me when you do spells. I need to concentrate.'

'Okay. Good luck.'

'You too.'

Simon closed his eyes and once again summoned the strength within him, yet again focusing on the terror that trembled him. Any other Malant would need several extraordinarily potent elements to even have a chance of conducting such a spell, not to mention the remarkable concentration, patience and vigour they'd have to have just to survive the might of the magic. But to Simon and Beth it was simply a matter of tapping into the incredible innate power that coursed through their bodies every second of every day.

He summoned a picture of Carly in his head as he channelled the force within him. He only needed to utilise the natural properties of the stone a tiny bit to enhance his ability and make up for the short term weakness he was experiencing following the teleportation spell.

As the images of Carly grew more vibrant in his mind, the stone began to glow, and seconds later Simon's body mirrored the same ruby radiance. The bright aura soon erupted into a fiery red blaze, which rapidly intensified until an entire inferno engulfed the whole of the garden and dazzling beams shone out like the rays of the sun swallowing up every inch of green.

An image hit him. He dropped the stone with horror as he got a glimpse of Carly in the exact place she was at that moment.

'No!' Beth screamed from across the garden.

Simon raced over to her as she collapsed to the ground in anguish.

'No!' she cried.

Simon grabbed her in his arms.

'Did you see her?' he asked, barely able to control how scared he felt. He knew what she was about to say, but he didn't want to believe it.

'I don't know where she is. Some room. It could be anywhere. But he's got her!' Beth shrieked. 'That bastard's got her!' She was almost choking she was crying so much. 'Damien has got our girl. She was sitting there next to him, like they were playing happy fucking family. He's got our daughter.'

'I know,' Simon said, hugging Beth tightly, trying to soothe her. He had to put his fear behind him now. He had to be strong. He had to find a way to get through this, support his wife and get his daughter back. There was no room for any more weakness.

'Did you see Carly?' Beth sobbed. 'Do you know where she is? Please say you know where she is.'

'I saw her. It looked like a hotel room. It could be anywhere.'

'Was she...'

'Yes. She was with Damien too. She was standing in the middle of a room looking at him. Damien's got them both.'

SIX

Beth sobbed heartily into Simon's shoulder for a few minutes. She needed to let it out. This was her worst nightmare.

But as the pain seeped out through her tears, she quickly realised that she needed to grab a hold of herself. She couldn't be a wreck. She needed to focus and fight this. Crying wasn't going to get Scarlett back.

She took a few calming breaths before she looked up to Simon's face. 'What can we do?'

He helped Beth to her feet. 'We're going to find her and we're going to bring her back. And then we're going to find out how Damien managed this and stop whatever he has done. He will not get the better of us. Do you understand?'

Beth nodded as she wiped her face with her cardigan sleeve. 'Tell me what to do.'

Simon was the smartest person that Beth had ever met. His problem solving abilities were the main reason why Bird Consultants had been so successful. He had never been beaten by any issue, and Beth felt sure that he'd find a way to resolve this. She put all her faith in him.

As she watched him, she could practically see his brain

churning over thoughts and plans; his chocolate brown eyes deepening with the intensity of his concentration.

'We need to repeat the location spells,' Simon said. 'I thought it seemed like they were in a hotel room. What did you think?'

'Yes, I suppose,' Beth said, her heart hurting as she recalled the image she'd seen of Scarlett with that horrible man. 'Yes, actually, yes. It didn't seem like a home. I'd definitely say a hotel room.'

'Right, well we need to redo the location spells, but this time not focus on the people, instead focus on their surroundings. If we concentrate hard enough, we should be able to extend the spell a little longer, giving us more time to explore the room. I know the image is limited, but look for any clues you can. Any sort of branding at all. Anything that gives it away as a hotel chain or an independent. A large hotel or a bed and breakfast. Some places have local information on the desk. Pull together as many details as you can and we'll compare notes.'

Beth felt sick at the prospect of seeing that man with her daughter again. Her lip began quivering as she nodded in agreement with Simon's idea.

'I'll do Scarlett this time,' he said, understanding.

'Is that okay? I just can't...'

'It's probably better anyway that we see the room from a different perspective. You do the spell to locate Carly and I'll locate Letty. Are you okay with that?'

'Yes. Yes. We just need to draw out the image as much as we can to see anything in the room that could possibly help.'

'That's all we need to do for now. We're just going to take it one step at a time. Are you ready?'

Beth nodded and Simon went to pick up the stone she'd dropped.

'I don't think I need that,' she said. 'I feel so charged up, I could probably teleport about five times in a row and not even take a breath. That bastard doesn't know what's coming to him. I've never felt the power electrify me like this before.' When they'd sucked the power out of the rooms in the office, Beth had felt irritated by the sensation. But this time she was buzzing, as if someone had plugged her into the Malancy mains and she was ready to explode with magic. It would have been exhilarating were the circumstances not so dire.

'I know,' Simon said, grasping Beth's hand. 'The green in your eyes is sparking. It connects with your emotions. Don't let it get out of hand, though. It can easily start to control you if you let it. Stay in charge.'

'I can feel what you mean. It's like it's got a life of its own within me. It's ready to burst.'

'Use it in the right way, Beth. Together we're an unstoppable force, but we need to use it correctly.'

'You've said that so many times before. I'm only just understanding now exactly what you mean. Let's get this spell done before I take off.'

'Okay. I'll go and stand over there again.'

Simon squeezed her hand one more time before backing away.

Beth closed her eyes quickly. She conjured up images of Carly, letting her brain flick through everything she knew about the woman. At the same time, she let the extraordinary power build up inside of her chest like a flaming ball of anger and fear. Her body quickly ignited into a golden glow as the power took charge. Her images of Carly strengthened as deep crimson swathed her body, before it reached its intensifying peak and blasts of red illuminated the entire garden.

It was at this point that the image of where a person was located normally popped into the spellmaker's head. But all Beth got was an empty hole. It wasn't even blackness - it was nothingness. She held it there for a few moments, hoping there was just some sort of weird delay, but nothing came to her mind at all.

She snapped her eyes open, releasing the spell and

immediately extinguishing the ruby highlights around her. She turned to Simon who was looking straight back at her, an equally concerned expression covering his face.

'I couldn't see anything,' she said. 'What does that mean? Did I do it wrong?'

Simon walked over to her with steady, meaningful steps. 'I saw the same.'

'It wasn't blackness, like she was in a dark room. It was nothing. There was just emptiness in my head.'

'I know.'

'What does that mean?'

'I know exactly what that means.'

Beth's heart pounded as she asked, 'Are they dead?'

'No. Don't worry. Not at all. All it means is that someone has blocked the spell. Damien can't be working alone.'

'Carly's a Malant. Do you think he made her do it?'

'He clearly has something over her. As we both know, Carly is a strong willed woman. I can't see anyone easily getting the better of her. But this can't be Carly's doing. It takes immense power to be able to conceal people from a location spell. She'd either need some serious elements behind her or a team of Malants.'

'So you think Damien is being helped out by someone else?'

'I'm thinking more than one person. But either way, if enough power can be rendered to conceal them, then I'm guessing the same level of magic was used to teleport Damien out of prison. The only way any of this could be possible is if he has a strong force supporting him.'

'What are we going to do?'

'He has strong support, but we're the most powerful Malants in existence. One of us alone has more power than the entire Malant population put together. Do you think he stands even a remote chance against us both?'

Beth took a deep breath as she felt a small drop of relief from Simon's words. This was bad, but they had the power to stop anything. And with Simon's clever thinking added into the mix, she knew it was just a matter of time before they defeated this threat. She had to think rationally.

'Okay, but if we can't see where they are, what do we do next? Would it be worth locating Damien?'

'If he's concealed the two people with him, I'd say he's neatly concealed himself too. This is typical behaviour from him. I think next we need to leave magic aside and start building together some facts. Firstly, let's find out how Carly left. I'm going to check the CCTV footage. Then we'll go and see Jim. Maybe he's heard from Carly. Let's explore every avenue we can.'

'Right.'

The pair dashed towards the study at the front of the house and accessed the camera footage. Simon simply placed his hand on the recording device and it scanned through to the moment that Carly left.

Beth was only capable of short, sharp breaths as they watched Carly make her way out of the door, carrying Scarlett in her arms. She headed towards the gate, stood back as it slowly opened, and then she stepped out onto the road, turning left.

'What's she doing?' Beth asked.

'Taking Scarlett out for a walk, maybe?'

'No, she'd use the pushchair. She wouldn't carry Scarlett around. That's ridiculous.'

'Maybe they spotted something. Maybe she heard something and she was going to check. She wouldn't leave Scarlett on her own.'

'But she's got her bag with her,' Beth said. 'She looks quite prepared. Far from just popping out to check on something. It's really odd. There's absolutely nothing around at all. The nearest shop is a few miles away. Where on earth can she be going?'

'Whatever the case, Damien must have been nearby. He must have picked them up.'

'Maybe he hypnotised her or something. She could be in a trance. She's walking calmly. She doesn't seem distressed.'

'You said this is odd,' Simon noted.

'Yes. Well it is.'

'We don't actually know that for sure, though. Maybe she often carries Scarlett in her arms and goes for a walk. Let's see.'

Simon closed his eyes and concentrated, his hand once again pressed on the computer system.

Hundreds of images quickly flicked through the screen of Carly leaving the house. And every single time she left in the car. There wasn't one incident of her leaving on foot through the gate.

'She hasn't got her car today,' Beth reasoned. 'Maybe that's connected.'

'All we're getting at the minute are a lot more questions and very few answers,' Simon said. 'We need to speak to Jim.'

'I think you're right. You get the car started, I'll lock up.'

Simon nodded. He kissed Beth swiftly before heading out to the car. As Beth made her way to the doorway behind him, she thrust her hand out towards the back of the house, ensuring that the back door was properly locked, and then she summoned her bag onto her arm, not able to remember where she'd left it. Finally she grabbed the house keys from by the entrance.

She pulled the front door tightly shut, pressing her hand against it momentarily to ensure the security system flicked on. Being magic certainly saved a lot of time.

She then headed to Simon's Jaguar F-Type Coupe that was already facing the opening gates, ready to leave. She jumped in the passenger seat and Simon accelerated forward.

Jim lived closer to London, on the edge of Buckinghamshire, just before the greenery rolled into the boroughs of the city. Simon drove quickly, albeit safely, willing a few green lights along the way, such was his privilege.

They made it there in an impressive eighteen minutes. They pulled up onto Jim's drive, next to his Mazda. It was a far humbler two bedroom house compared to the Birds' mansion, and it sat nestled in the middle of a modern estate.

They rang the doorbell, but there was no answer. Simon placed his hand on the door.

'I can sense he's in there.' Simon knocked on the door and rang again. 'Jim,' he called. 'Jim, it's Simon and Beth.'

'I hope he's okay,' Beth said, concerned for one of their dearest friends.

The door clicked and Jim let it fall open. He backed away. 'Come in,' he muttered.

He disappeared into his living room and Beth and Simon turned to one another. This was extremely unusual. Jim was always nothing but the perfect host.

'Are you okay?' Beth asked as they entered the house, closing the front door behind them.

They headed into the small, homely living room to find Jim slumped on the settee, dressed casually in jogging suit bottoms and a t-shirt. Jim was normally so formal and bright, and Beth felt her heartbeat quicken as she sensed something else was deeply wrong. This day hadn't been a rollercoaster. It had been a full on terrifying adrenaline assault course.

Beth moved around so she could see Jim. His head was hung low. He couldn't look at them.

'Have you been crying?' she asked, catching the slight puffiness to his cheeks.

'She's left me,' Jim mumbled.

'What do you mean?' Simon asked, standing firm towards the back of the room, giving Jim some space.

'Carly. She's broken up with me.'

'What?' Beth asked, barely able to believe it. 'But we

saw you yesterday. You seemed so loved up.'

'I thought we were. Things were going really well. We'd even started talking about moving in together. Then suddenly out of the blue this morning she messaged me to says it's over. She didn't even have the courtesy to break up with me to my face.'

'What?' None of this was making any sense to Beth. These weren't the actions of the Carly they knew. Damien was definitely interfering somewhere.

'I thought something was up last night,' Jim continued. 'I should have known. She was acting very weirdly. She stays here quite a lot, but last night she said she needed to be at home. She said she was tired and her place is so much closer to yours for the morning. I offered to stay at hers, but she wouldn't let me. She said she knows I hate the longer commute on a Monday. It is a fair way to London Bridge from hers, but I'd do anything for her. I suppose I didn't think too much of it at the time, but now I'm questioning everything. Did I upset her or something? She won't tell me. She won't answer my calls. All I got was a text from her telling me that she is in love with someone else and that was that. I don't know what to do with myself.'

'She's in love with someone else?' Beth queried dubiously, now more sure than ever that Damien was manipulating this whole situation. 'I don't believe it. You've been together for eighteen months. This isn't Carly.'

'I wouldn't have thought so, but...'

'Things are more complicated than you know,' Simon said.

Jim turned to look at him as Simon walked around to address Jim properly. 'What do you mean?'

'Jane's been trying to call you all morning.'

'Sorry. I know I should be on the ball with Malancy stuff. I just...'

'This morning non-Malants started to develop powers,'

Beth said.

'What?' This clearly caught Jim's attention.

'Then we found out that Damien has escaped from prison,' Simon added.

Jim's jaw dropped open. He took a breath before saying, 'Not a coincidence, I'm assuming.'

'It gets worse,' Beth said.

'How can anything be worse than that?' Jim asked.

'We got home to find Carly and Scarlett missing. We did a location spell and they were both with Damien.'

'Damien's kidnapped them? Where are they?' Jim snapped to his feet, ready for action.

'All we know is that they're in what we think is a hotel room,' Simon said. 'When we tried to repeat the location spell, we found out they'd been concealed.'

'Concealed? That takes quite a lot of power.'

'Power that Damien couldn't have.'

'So there's a team?' Jim asked.

Simon's phone started to ring from his pocket. 'It would appear so,' he said as he pulled it out. 'It's Ralph,' he told them before he answered it. 'Simon speaking.'

Beth watched Simon's face turn from interested to alarmed as he listened to Ralph.

'There's absolutely no way that can be true,' Simon said into the phone. 'How can that be possible?' Beth felt the terror tremble her again. It was so rare that Simon sounded distressed. 'I see. I know. You have to find out more. This couldn't be any worse. This is exceptionally dangerous. I want every single person at Malancy HQ working on this. Nothing else matters, do you understand. This is our worst nightmare playing out. We have to stop this, and I mean now.'

Beth's legs almost gave in on her. She sat down on Jim's armchair that was just behind her as she tried to process what could possibly be so bad that the strongest man alive was quivering at the prospect.

'What do you need from us?' Simon asked into the

phone. 'Right. No problem. Just get working. I want updates whenever you have them. This has to end.'

Simon hung up the phone and he turned to Beth and Jim. His face was pale and fierce. Beth could see the flesh of his hands pulsating under the force of his emotion, and his eyes seem to swirl in a fiery rage.

'What did Ralph say?' Beth asked, although she could hardly bear to hear the answer.

'It's Damien,' Simon said.

'What about him? Have they found him? Is Scarlett all right?'

'I'd say our daughter's in about as much danger as humanly possible.'

Beth wobbled to her feet. 'Oh God. What's he done?' She could hear her heart pounding; thick and fast pumps that made her energy spike in a way she worried she would struggle to control. And from the throbbing flesh of Simon's hands, she knew he was feeling the same way.

'Ralph can't find any reason as to how this is even possible... but Damien's got his powers back.'

'What?'

'Not just his powers back,' Simon added, before a slight gulp of hesitation. He turned to address Beth very directly. 'Almighty power. It seems his powers now mirror our own. Ralph's tracked the thread. Damien now has innate abilities just like us. He's now our equal and he has our little girl.'

SEVEN

'That can't be right,' Beth stated, flatly refusing to believe it. 'That can't possibly be true. We're unique. We're special. We were born this way. How can he just adopt such incredible power, just like that?'

'I don't know. But there was no doubt. Ralph said he'd checked it a hundred times. Damien has unstoppable power.' Simon began pacing around, as if the steps would somehow give him answers.

'No he doesn't,' Beth argued back. 'Don't be stupid. For starters, he doesn't have a partner. There's only one of him. There are two of us. Together, combined, we're amazing. How can he ever be as powerful?'

'Because we're still two individuals. We draw off each other's strength, and there's nothing to say that he won't be able to do exactly the same. He might not have figured it all out yet, but we only have to touch each other and we both get a surge in energy. It's very possible that he'll be able to do exactly the same.'

'Then I won't let him touch me. He won't get near me.'

'We're going to have to get near him to get Scarlett back. This is Damien we're talking about. Everything will work in his favour. It always does. We had to strip him of all his power before just to have a fighting chance. Now he's our equal in every way.'

'Then how are we going to win?' Beth asked.

'We can't,' Simon said with a fear in his eye. It was the sort of fear that Beth thought she'd never see in her husband and it sent chills through her.

'There must be a way,' Beth reasoned. 'There is no way that he can be better than us. We're smarter, and we have more experience. How on earth can you say he's our equal?'

Simon paused. He took a breath and his face became grave. 'You're right. He isn't our equal. We have morals guiding us. We actually care. Damien has nothing guiding him at all. I'd say literally anything is now possible.'

'No!' Beth snapped back at him. 'I refuse to believe that he could be more powerful than us. That's just ridiculous. He's one man. Besides, it takes a lot of getting used to these powers. From someone also new to it, trust me, it's not easy.'

Simon shook his head. 'He's been a Malant his whole life. He knows how it works. You've only known about your powers for a few years. He's had a lifetime of experience and now nothing is stopping him.'

'Don't say that. You sound defeated before we've even started. No one knows our power like you do. There must be some way that we can increase our abilities. Work together somehow to get one over him.'

Simon stopped moving and Beth could tell that an idea had just struck him.

'There is one way that we can increase our power,' he muttered.

'How?' Beth asked.

'No,' Jim warned, but Beth was too focused on the hope that Simon was giving her to truly acknowledge the concern in Jim's tone.

'It's the only way to beat him.' Simon paused and took a heavy breath. 'After all this time, no matter how powerful we seem to be, he keeps getting one over us. There is now only one way left to beat him.'

'What is it? Whatever it is, let's do it,' Beth said, desperately.

'We've always been at a disadvantage. It's time to fight fire with fire.'

'Simon, no!' Jim yelled, standing up. He glared at Simon fiercely, but Simon just turned away and ignored him.

'What are you going to do?' Beth asked, cautiously.

Simon glanced at Jim just once before he turned to Beth and said in a calm and measured voice, 'I have to turn to dark magic. It's the only way to ensure that we get Scarlett back. It's the only way to keep us safe. To keep everyone safe.'

'No!' Beth said with shock. 'No, you're not doing that. That's the one thing we should never do.'

'I have to,' Simon reasoned. 'Don't you see? It's always been calling me. That intensity you feel, it's the dark magic wanting you to give in. All I have to do is let go.'

'No!'

Beth watched as Simon's frame seemed to relax.

'No! Let's talk about this,' she said as panic jolted her. 'There has to be another way.'

She tried to get her brain to think. There had to be a million other things that they could do. She knew virtually nothing about dark magic, other than the fact that it was completely illegal and it meant very bad things. Damien had been imprisoned for using dark magic against them. Simon couldn't do the same. They had to be better.

Her body froze as the pulsating across Simon's hands and arms immediately stopped. Everything in the room seemed to grind to a halt and all Beth could do was watch. She didn't know what was about to happen, nor what on earth she could do about it, but she knew she was right to feel afraid.

Red flecks began sparking across Simon's skin, as if to mark the eerie beginnings of a new era. His eyes became jet black pools, as if deep, deadly ink had dripped into them.

'Simon, don't do this. Stop this now!' she cried.

'It wants me, Beth. I have to listen to it. It's the only way to get Scarlett back.'

'No!'

Beth stepped over to Simon, desperate to make him see sense, but before she had a chance to grab him, he pushed her away. She fell backwards against his tremendous force, although he'd barely touched her.

As she scrambled to her feet, she felt the change. The man before her wasn't the man she'd married. Everything felt so different. It was like she was losing him.

'Simon, stop this!' she pleaded, desperate tears now filling up her eyes. 'Simon, this isn't the way to win. This isn't how you'll get Scarlett back. We have to be the better people.'

'No, Beth. We have to be more, not better. We have to overpower him, and this is the only way to secure all our futures. Can't you understand how dangerous this is?'

'What you're doing is dangerous!'

Simon's veins became a fiery red colour, highlighting the crimson poison that was now flowing through his body. As the darkness slowly devoured him, his whole expression became violent. He may have been stern naturally, but Beth had never seen him look so brutal. This could not end well.

'Simon, stop this now,' she said, moving over to him again and grabbing his arms. 'Listen to me. Listen to me! You need to stop this. This isn't you. You're letting the power take charge. What you've always warned me not to do.'

'Get off me, Beth,' he said, his voice stone cold.

'No. Not until you come back to me.'

'I'm warning you. I'm doing this to save our daughter and I won't let anyone, including you, stand in my way. You're clearly too stupid to understand this. But you will.

When we defeat Damien once and for all, you will.'

'What are you doing?' Tears pricked at her eyes as she felt the man she loved disappear right before her.

'Let me go,' Simon hissed.

'No. Come back to me. Stop this now!'

Simon pushed her away again, sending her flying across the room using just the mere tips of his fingers. She landed awkwardly on the carpet with a heavy thud.

'What are you doing, Simon?' she cried, as she stared into the black heart of the man that she barely recognised as her husband.

'I'm doing what I should have done a long time ago. I'm doing what needs to be done. I'm doing this to save everyone.'

With that, Simon vanished. He just disappeared clean into the air.

'Where's he gone? Where's he gone?' Beth said as she tried to find her feet, despite the agony of her fractured arm.

Jim helped her steady herself.

'Are you okay?' Jim asked. 'That wasn't Simon. I know he didn't mean to hurt you.'

'It's nothing. I'm fine. I'll self-heal in a moment. I just need to take a second to process everything. You have to tell me about dark magic. What has Simon done to himself?'

'Oh Beth, this is bad. I can't believe he's done this. We have to get him back.'

'What is dark magic? I mean really.'

'There's a reason why it's illegal to use. It's not just power, Beth. It's limitless power. Whereas the power we're all familiar with taps into our emotions, this goes to a darker place. It taps into all the things we want to do but we never dare. It will wipe him of his inhibitions and all the ethics that guide his use of magic. An average Malant could cast spells far beyond anything they'd normally be able to manage. That's why we made it illegal. But with

Simon… Simon will literally be unstoppable. Who knows how far he'll go. He won't have any restraint in him at all. He's tapped into his deepest, darkest desires and he's set it all free. This could be absolutely chaotic.'

EIGHT

Simon appeared in his living room. Despite the immense power needed for his teleport spell, he didn't even feel an ounce of weakness. It was incredible. He had more power than he'd ever been able to imagine and it was utterly invigorating.

He knew he'd just broken down all of his barriers. It was something he'd feared for so long, but now he'd done it he couldn't believe how liberating it was.

A flash of his daughter came into his head and Simon took a breath. He felt a small part of his good side latch onto reality, and the regret of how he'd pushed Beth away flittered through him.

He battled within himself to keep the darkness under control. As glorious as it felt, his logic told him he could not afford to sink too deep into it. He needed the extra resource that the darkness gave him, but he knew he had to utilise its power without surrendering to it completely. He was confident he could control it. It would be hard, but very possible.

Even as he was telling himself this, his desires were calling to him. He felt such a yearning to let go of everything. It would be so easy. It would feel so good.

'No!' he said aloud, pushing the darkness back down. It would take immense inner strength to find the balance, but it would be worth it to see Damien back in prison.

The memory of Jim's eyes staring at him sparked through his brain. Determination, desperation... pleading? But of course Jim would warn him off this road. Jim didn't understand.

The exhilaration of the darkness delighted him, almost whispering at him to give in. There was just one part of his brain that refused to let go of his morality. But the darkness fought with it, reasoning that this was Simon's only chance of success, and Simon was only too happy to listen.

He told himself that the threat had become insurmountable, so the side of good must rise to the challenge. He'd literally been left with no other choice. Then he justified that he could still acknowledge the decency within him. He wasn't going to turn to a life of crime. He was just going to use his new immeasurable force to combat the biggest threat the Malancy had ever seen. That was all.

Having convinced himself that he was doing the right thing, Simon delayed no longer. He closed his eyes, ready to track down his nemesis.

There had never been a time when he hadn't been able to sense whether someone was a Malant or not. It was one of the gifts that came with his supreme ability. He could feel their magic just by being near them. But now he'd stripped back all of his boundaries, Simon knew he'd be able to sense them from anywhere.

He stood tall as he attempted to track down Damien's aura. As he focused, though, he was overwhelmed. He could sense about a million people, and those were just the relatively local ones. Of course! The whole bloody world had become Malants. How was he supposed to decipher Damien out of all of this madness?

He marched through the house, fuelled by a sudden

rage at how inconvenient this was. He entered the kitchen, threw out his hand, and the back door flew open at his command. He charged out into the garden, the throb of the world's power now suffocating him.

It was unbearable. It was too distracting.

He could normally sense Beth above everyone else. Whenever he concentrated, he could hear her heartbeat, such was their unique connection. Now Damien had joined their exclusive club, Simon was sure that he should also be able to easily pinpoint Damien. But with the confusion of a whole world of magic, it made it impossible to get any clarity.

Maybe that was why Damien had done it. Dark magic must definitely be involved from his end, and Damien was surely going to use any trick possible to distract Simon from finding him.

But Simon now had power that Damien wouldn't dare believe he was capable of. And Simon knew just how to use it.

Simon bent down to touch the grass. He drew up power from the ground, absorbing more energy from every natural source around him than he had ever needed before.

As the power surged through his fingers and across his body, it pushed him up and raised him into the air. He was levitating high above the ground, such was the force of the magic he was conducting.

The potency intensified and ignited his frame, making him a fiery God hovering above everyone and everything. He enjoyed the feel of the astonishing strength that he now commanded, and he took a few moments to relish in the ecstasy that tantalised his skin; his soul. How he wanted this moment to last forever.

He finally let the spell reach its peak, immediately shooting electrifying bolts of red through the air in every conceivable direction. The world began to shake and Simon let out an immense scream - a reaction to both the pleasure and the ferocity.

The violent red beams vanished as the spell completed, and Simon landed firmly on his feet. Even despite all that power, he still wasn't so much as out of breath. He closed his eyes and smiled.

His body slowly calmed from the high and he opened his ears to listen.

He'd sent a beacon out across the world, making it easier for him to tap into the stronger force of Beth and Damien. It need not have been such a dramatic spell, but he hadn't been able to resist trying out his new capabilities. It was such a rush.

As always, he sensed Beth straight away, and he was instantly irritated. The sound of her grated at him. That heartbeat that was constantly near him, pleading with him, needing him. She was like a shackle around his ankle that constantly prevented him from moving forward. Always moaning about being right, being moral. Where was her sense of fun?

Shaking at how much she peeved him, he closed his eyes, but her erratic heartbeat was too dominant in his ears now. He couldn't hear anything else. She was always blocking him from doing things!

She was still with Jim; he could sense that.

Poor Jim.

It was then, quite unexpectedly, that he also sensed how scared she was.

A faint tinge of love thawed Simon's new found loathing as he pictured the bravest woman he'd ever met frozen with fear.

His love slowly fought back, and, as it did, he didn't notice the red flecks across his skin fading away, and he wouldn't have known that the chocolate essence of his eyes began to dissolve away the black.

Simon Bird seemed to be returning to his old self.

Then a second loud, throbbing heartbeat started to pump through. It was just as noticeable as Beth's, but this sound made Simon's blood boil, and the crimson poison once more marked his skin.

He brushed Beth's heartbeat aside and focused on the other pounding. The only other force that was equal to his own.

It had to be Damien. And he could sense exactly where he was.

Simon's veins charged with red lava as the thought of Damien amplified the dark magic within him.

Damien wasn't far. He wasn't far at all. He was in Buckinghamshire. He couldn't be more than a few miles away.

Simon tapped into the sound. He closed his eyes and let all other thoughts disappear from his head. He had to get to Damien and he had to get there now.

NINE

Beth opened her eyes as her self-healing spell completed. The pain across her arm slowly started to vanish and she sat quietly for a moment on Jim's settee, not knowing where to start processing all that had happened.

Every Malant had the ability to self-heal. It was far easier for Beth and Simon with their stronger innate power, but it was a simple enough spell for any regular Malant to conduct as long as they had a reasonably potent element in their grasp.

It was one of the special gifts that Malants had, and for a fleeting moment Beth considered how it might be a positive that every single person alive now had this same ability. The Malancy might be dangerous in the wrong hands, but it also offered so much goodness.

Beth found herself shaking her head. She'd just been cruelly shown that the Malancy wasn't just dangerous in the wrong hands. It had shocked her how her own husband, who was fundamentally a very decent person, could so easily submit to the darkness of the magic. She quickly decided that it wasn't a good thing for the world to have access to this power. She knew they had to remedy the issue as soon as possible. As soon as Scarlett was safe. Whether that was working with her husband or not.

If only Simon hadn't taken such drastic action. If only he hadn't just vanished.

Beth simply didn't know what to do next.

She looked up at Jim who was watching her with concern.

'What did you mean by deepest, darkest desires?' she asked. 'Simon already has enough money and power to literally do anything he wants. What more could dark magic give him?'

'The ability not to care,' Jim said, sitting down next to her. 'The complete eradication of restraint. The chance to conjure up spells that cause pain and anguish. Simon's a good person - a really good person - but he's suffered a great deal by being different, and he's got a lot of pain and bitterness within him. If he even takes an ounce of it out on Damien, who knows how bad this could get. Then let's not even mention the fact that the head of the Malancy has turned to dark magic. If anyone finds out, this could cause a catastrophic wave across our community.'

'There has to be a way to stop him.' Beth shook her head again with frustration. 'He wouldn't listen to me, though. He just let himself go. How could he so easily just let go like that? What was he thinking?' Beth was halted by a sound. 'Is that my phone? Maybe it's Simon. Maybe it's Carly!'

'I can't hear anything.'

As Beth stood up to find her bag, she suddenly realised that she was more in tune with everything around her than she'd ever been before. Her bag was across the room and her phone was on silent. There was no way she should have been able to sense it.

She grabbed it from the side pocket.

'It's just Gayle again,' she sighed. 'Surely she can get the hint that I'm busy.' Beth noted that there were three voicemails, but work could wait. It really wasn't important right at that moment.

'Oh God, Jim, how are we going to get him to stop taking this terrible path that he's going down?'

'I don't know. That's the problem with Simon. He's always been the cleverest and most powerful person in the room. He's never had to listen to anyone. But he does listen to you.'

'He wasn't listening a few minutes ago,' Beth said before an idea sprang into her mind. 'Paul!' she screeched. 'I bet he'll listen to Paul. He's the only person in the world that Simon looks up to. We have to tell Paul.'

As the words left Beth's lips, the earth around them trembled.

'That can't be good,' Jim said. 'That's the second time we've had a tremor in the last twenty-four hours.'

'I'm sure it's not important,' Beth said, knocking Jim's concerns aside. 'These things come in waves, don't they.' But Beth didn't believe her breeziness. She was terrified that all hell was about to break loose, and a darkness in the pit of her stomach signalled just that.

'Something tells me we need to take action now,' Jim said. 'I think you might be right about getting Paul involved. He's practically a father to Simon, and Simon respects him as just that. Paul could be... Oh my God.' Jim's face turned pale with fear.

'What is it?' Beth asked.

'Your skin.'

Beth looked down at her hands. Red flecks were spotting across the flesh.

'What's happening to me?' she shrieked.

'Your eyes,' Jim gasped. 'They're flitting between green and black. Don't go to the dark side too, Beth. You can't do it.'

'I don't want to. What's happening? Why can't I control it?'

'My guess would be that you're connected with Simon so him turning to dark magic is dragging you down with him. I need to get to Malancy HQ. We need some extra resources if we're going to combat this.'

'Is that what I can feel? It's almost euphoric. I thought it was the healing spell.'

'Don't give in to it, Beth. Fight it. You have to control it or it will ruin you.'

Beth suddenly feared the exhilaration that she'd been welcoming not seconds before as her new found power attempted to take charge. It seemed to be playing with her; pulling her away from the horror of reality. It was making her want to revel in the release of letting go.

If only it had banked on how stubborn she was. 'I think I can control it for now,' Beth said, refusing to acknowledge both to herself and Jim how formidable the desire to sink was. As she battled internally, an idea came to her. 'Can I use it?'

'What do you mean?'

'I must have extra power now. If I use it, will that be bad?'

'Why do you want to tap into dark magic?'

'I don't. Not like that. I want to teleport you to Malancy HQ and then I'm going to track down Simon. I can keep him calm until you've had a chance to explain everything to Paul and you've come up with a plan.'

'I don't know.'

'Time is not on our side right now. We need to get to Simon.'

'Okay, you're right. Well, it's possible you could use it. But you must remember it's dark magic. You'll have to exercise incredible strength or it could suck you right under. You must only use the power that you require. And only in short bursts. It will take deep concentration. Can you do that?'

'I think I can manage it.'

'Do not give in to it. It is imperative that you remain in control at all times. This is highly dangerous.'

'I know. I don't want to do this, but we're running low

on options. If you think I've gone too far, you must let me know.'

'Oh, I will.'

'Right. Let's give it a go. Hold my hand.'

Beth took Jim's hand and she closed her eyes. She could feel the power snaking through her. It was enthralling; almost too tempting to give in. But her head was staying strong.

She imagined Jane's office at Malancy HQ, where she had no doubt they'd find Paul and Jane. She barely had to summon any emotion at all and within seconds they appeared.

'Beth?' Jane said with surprise from her desk, where Paul was sitting next to her. They were studying her computer. 'Is everything okay? Where's Simon? Is Scarlett okay?'

'Things are not okay,' Beth replied. 'Simon's turned to dark magic.'

'What?' This made both Jane and Paul stand to their feet.

'And Damien's got Scarlett.'

'Oh, Beth,' Jane said with a mixture of sorrow and fear.

'The bastard!' Paul yelled. 'Why can't he leave you alone? What is he thinking? What is Simon thinking? He can't beat Damien by turning to dark magic.'

'On the contrary, I think he has every intention of bringing Damien down once and for all,' Jim said.

'But at what cost?' Paul snapped.

'We did a location spell to find that Carly and Scarlett are with Damien,' Beth explained, 'and then we found out about Damien's increased power. It sent Simon off the rails.'

'You're turning too,' Jane gasped, focusing on Beth's hands where the shards of red were teasing her.

'Not through choice,' Beth replied.

'I think her connection to Simon is pulling her down with him,' Jim said. 'We need to find a way to sever it. We cannot have both of you turning to dark magic. It's devastating enough that one of you has.'

'I need to go to him,' Beth said. 'I can feel him. I can hear his heartbeat. And I am pretty sure he's with Damien too as there are two very loud heartbeats in my head that are very close together.'

'Can you tell where they are?' Jane asked.

Beth closed her eyes to concentrate. 'I think he's near our home. I don't know, but I know I can teleport straight to him. I can tap into the sound.'

'Are you using dark magic?' Jane asked with caution. 'You can't.'

'Jim said if I just use it in short bursts then I can control it. I won't use it unless I absolutely have to. I don't want to go down that path.'

'Beth, this is illegal. Jim, what were you thinking?'

'I don't think we've got any choice at the minute,' Jim stated. 'If we want to save Simon, and keep the whole of the future of the Malancy intact, we need Beth to do this.'

'And I need you to work through a plan,' Beth said. 'Paul, you're our best chance of getting through to Simon. He wouldn't listen to me. He threw me across the room—'

'What?' Paul seemed horrified.

'But he's always listened to you. I'm going to go and be with him and stop him from getting out of hand. You need to come up with a plan to talk him out of this. You're our only hope.'

'What am I supposed to say to him?' Paul asked with concern. 'He threw you across the room?'

'We'll think of something,' Jane said. 'If you can buy us a bit of time, Beth, we'll come up with a plan.'

'Even if we do come up with a plan, how will we know where you'll be?' Paul said. 'You don't even know where he is.'

'I'll have to send you a message somehow,' Beth said, thinking through her options.

'But what if you don't? What if you can't?'

'You controlled the dark magic to get here?' Jane asked Beth.

'Yes. I just tapped into the smallest slice of it and now I'm keeping it at bay.'

'Can you repeat that?'

'I hope so.'

'Good, because I know a trick.' Jane picked up her phone and dialled a number. 'Ralph,' she said after a few seconds. 'I want you to bring up one of your most potent elements. I mean now.'

'What are you doing?' Beth asked.

'Whatever he brings up, I want you to put some magic into it. Pour it into the element. Link it to the teleport spell you're about to do and give it some gusto. The idea is that wherever you go now, to be with Simon, we'll be able to use this element to follow you. You'll be heightening the power of the element with your magic and we'll use our powers to complete the spell.'

'I can do that?' Beth asked, gobsmacked.

'How do you know about that?' Paul asked Jane.

'You learn a few things in this job.'

'Here's your element,' Ralph said, breathlessly appearing at the door. He certainly understood the word "now".

'Give it to Beth,' Jane instructed. Ralph placed a rock in Beth's hands. It appeared to be covered in silt.

'A rock?' Beth asked.

'It's not just any rock,' Ralph explained. 'It's a rare element that a Malant once came across in the Gobi Desert. I only have a few of them and it's about as potent as you can get without turning to dark magic.'

'Thank you, Ralph,' Jane quickly responded. 'Any progress from your end?'

'We're still trying to track down Damien. I've also got a team looking into exactly how he managed to get these new powers, and how he escaped from prison. Every resource I've got is focused on this.'

'Good to hear. Keep us posted.'

'Will do.'

Ralph scurried off.

'No one out of this room can know what Simon's done,' Jane said. 'Do you understand? If anyone else finds out, I'll be left with no choice but to arrest him. He can't be above the law.'

'You can't arrest him!' Beth said with shock.

'Then we'd better sort this out quickly and discreetly.'

'Tell me what I need to do.'

'Think through the spell in your mind. Where Simon is and how you're going to get there. But focus the spell on the rock.'

'So imagine I'm casting the spell, but sort of throw it towards the rock instead?'

'Exactly.'

Beth looked down at the rock in her hands. She summoned up her power, although it was flowing more freely than ever before. She zoned in on Simon's heartbeat and set herself to track it. She focused on the sound, and she readied herself to teleport. Only instead of closing her eyes and willing herself away, she instead pushed the power down to the rock in her hands.

It glowed a vibrant red colour and then black smoke puffed out of it as it crackled. The spell was done.

'I hope I did it right,' she said as she placed the rock down on Jane's desk.

'I have every faith in you, Beth. Now go to Simon. Stop him from doing anything he'll regret and we'll be with you as soon as humanly possible.'

'Just give us a few minutes to assess what he's done and what I can possibly say to him,' Paul said. 'I never thought this would ever happen. We can't afford to cock this up.'

'I'm going to start looking into how we can sever the two of you with regards to the dark magic,' Jim said. 'I'm afraid we're going to lose the both of you.'

'Okay, but don't do anything without my permission

first,' Beth said. 'At the moment, the dark magic I'm feeling may be our only way to keep in contact with Simon. Let's not do anything rash. Making snap decisions is what got us into this mess in the first place.'

'Be prepared for anything, Beth,' Jane warned. 'Just keep him under control until we can get there with some sort of plan. If anything happens to Damien, Simon will have to pay. I can't make an exception for him. As much as I really want to, he must be responsible for his actions, just as any Malant is. Remember that, Beth.'

Beth wanted to cry. The idea of her husband being locked up in prison was horrendous. She was terrified about what she was going to appear into, but she really was left with no choice.

All she had to do was keep things neutral until back up arrived. That was all she had to do.

This was Simon. The love of her life. Surely it couldn't be that hard.

Beth took a deep breath. 'Don't be long.'

'Give us a few minutes to pull up some facts on dark magic and get our heads around what we're facing, and we'll be with you,' Paul said. 'A few minutes.'

'I'm holding you to that.'

'Good.'

'Right. See you in a few.'

With that, Beth closed her eyes and tapped into her new found strength, focusing on Simon's heartbeat. As much as she hated that any of this was happening, her husband needed her. It was time to go.

TEN

'What the fuck? How did you find us?' Simon heard Damien's words before he opened his eyes to see the man. He was clearly in a hotel room somewhere. Damien and Carly were both sitting on the bed: Carly with Scarlett wrapped in her arms and Damien studying an iPad.

'Give me my daughter back,' Simon said as Damien stood up. Simon wanted to run forward and grab Scarlett from Carly's arms, but he was aware of how delicate a situation this was. He couldn't take the risk of any harm coming to Scarlett.

'What?' Damien shouted, glaring at Carly. 'This is Simon and Beth's daughter?'

Carly just shrugged and Simon instantly detected that things were far from how he'd expected.

'Yes. And I want her back,' Simon said.

'Give him the girl back,' Damien said to Carly, a noticeable panic to his voice.

'No,' Carly replied.

'Why did you tell me she was your daughter?'

'Because she might as well be. She spends more time with me. You're bad parents,' Carly said to Simon. 'Always working. Always leaving her with the nanny. Too busy with your Malant business. I don't think she'll miss you. Hell, in a couple of years she won't even remember you.'

'What have you done to her?' Simon accused Damien.

'Done to her?' Damien replied with genuine shock.

'Am I not capable of making my own decisions?' Carly said, shifting off the bed and standing on the other side to where Simon was, still with Scarlett in her arms.

'What is going on?' Simon asked.

'Carly helped me escape,' Damien said. 'She told me she was your cleaner. She said she was a struggling single mum and we were going to run away and start a new life together. I really thought it was her daughter.'

'Didn't you think it was a coincidence that the girl was also called Scarlett?' Simon asked.

'I don't know what your daughter's called. I don't care,' Damien said. 'All I want is to put the past behind me. I needed to get out of that prison. I want a fresh start.' Damien turned to Carly. 'Give him the girl back. We don't need this. I don't want this. Give him the girl back and then we can properly disappear.'

'He doesn't deserve her,' Carly said.

'She's my daughter. My flesh and blood!' Simon raged, his anger now upsetting Scarlett who started to cry.

'See what you've done now?' Carly said, gently bouncing Scarlett to try to soothe her. 'She might be related to you, but you have never been much of a father.'

Simon refused to respond.

'Throwing money at things doesn't make up for love,' Carly added.

'I'm not having this argument with you,' Simon said. 'Give her back.'

'No. She's staying here with me. With us.'

'What is going on?' a voice said. Simon turned to see Beth standing next to him. He saw the black swirling in her eyes and he didn't know whether to laugh, push her away or hug her. He was feeling extremely confused and he didn't like it.

'Please, Carly,' Damien pleaded. 'We don't want to get on their bad side. Trust me, this can't end well.'

'Carly, give Scarlett to me,' Beth said.

'No. As I was just telling your husband, you aren't fit parents. She's going to be much better off with me.'

'What?' Beth gasped. 'How dare you!'

'It seems Carly helped Damien to escape,' Simon explained.

'What? Why would you do that? What about Jim?'

Carly rolled her eyes. 'Jim is nice. I kind of liked him. But Damien and I are in love.'

'How can you love Damien? Do you know what he's done?' Beth screeched, making Scarlett cry even more.

'We've all made a few mistakes-'

'Mistakes?! Damien has lied to, manipulated and hurt so many people. He is all about self-gain. He's the most selfish person I've ever met.'

'I was,' Damien said. 'I was. I know I was. I've made some terrible mistakes. But prison has made me re-evaluate everything. Carly has made me happy. All I wanted was to get out of prison and run away with her. She told me Scarlett was her daughter.'

'How do you even know each other?' Simon asked.

'I used to go with Jim to visit his brother in prison,' Carly explained.

'Jim visits George?' Simon asked with surprise.

'Yeah, every month or so. I know George is like the evil twin-'

'Not like. He literally is Jim's evil twin,' Beth corrected.

'Either way, they're still related. Jim's a nice bloke. A bit boring, but he's decent.'

'And on one of these visits, you met Damien?' Simon said.

'Yeah, he was sitting across the room with his folks. I was immediately captivated by him. I mean, I'd heard of him. What Malant hasn't? The only man to ever rock the almighty Simon Bird. I had to get to know him better.'

'It started out with some innocent letters and developed from there,' Damien said. 'If I'd known this was your daughter.' Damien turned to Carly. 'Will you just give her back?'

'No!'

'Right, I've had enough!' Simon had no choice but to raise his voice now as Scarlett's bawling was getting louder and louder. He turned to Damien. 'Are you going to end this or am I?'

'What do you want me to do? Believe me, I want what you want. I want you to take your daughter and I want to go. I don't want any more trouble with you.' Damien was almost trembling and Simon decided to believe him. As much as Damien could never be trusted, Simon could clearly see his endgame here wasn't to take Scarlett.

Now knowing that Damien was no threat to them, Simon took actions into his own hands.

'Be ready,' he ordered quietly to Beth before he turned to Carly and concentrated on her arms.

'Ow!' Carly screamed. Simon was burning her flesh – all under control so it would never hurt Scarlett.

Carly dropped the girl, the pain so intense, and Simon re-focused his attention to halt Scarlett in the air, not letting her fall.

Beth, always in tune with Simon's actions, raced forward to grab Scarlett, knocking Carly - who was recovering from the pain - out of the way.

'We've got her,' Beth said, deep relief in her voice. She kissed and cuddled their sobbing daughter as she turned to walk back to Simon, when Carly suddenly lunged forward.

'You bitch! She's mine!' Carly stabbed Beth right in the back. Beth yelped in agony before she began falling helplessly to the floor.

Panic jolted Simon. Without thinking about it, he used his power to speed across the room, catching his wife and daughter just before they hit the ground.

Blood started pooling across the carpet and all the red

flecks vanished from Beth's skin as she grew eerily pale.

Simon's head span at a million miles. There was so much going on.

'Heal, Beth. Can you heal?' he begged, grasping Scarlett with one hand and caressing his wife with the other.

Beth could barely speak. The blood was seeping out of her so fast and Simon knew he had just seconds to help her.

He looked across at the shocked faces of Carly and Damien and cast a quick spell. Both of his enemies flew to the wall on the other side of the room and Simon used his magic to pin them against it. He then popped Scarlett down. She was so desperately upset and in need of attention, but there was nothing he could do.

'Just stay here a minute, darling, while I help mummy out.' He put both of his hands on Beth, ignoring the blood that was now soaking up into his trousers.

He closed his eyes and summoned the force, casting his healing spell.

'She's got the knife!' Carly suddenly shouted out.

Simon flicked open his eyes to see Scarlett. Her tears now halted, she had crawled to the other side of Beth and was holding Carly's dagger in her hand.

'Put it down, Letty,' Simon said in the softest voice he could manage. His hands were holding Beth in a state of flux. He couldn't let go. He knew how close he was to losing her. His hands were the only things stopping Beth from slipping away, but he needed to concentrate to complete the spell.

'Letty, put it down. Listen to daddy.'

Scarlett began to study the knife, her upset now replaced with curiosity. She wiped drops of blood onto her hands and Simon's heart stopped beating.

'What were you doing with a knife?' he yelled at Carly, as he contemplated what his next move should be.

'Let me go,' Carly said. 'I'll take it off her.'

'And take her as well. I don't think so.' Then Simon

saw his only option. 'Damien, you do it.' He let Damien loose from the wall; the lanky man instantly lurching forward against the force of the freedom. Simon never thought he'd see the day he was trusting Damien with something, but this was a desperate situation.

'Damien, get the knife off Scarlett.'

'No,' Damien said.

'Get the fucking knife!'

'You want to frame me. I know. You want my fingerprints on it.'

'You can wipe them off after. You can keep it. I'll never track you down. Just get that knife away from my daughter.'

'You'll let me go?'

'Yes. If you get that knife away from my daughter, I'll let you go. I promise. But do it now!'

Damien cautiously headed over to Scarlett.

'Can I have that?' he said to the girl. He took the knife easily from Scarlett's hands and then held it like it was poisonous. 'What do I do with it now?'

'Anything. Just get it away from her.'

'I don't want my fingerprints on it.'

'Throw it away. I don't care! Just get it away from her.'

Damien threw the knife across the bed, across to the other side of the room, and Simon focused back on Beth.

He was instantly pulled from his concentration again when he heard a blood-curdling scream.

He looked up in horror to see Paul dropping to the ground, the knife right in his chest.

ELEVEN

'No!' Jane screamed. 'Save him! Simon, save him!'

'I'm here with Beth,' Simon shouted desperately as he drew on all the power within him to speed up the healing spell. Luckily, healing spells only worked with good magic.

'I didn't mean to. I didn't mean to,' Damien said, sheer panic in his voice. 'Where did they come from? I can't control it. This bloody power is so intense. I didn't want any of this.'

'Paul!' Jane screamed, kneeling down to be with him. 'Simon, help!'

Simon blocked everything out as he centred his thoughts on Beth. He couldn't lose her.

Finally the spell began to work. The colour flourished back into Beth's face and Simon felt her wound disappear. 'Are you okay?' he said.

She nodded and sat up, a little breathless.

'Keep an eye on Scarlett.' Simon raced over to Paul's side. He dropped to his knees to begin another healing spell, when he stopped.

'No,' he gasped.

'Heal him!' Jane ordered.

'Paul?' Simon put his hands all over Paul, trying to

sense some life. But it just wasn't there. 'No!'

'Heal him. Why aren't you healing him?'

Simon pressed his hands on Paul again, desperate for his magic to work. But he couldn't sense anything at all. Not one spark of existence.

'No,' Simon whimpered.

'Simon, help him.'

'I can't.'

'Heal him! Do it now!'

'I can't!'

'Why not? Why won't you help him?'

'He's dead.'

A chilling silence grasped the room as Simon fell back. He kept blinking, praying for this not to be true. Praying that this was all a horrid nightmare and reality would soon kick-start around him again, like any normal day.

'Heal him!' Jane screamed, touching Paul all over frantically.

Beth raced over to Simon. He could see she wanted to do something or say something, but there were no words. No words.

He pushed Beth away and scrambled to his feet.

Deep, agonising pain flared in patches as he swiftly moved between the terror of the truth and total disbelief.

Paul couldn't be dead.

Paul couldn't be dead.

His uncle could not be dead.

Simon looked at Paul lying on the carpet. He was like a hollow shell, the life in him having all been extinguished. The emptiness was so apparent to Simon with his heightened senses.

He wanted to throw up.

Tears started blocking his vision and he paced around, not knowing what to do with himself.

It hurt. It hurt so much.

He flicked his head towards Paul again, determined to find a way around this. But when he witnessed his uncle's lifeless body, he had to realise all over again that there was nothing he could do. He was utterly powerless for the first time in his life.

There was no way to control this. It was final.

'Where's Scarlett?' Beth asked, snapping around, looking everywhere. 'Where have they gone?'

Carly, Damien and Scarlett were all missing. Simon realised he must have let her go when his focus had been taken by Paul.

He couldn't breathe. He couldn't find any air. He felt totally lost and bitterly terrified.

'Where are they!' Beth yelled.

He couldn't think. He couldn't tap into his normally clear, sharp mind. It was like a junk yard of distress and, at best, he could trudge through his sorrow. Nothing else was there. His brain was clogged up and everything was gone.

He grabbed his head, the pain almost too much to bear.

He screamed, trying to release the agony within him, but nothing was easing. It just kept increasing, like a relentless tsunami of misery that kept beating itself against him.

He could see Beth looking at him. Hoping for the answers that he normally gave her.

Carly had been right. They were terrible parents. And he was a terrible husband. There was no way he could help now.

He glanced down at Jane, sobbing over Paul. She too glared up at him, the same look of hope. Simon always had a solution. He was always the one who could find the loophole.

But he knew that this time it was most definitely unalterable.

It was too much.

Paul couldn't be dead.

What was he going to do without his uncle?

He felt the tears drip onto his lip as he cried.

There was nothing Simon could do.

Scarlett was gone and Simon didn't know if he had the fight in him anymore.

He grabbed his head and screamed again, before everything became far too overwhelming.

He summoned all the power within him and he flashed images of anything in his head. He had to get away. He had to get out of there. He had to think!

In the blink of an eye he was gone.

TWELVE

Beth watched the empty space where Simon had been. Her immediate instinct was to follow him, wherever he had gone. She wanted to be there for her husband and they needed to find Scarlett. She'd never seen him in such a state, and she wasn't feeling much better herself. But then her eyes fell to Jane, who was sobbing over Paul's body on the floor.

It was devastating. There was no way she could leave Jane all alone.

Beth took a calming breath as she rationalised her thoughts. Maybe Simon had gone to find Scarlett again. Even if he hadn't, surely Carly wouldn't allow any harm to come to Scarlett. She'd always seemed to love Scarlett.

Beth watched as Jane removed the knife that was buried deep in Paul's chest. Jane threw it aside and Beth felt grateful that at least Carly didn't have it anymore. Then she felt dreadful.

Beth battled with her tears as she tried to decide what to do. Her first priority should be Simon and Scarlett. But how could she leave Jane right now?

Jane was gasping for air, she was crying so much. It tore Beth to shreds. She glanced at Paul's body and a wave of realisation smashed over her, leaving her winded.

It didn't make any sense. How could Paul be gone? Just like that.

Beth slowly knelt down next to Jane, choking back her sobs as the events all became more and more real.

For the first time, Beth noticed that her smart work clothes were drenched in her own blood. She looked horrific. She'd almost lost her own life.

A chill grasped her. Saving her had meant Simon hadn't been able to save his uncle.

It should be her lying on the carpet, not Paul.

She felt sick with grief.

Jane turned and cried into Beth's shoulder. Beth wanted to say something, but nothing seemed appropriate. All she could do was let Jane cry, and the pair sat there for what felt like an age doing nothing but letting the sorrow soak through them.

Eventually Jane's tears eased. She sat back and took a few deep breaths. It was then that Beth recognised Jane's innate formality taking over. Jane was so often in business mode, and Beth assumed that it was probably a helpful way of distancing herself from the pain.

'I should call someone,' Jane said, standing to her feet. 'The Malancy can deal with this. We don't need to involve the mainstream authorities.'

'Do you want me to call them?' Beth asked.

'No. I'll do it.' Jane didn't move as she stared down at Paul. 'What happened? Why would Damien do this?'

'I don't know. It all happened so quickly. It was Carly who stabbed me, not Damien. All I really remember then is Simon trying to heal me. I think Damien was trying to get the knife away from Scarlett. I don't actually think he meant to cause any harm. It's all Carly. As much as I find it impossible to believe, I think Carly was behind all of it. Damien actually looked terrified.'

'There's still a warrant out for his arrest. We will have to add new charges now. Manslaughter maybe. We'll need to establish the facts.' Jane's lip wobbled as she said this, but she gripped firmly onto her composure.

'Magic didn't do this. Are you sure you don't want me to involve the mainstream police?'

'No,' Jane firmly replied. 'Firstly, I want to be the one to punish Damien when we find him. Secondly, I want to know exactly where he is at all times. And finally, magic is still involved somewhere along the line. How could we possibly explain how the killer got away?'

Jane's whole frame trembled as she finished her sentence. The tears were battling for their freedom but she stood tall.

'Shall I cover him up?' Beth said, reaching for the bed covers.

Jane nodded as she pulled out her mobile from her trouser suit pocket.

Beth placed the duvet over Paul's body, her own tears silently mourning him as she did.

She couldn't feel him, as if his soul had indeed departed. It didn't seem like Paul anymore. It was just the empty shell of one of the best men she'd ever known.

She turned around as she wept a little. She didn't want Jane to see her, and thankfully Jane was pre-occupied on the phone to some Malant contacts, giving them orders to come down, collect the body and clean up.

Beth felt so desperately sad and totally panicked.

Her mind flicked to Simon and Scarlett. She really should be with her husband, and they should be tracking down their daughter again. But she couldn't leave Jane on her own.

Jane was now a widow. They'd only been married for a couple of years.

More of Beth's silent tears streamed down her face. She stepped into the bathroom to get a tissue and she took a few deep breaths.

Her time for crying was later. She had to be strong for now.

When Beth reappeared, Jane was sitting on the bed, staring at the duvet covering Paul's body. She looked half missing, such was her grief.

'Everything okay with Malancy HQ?' Beth asked.

Jane nodded. 'They're on their way.'

Beth moved over to sit next to Jane and the pair waited in silence. A wretched, sorrowful silence. Nothing else seemed appropriate with Paul still there on the floor. All they could do was wait.

Beth ran through ideas in her head as to how she could excuse herself. But every time she looked down at Paul's covered up body, she knew she couldn't do it. She couldn't leave Jane alone with Paul.

Maybe Simon was rescuing Scarlett right at that moment and he was taking her back to their house. It could all be okay. It could all be over.

At least Beth's family was alive.

It was nearly an hour later before there was a knock at the door. Beth quickly stood up to answer it.

She recognised the faces of some of the Malancy government team, but she didn't know all of their names.

'We're very sorry for your loss, Mrs Bird,' the man who seemed to be in charge said to Jane as he entered the room. 'We'll deal with this now.'

'Look after him,' Jane ordered.

'Of course. There's a car outside ready to take you both back to Malancy HQ.'

'Wouldn't you be better going home?' Beth said, before she immediately shook her head. 'No, perhaps not. Malancy HQ it is.'

Beth still couldn't find her escape. She was getting desperate now.

A moment of terror swept through her as her mind quickly processed the idea that Simon might have done something stupid. She knew how his anger could overwhelm his judgement. Even more so now he'd let the darkness in.

What if he'd attacked Damien in revenge? What if Scarlett had got caught up in the crossfire this time?

Beth took a deep breath. She couldn't think like that. She clenched her fists as she pushed those thoughts from her mind. She had to stay positive.

'Are you ready?' she asked Jane.

All Jane could do was nod.

Beth took Jane's arm and led her out of the room. They headed outside the hotel to find a car waiting immediately at the entrance.

The journey back to London was again silent, and Beth started to feel awkward. She wanted to offer kind words. She wanted in some way to make Jane feel better. But then she put herself in Jane's shoes and she couldn't cope. Losing Simon would be the end of Beth's world. How could any words possibly soothe Jane at this moment?

It took them about an hour to get back to Malancy HQ, and Beth was fidgety with how much she needed to see Simon.

The car pulled up outside the entrance of the building and Beth finally saw her chance to escape. But just as she was opening her mouth to tell Jane that she'd be leaving, Jane exited the car without a word and entered the premises.

Sighing, Beth ended up following Jane right up to her office.

Jane sat down at her desk and seemed to get straight into work. This had to be it. The words "I need to go and find Simon and Scarlett now" were just about to flow out of Beth's mouth, when Ralph came running in.

'Reception told me you were back,' he said, breathlessly, clearly having run upstairs again.

Jane just glanced at him from behind her computer.

'Firstly, I heard the news,' he continued. 'Please accept my deepest condolences. It's horrendous to think that something so awful could happen.'

Jane didn't reply. She just flicked her eyes back to her

monitor.

'There is no way I'd be coming to you with this if I didn't think you'd absolutely want to know,' Ralph continued.

'Perhaps it's best if you come back later,' Beth said. 'I don't think Jane's in the right frame of mind to process work at the minute.'

'I understand,' Ralph said. 'But I know you'll want to hear this. I know how Damien got his powers back. I know why he's so strong.'

This caught both Beth's and Jane's attention. Ralph walked closer to Jane's desk, to address her properly, and Beth followed to stand next to him.

'We don't know how Damien got his hands on it yet, but we traced that an element was used in some sort of spell to give Damien his immense power.'

'Well obviously magic was involved,' Jane bit back. 'How is this useful information?'

'Because it isn't just any element that was used. I've been testing it in my lab.'

'What were you testing?' Beth asked. 'What sort of element is it?'

'It's a stone. What would seem to anyone else just your average, everyday stone. It's fairly large, and beautifully smooth and round, but in no other way would it render any sort of attention.'

'What makes it so special, then?' Jane asked, impatiently.

'The stone had been made potent. You could say manufactured so. Resulting in it being more potent than it naturally should have been.'

'What?' Jane sat forward, her attention engaged. 'How?'

Ralph gazed towards Beth, seemingly a little uncomfortable. 'Erm... We have some answers. But we still need to do a lot of further analysis-'

'Spit it out, Ralph,' Jane barked. 'What made this stone so potent?'

He cleared his throat. 'It would seem to be... Mr Bird. Simon Bird. I have tested it thoroughly and there's no doubt. The stone was laden with Mr Bird's power. It's one of the most potent elements I've ever seen, and it was definitely made so... by Mr Bird.'

'What?' Jane asked, confused.

'That can't be right,' Beth argued.

'There are a lot of gaps in our knowledge,' Ralph said, cautiously. 'We're yet to know a great deal of what has happened here. But what I can tell you with absolute certainty is that a stone wielding an abundance of Mr Bird's power somehow got into Damien's hands, and Damien found a way to use this element to give himself Mr Bird's abilities.'

'Did you know about this?' Jane said, snapping to her feet and glaring at Beth.

'Of course I didn't,' Beth replied. 'This can't be right.'

'You heard Ralph. He is absolutely certain. And I trust him. Far more than I trust that husband of yours.'

'What?'

'He's clearly involved in this somewhere.'

'No. No he's not. There's got to be a simple explanation.'

'Simple? How is any of this simple?'

'I meant straightforward. I meant logical. Simon would never, ever, ever do anything that would give Damien powers.'

'Not the Simon that Paul and I knew, no. But now he's turned to dark magic.'

'What?' Ralph asked with shock.

'He only did that today,' Beth explained. 'To save our daughter.'

'And where is Scarlett? She's not saved is she?' Beth's stomach churned at Jane's words. 'No, he turned to dark magic for his own selfish reasons.'

'How can you possibly say that?'

'Because my husband is dead!' Jane shouted. 'And

when you track it back, Simon is ultimately to blame.'

'Simon has lost just as much as you.'

'And he cares about it so much, he could just disappear and leave us to it. What a nice man you've got there.'

Beth didn't know how to respond. She wasn't delighted that Simon had disappeared on them, but things were far from black and white. Simon only had two blood relatives alive, and both had disappeared in the space of minutes. One had been kidnapped and the other tragically murdered. She couldn't blame him for needing to escape.

If only Beth could be so bold as to do the same.

'What is going on?' Jim said, coming through the doorway. 'I can hear shouting from my office.'

'Paul has been murdered,' Jane stated.

'What?' Jim gasped.

'It was an accident,' Beth insisted.

'And Simon is to blame,' Jane said.

'No! No he's not.'

'Simon killed his uncle?' Jim asked, turning pale.

'No he didn't,' Beth yelled. 'Damien did it. But I don't think he meant to.'

'Damien might have wielded the knife,' Jane said, 'but the only reason he was out of prison and able to do that was because Simon gave him the power.'

'We don't know what happened!' Beth screamed, desperate for Jane to see sense.

Jim took a seat, overwhelmed by the information being thrown his way.

Jane picked up her phone, her stone cold eyes burning into Beth.

'I need some arrest warrants putting out,' she said to whoever answered. 'Firstly, for Miss Carly Adams.'

'What?' Jim asked, now looking dizzy.

'We'll explain,' Beth said. 'I'm so sorry, Jim.'

'For both attempted murder and she's an accomplice to murder. Yes, that's right. Next I want Mr Simon Bird arrested immediately.' Her voice was steady and bitter.

'Yes, Mr Simon Bird.'

Beth gasped for air. She froze still as she couldn't believe what she was hearing.

'He's used dark magic, he's been instrumental in helping Damien Rock escape from prison, and he's also wanted in association with the murder of Paul Bird.'

'That's not true!' Beth exclaimed. 'How can you say that?'

'I also want a security team up in my office now to arrest Mrs Bethany Bird. She has also used dark magic and may be an accomplice.'

'What? I haven't done anything.'

'Jane,' Jim warned, rising to his feet.

'I mean now!' Jane said before slamming down the phone.

'Jane, be careful,' Jim said.

'If you haven't done anything, you have nothing to fear, do you?' Jane said to Beth, a coldness emanating from her that Beth didn't recognise.

'You told me to use dark magic,' Beth said.

'You made your own free choice.'

'We did it to save our daughter.'

'Who strangely is still with Damien.'

Three men appeared at the door. They were hesitant as they approached Beth.

This was madness. Beth couldn't be arrested. She hadn't done anything wrong. Nor had Simon. They were merely guilty of trying to save their family; a family that was now being torn apart.

Beth's heart started to throb uncontrollably as the officers grabbed her wrists and handcuffed them behind her back. They were reading out her rights, but she couldn't concentrate.

This could not be happening.

She closed her eyes and thought of home. The only place in the world where she hoped she would be safe, and where she hoped she might find her husband.

Home. Their safe haven. Their wonderful home.

Her heart pounded more, tears were filling up in her eyes and her whole frame started to panic as the images of home intensified in her head.

In a flash, she appeared in her bedroom.

Everything was calm and silent and Beth fell to the floor, still handcuffed, and sobbed.

THIRTEEN

After a few minutes, Beth composed herself. She'd needed to cry, to let it all out, but now she had to get on and find Simon and Scarlett. She could fall to pieces again later. She just had to hold it together until she found Simon.

She clambered to her feet and she closed her eyes to cast a simple spell. A few seconds later, the handcuffs fell to the floor with a thud.

She rubbed her wrists, but her dignity had been hurt more than anything. How could Jane be so cold as to arrest her own family? Paul will be horrified.

Beth stopped.

Paul will never know.

Beth took a deep breath before she headed down the stairs.

'Simon,' she called. She poked her head into the living room and the kitchen, and she made the effort to look out into the garden, but she knew Simon wasn't there. She couldn't sense him anywhere nearby. She could always sense Simon when he was close.

She knew she had to find Simon first. If they were going to successfully overpower Carly and Damien and get

Scarlett back, they needed to do it together.

Beth took a few more calming breaths. She needed to concentrate. She might not have a clue where Simon was, but she felt confident that she could easily track him down. They had a special connection, and she could always hear his heartbeat if she listened hard enough.

She stood in the silent kitchen and tried to find her husband's sound.

Immediately she was blown away by how loud everything was when she tapped into it. The world of people with new Malant abilities was very intense. But one heartbeat was louder than them all.

Beth felt herself flop. She instantly knew that wasn't Simon. It wasn't a warm sensation. It was cold and hard. It clearly had to be Damien's heart that was pounding through.

Beth felt stabs across her chest as she contemplated how Damien was with her daughter. She could tell he wasn't that close anymore, but he was still out there somewhere, causing more pain. How she prayed that Scarlett was being looked after.

That was when she realised that she didn't know whom she was more afraid of: Carly or Damien.

It was a fearful day when someone was worse than Damien.

As that fear chilled her, she put Damien's heartbeat aside in her mind and she searched for Simon.

She opened her heart and her mind and she willed the sound of him to break through, but it was proving more difficult than ever before.

Finally she did hear something. It was weak, though. She could barely sense the loving feeling of her husband that she was so familiar with. It all seemed too distant and feeble.

What could that mean?

Trembling at the worry of what else was going wrong, Beth quickly decided she should check with a location spell. Whilst her head warned her that Simon might have blocked himself, she couldn't shake the fear that something else bad had happened. Whatever state Simon was in, a location spell would show her. Even if she could see nothing and he'd blocked himself, she'd get some answers. If he'd blocked himself at least it would mean he was still very much active and in control.

Beth stood in the centre of the kitchen and closed her eyes. She thought of Simon as she summoned up the power to cast the spell.

Within seconds, beaming rays of red light suffocated the kitchen and Beth had her answer.

She'd seen nothing but emptiness. The same kind of emptiness she'd seen when she'd tried to locate Carly. He'd blocked himself.

She felt both deflated and relieved.

She flopped back on a chair at the kitchen table as she contemplated her next move. If Simon was active but had a weak sounding heart, what else could that mean?

Her brain span for ages, churning through possibilities, when a very simple answer finally popped up.

Maybe he was just far away. Very far away.

She stood up. If he was just far away, that shouldn't prevent her from being able to tap into him. It would make it more difficult, and she knew she'd have to use dark magic. But she needed to be by his side.

She just had to make sure she didn't use too much dark magic.

But how much extra power would she need to connect with such a weak link? Terrified goose bumps scattered across her as she remembered what the darkness had done to Simon.

Then, out of nowhere, something Simon had once told her jumped into Beth's head. He'd once found her by just focusing in on her. He'd thought about her so much that he'd become lost in his own mind and it had pushed through the barriers.

If he could do it, she should absolutely be able to do it. Their connection ran deeper than magic. Didn't it?

Maybe she could give that a go instead. She couldn't risk using too much of her dark power, so why not utilise their sensational bond?

Beth closed her eyes and conjured up images of Simon.

She thought about his gelled brown hair that always looked perfect. His chocolate eyes and square jaw that were always hiding how he was really feeling, and that gorgeous smile that so few people ever got to witness.

She thought about how loving he was, and how protective he was of her and Scarlett. He'd give up all his money and power in an instant if it meant saving his family. Ultimately, his family meant everything to him.

And Paul had been his only family for years. After his parents had died, right up until the moment he was in his early thirties and finally met Beth, Paul had been all Simon had had.

Beth considered how devastated Simon must be. She imagined him sobbing or angry, or probably both.

Or no, he'd be staring out into space, looking lost, looking detached.

Beth opened her eyes. That wasn't her imagination. That had been him. That had been Simon!

Wow!

She closed her eyes again and recalled the image. She could see him, just as he was at that very moment. He really was so very far away.

She looked around the room he was in. It had an oak wooden floor, bright, elaborate curtains, a huge mirrored wardrobe in the corner and there were paintings all over the walls. Simon was sitting on a large bed that dominated the centre of the space.

She knew she'd been there. Where was it? It wasn't a hotel. It seemed far too lived in. She studied the room some more.

There were books all over a bookcase towards the back

wall. Books and Blu-rays.

She scanned her eyes around the image in her head and she focused in on the bookcase.

Action movies. The bookcase was covered with action movies and horror novels.

It was Paul's room! Definitely Paul's room. But where? Paul and Jane's house had carpet throughout upstairs.

New York!

It came to Beth like a flash. Simon had teleported to New York. He'd lived with his uncle in a flashy apartment on the Upper East Side for years, while his uncle had set up the American branch of the company. Simon had run the UK office from New York for many years, just coming back when he needed to.

Beth had only been there once, when she was pregnant with Scarlett. She'd been desperate to know what Simon's American life had been like, and both Bird men had decided to keep their expensive US abode for when they travelled back.

Paul had loved his New York life. It was marrying Jane that had convinced him to return to England. And as soon as Beth had arrived there, she'd been able to see why. It was such a magical place. She knew she wanted to go back. She never imagined it would be in such dire circumstances, though.

She also knew that there was only one way she was going to get there realistically. A flight would take her about a day, from booking it, to getting to the airport, to getting to the apartment at the other end. That's if she could even remember where it was.

She had to get to Simon now. Every second they weren't looking for Scarlett was a second more their daughter was in danger.

That left Beth with one option. She must tap into her dark magic again. Using good magic, they could only just about manage teleport spells when they worked together. It would completely wipe her out for hours if she tried to do it on her own, and she needed all of her strength to deal with what came next. Getting there was the easy part. Comforting Simon and finding Scarlett were her ultimate goals.

Jane's cold eyes flashed through Beth's head. Beth shouldn't be using dark magic. Jane was angry enough as it was. But she had no other viable way. And at least she knew she could do it and control the amount of darkness used.

Beth relaxed as she let the shadows seep in. Within seconds she saw the red specks scatter across her skin. She fought hard within herself to limit its effect. She just needed enough to cast the spell. But it would be so easy to give in completely.

It would feel so good.

Beth shook her head as she fought for control.

She closed her eyes and focused on the image of Simon in Paul's bedroom. She summoned up her power and she lost herself in the image of New York.

Seconds later, she was there.

FOURTEEN

'Are you okay?'

The soft words pulled Simon from his trance. He looked up to see Beth standing on the other side of the room.

She'd made it. He felt instant relief.

He jumped off the bed and raced to her, throwing his arms around her. He had never needed anybody more.

Beth slowly wrapped her arms around him in return and it immediately set Simon's tears free. He sobbed on her shoulder as the pain of his loss tore away at him.

'I couldn't save him. I couldn't save him.'

'I know,' Beth soothed. 'I know. You really couldn't. There was nothing you could do.'

'I couldn't lose you. But I didn't know it would cost Paul his life.'

'I know. It all happened so fast.'

'Scarlett had gone too. I didn't know what to do. I just didn't know what to do. We need to get to her. I'm so sorry. I just couldn't...'

Simon felt Beth pull away and he expected to see anger on her face. But instead she calmly looked at him, trying to seem strong, trying to hide the deep sorrow that was so obviously there. It almost choked him to see her so sad.

'Let's just calm down. Both of us,' she said, stroking his cheek. 'We're not going to be able to do anything if we don't take a few breaths and get our heads in gear.' Beth took Simon's hand before she hesitated. 'Do you want to stay in this room?'

Simon thought for a second. Everything hurt. Absolutely everything. It was like he'd been winded from a harsh strike and the pain just wouldn't subside.

'How about I make us a nice strong cup of tea?' Beth said. 'Perfect for clearing the mind.'

'I think I'd prefer a whiskey.'

'A whiskey it is.'

Simon tightened his grasp of Beth's hand as they left Paul's room and headed through the spacious apartment to the living room.

It was a stylish and modern residence, far funkier than Simon's mansion in England. In reality, it had always been Paul's apartment more than Simon's. Simon was initially only a visitor, but he'd preferred his US escape to the dullness of his lonely UK life at the time, and so he'd stayed on a pretty permanent basis. That was, until he'd met Beth.

Simon sat on the sofa while Beth inspected the large drinks cabinet. Paul had never been short of anything.

'Is a Macallan okay?' Beth asked.

Simon found a tiny smile. 'Paul's favourite. We only touched it on special occasions.'

'Maybe not then.'

'What are we saving it for now? He'll never drink it again.'

A tear caught Simon's eye but he refused to give in to it.

'Perhaps just Glenfiddich for now,' Beth said, pouring a small glass for Simon. She brought the glass over to him before pouring a small Grey Goose vodka for herself.

She came over and joined him on the sofa.

Simon took his first sip, and he enjoyed the heat as it slivered down his throat. It felt calming.

As the alcohol soothed his agitation, clarity returned to his mind. 'We need to go and get Scarlett,' he said. 'I couldn't think straight before. I shouldn't have come here. I just...'

'It's okay,' Beth said. 'It's quite understandable. You've been through a lot. Today has been horrific.'

'I thought I'd lost her. Then I thought I'd lost you. Then...'

'It's fine. We're going to get her back,' she said. 'Tell me what happened before I got there. Was Carly really saying she was going to keep Scarlett as her own?'

'Yes. It was all backwards from what I expected. Damien seemed utterly shocked. He was telling her to give Scarlett back to us. I don't think he was pretending.'

'Why would Carly do that?'

'She was saying we were bad parents. I couldn't believe it. What a bitch! She'd kidnapped our child!'

'We're not bad parents, are we?'

'Absolutely not. Our daughter wants for nothing. Including love. We couldn't love her more. But we also need to work. We have huge responsibilities and a lot of people counting on us. Therefore we need help to manage it all. We're good people and good parents. Don't you dare think otherwise. Letty will have a brilliant life. We'll both make sure of it. And Carly will not be allowed within ten miles of her ever again.'

Simon felt the rage eat away at him as he sipped at more of his drink.

'You're right,' Beth said. 'She won't get away with this. Even when we get Letty back, I want Carly to suffer.'

'Oh, she'll suffer all right.'

'Simon, stop it.'

'What?'

'Look at you.'

Simon looked down to see red flecks flashing across his

hands. The dark magic was still taunting him, and the surge in power was something he was increasingly welcoming.

'I have it under control,' he said, although he refused to acknowledge to himself whether that was true or not.

'I hope so, because we need to think more carefully about how we get Letty back this time,' Beth said. 'We can't just go bursting in there. We need the upper hand.'

'The element of surprise works well.'

'It didn't last time. Look at what happened. Besides, I'm sure they'll be expecting us to just turn up again. It will hardly be a surprise anymore. They'll be ready for us.'

'You're forgetting. Damien must have teleported. He'll be exhausted. He won't be able to defend himself.'

'It wasn't Damien we were defending ourselves from last time, as I remember it.'

'No, but...' This threw Simon. Beth was right. It was Carly who had been the main threat. She wasn't even that powerful. She just had no scruples.

'We need to cover ourselves for every possible eventuality,' Beth said. 'I think we need to assume that Carly could be ready for anything.'

'Yes, I suppose you're right. I should know by now that when it comes to anything related to Damien, always expect to be at a disadvantage. A vast disadvantage. This is the man who not only defies possibility by getting his power back, but goes all the way to getting unlimited power that mirrors our own.' Simon caught a fresh look of concern whiten Beth's face. 'What is it?'

Beth seemed lost for words. This must be bad.

'What is it?' Simon asked again, panic joining the rage in his chest.

'Things have got slightly more complicated than before,' Beth muttered.

'Complicated? In what way? How could any of this get any more complicated?' As Simon felt the flames of his emotion burn through him, he noticed Beth's eyes flick back to his hands, where the darkness was visibly tantalising him.

'I don't know where to begin.'

'Anywhere. Just tell me.' Simon's heart stopped. 'Is Scarlett in more danger?'

'No. No, I don't think so. For all her faults, I don't think Carly's out to hurt Scarlett. And at least she doesn't have that knife anymore.'

'So what is it?'

Beth exhaled. 'It's Jane.'

Simon froze. In all of his mourning, he hadn't once cast a thought to Jane.

'How is she?' he asked.

'Mad.'

'Mad?'

'She went into all professional mode. I quite understand it, but...'

'What?'

'We went back to Malancy HQ. That's when Ralph came running into the office.'

Beth paused again and Simon could feel his body tense up. 'Yes?'

'Ralph has found out how Damien managed to regain his powers. How he's managed to mirror your power.'

'Our power,' Simon corrected.

'Not quite.'

'What do you mean?'

'We don't know exactly how Damien did it, but we do know now what he used to do it.'

'What do you mean, Beth? Just tell me. Get to the point.'

'It seems that Damien was in possession of a potent element.'

'While in prison? How did he get that?'

'More than just potent. It was laden with... We don't know how...'

'What was it laden with, Beth?'

'Your power.'

'What?'

'It was... it was you. Ralph is yet to explain how, but Damien had an element full of your power and he used it to make himself magic again.'

Simon gripped the glass firmly in his hand. That seemed utterly ridiculous. How could Damien get hold of such an item?

'I haven't made any elements powerful,' Simon said, categorically. 'I haven't done anything. Do you realise how dangerous that is? I wouldn't be so stupid. There is no such element.'

'Ralph tested it like a hundred times. He was adamant. Whatever Damien had, somewhere down the line it came from you.'

'This is bullshit!' Simon shot to his feet. He knocked back the remains of his whiskey and slammed the glass down.

'I thought the same thing. But Jane believed it straight away.'

'Jane? Jane believed it?'

'She's in a bad way. Her husband has just died. Imagine if it was me.'

'My uncle has just died. In every way he was a father to me. I'm hurting too, but it doesn't give me the right to believe any old crap.'

'I know. I'm sorry.'

Simon stood back. He recognised that fear in his wife's eyes. There was still more bad news yet to come.

'Tell me,' he said.

She took a breath. 'I'm so sorry. There was nothing I could do. I tried to tell her, but she wouldn't listen.'

'What is it? Tell me.'

'Jane has put out a warrant for your arrest.'

'What?'

'Firstly it's for the dark magic, which you can't be surprised about. Then she said she suspects you to be... an accomplice.'

'That's crazy! How could she possibly think that I would help Damien regain his power, let alone make it match mine?'

Beth hesitated. She could barely look at Simon. 'It's not just that,' she mumbled.

'Well, what else?'

'I think she actually used the word association...'

'Association of what?'

Beth just couldn't find the words.

'What?' Simon pushed.

'Murder.'

'She's blaming me for Paul?' Simon roared.

'I know. It's ridiculous.'

'Is she insane? How could she turn on me like this?'

'It's not just you.'

'What?'

'I was being handcuffed when I teleported out of there.'

'What? What the fuck? What for?'

'Dark magic.'

Simon stopped. 'Which is my fault. But it doesn't excuse her behaviour. Paul would never want this.' Simon rubbed his forehead. He was beginning to get a headache.

He walked over to the window to look out across the New York skyline. Not that he was taking any of it in. His mind was sodden with how much was happening. He needed to try to regain some clarity. He took a few breaths as he let his brain churn through all the problems.

'So the Malancy is looking for both of us?' he asked, turning back to Beth.

'Yes. At least we're far away.'

'It's not that simple, Beth. Tell me you've blocked yourself. You blocked yourself straight away, right?'

'No. I don't know how to do that. I've never had to do that before.'

'Beth, you should have done this. It should have been the first thing you did.'

'But I don't know how to do it!'

'Okay. I can do it for you. Stand up.'

'Are you sure?'

'Yes, but then we'd better get out of here. Jane would definitely have asked Ralph to do a location spell. She'll have the US Malancy authority onto us.'

'Surely they won't come after us. We're ultimately in charge.'

'Theoretically, yes. But Jane and Jim have day to day control. We gave it to them. They technically run the world Headquarters of the Malancy. The US will do whatever they say.'

'I never thought about that. I never thought! Do it now.'

'Okay. Just stand still.'

Simon closed his eyes and summoned his power. Blocking spells were just like location spells until right at the end. Instead of beckoning an image of the person you wanted to find, you erased them out in your mind.

As Simon felt the power charge up inside of him, he erased the image of Beth in his head. Brilliant rays of red swallowed up the room as the spell took hold.

'Is it done?' Beth asked, opening her eyes the second the dazzling red vanished.

'Yes.' As if for the first time he was properly taking everything in, Simon noticed how Beth was still in blood soaked clothes. He looked down and saw his own trousers in the same state.

'We need to clean ourselves up and get changed,' he said. 'Then we need to get out of here.'

'Shall we go home?'

'No. They could be there. They could be anywhere. We need to go somewhere anonymous. We need to disappear for a while until we've come up with a plan. We need time to figure out how we're going to get Scarlett back.'

'Where could we go?'

Simon scanned his brain. 'There's a coffee shop down

the road. Let's go there for now while we get our heads together and formulate a plan.'

'Isn't that a bit close?'

'Exactly. They'll assume we're far away. It's our safest option.'

'Okay. Whatever you think is best.'

'We have to get Scarlett back and then we need to find a way to fight this. Jane cannot arrest us.'

'I should tell you there's also arrest warrants out for Carly and Damien,' Beth said, as Simon headed into his bedroom. She quickly followed him.

'Then we need to act very fast,' Simon said, searching through his wardrobe. He grabbed some jeans and a t-shirt and threw them on the bed. He always left a selection of clothes so he didn't have to pack much whenever he travelled between homes. 'Letty cannot go into care. Jane will hold her ransom until we give ourselves up. We'll never see her again.'

'Jane would never do that.'

'I didn't think Jane would do this. We can't take the risk.'

'Carly and Damien are at least blocked.'

'For now. I never thought I'd say this, but at least Damien having our power means he can more easily defeat Jane's attempts.' Simon stopped moving.

'What is it?' Beth nudged.

'What has happened? As it stands, I feel less threatened by Damien than I do by Jane. My own family.' Simon took a step back and sat on his bed. He needed a moment to process everything. 'Talk about dark magic.'

'What do you mean?'

'Her turning on us like this. It's a darkness. It's no different to what we did.'

'Although her actions aren't illegal.'

Simon shook his head. 'I know I shouldn't have done it. And I never considered for a second that it would drag you down too. I was just so angry and afraid for Scarlett.

Damien with equal power is the biggest threat we've ever faced. Although him not using that power, that was a curveball. I just don't know what's going on. I can't figure any of this out.'

'You shouldn't have turned to dark magic, no. But I understand. When your daughter is taken, you'll do anything to protect her. Jane doesn't understand that. She thinks it's a simple choice. The only thing we can do now is make sure the darkness doesn't get the better of us.'

'Come on. We need to get moving,' Simon said, standing up. 'You don't have clothes here, do you?'

'No, but I'll just summon something up from home.'

'Beth, I'm so sorry.'

'Don't be sorry. You have nothing to be sorry about.'

'I love you so much.'

'I know you do. I love you too.'

He scanned his blood soaked wife. 'I'll go and turn the shower on.'

'Will there be hot water?' Beth asked.

Simon couldn't resist a small smile. 'Ever the practical thinker. One day you might realise that you have the power to override such issues as cold water.'

'Right. Yes.'

Simon headed into the en suite. He touched the pipes, casting a spell to heat the water, and then he turned the shower on. He returned to the bedroom where Beth was undressing. He did the same, but the second he took his shirt off he noticed a look of horror haunt Beth's face.

'What is it?' he asked.

'You might want to wear a jacket as well.'

'It's really warm...' Simon stopped himself as he realised what Beth meant. He scanned his arms and chest and saw the flecks of the dark magic dancing across his skin. 'Good point.'

'It won't be like that forever, will it?' Beth asked.

'Of course not. But at the moment it's feeding off my anxiety. All I'm capable of at the minute is survival. Let's worry about anything else at a later date.'

'Okay. You know I'm here for you, right?'

'I know. We're in this together. Completely. It won't beat us, Beth.'

'Nothing beats us Birds.' The smile came and went quickly from Beth's mouth.

Simon had never felt this type of pain before. A pain he couldn't control. It was crushing.

'We'll get through this. We will,' Simon said. 'Paul would want us to.'

'He'd whip us right into shape.'

'He would. Let's fight this for Paul.'

'For Paul.'

FIFTEEN

Simon and Beth quickly showered and changed and then they swiftly left the apartment.

It was a short walk to the coffee shop Simon knew of. They'd made it there with no issues, and it didn't appear as if the authorities were looking for them right at that moment. But Simon knew it was just a matter of time. Jane was a determined lady.

'What do you want?' Simon asked Beth as they stood back from the counter and perused all that was on offer. It was a simple yet modern place, with wooden furniture scattered about and bright lights beaming from the high ceiling.

'Can I just get a normal cup of tea?'

'You can get tea, but it won't be like we have at home. Sorry. I hear the coffee is good, if you fancy trying that?'

Beth pulled a face. 'Ugh, no.'

'I know. You can't beat a good cup of tea.' Simon tried to smile, but too much darkness was consuming him.

'What about a hot chocolate?' Beth asked. 'Do they do that? That's probably the safest alternative option.'

'Yes. That sounds good. Definitely better than coffee.'

'We should get some food as well. I haven't eaten since

breakfast. I don't even know what time it is.'

Simon glanced at the clock on the wall. 'Half twelve here, so... half five at home. Half five to us.'

'Bloody hell. We'd better eat. We need to keep our strength up.'

'What do you want?'

'I don't know. Whatever they've got. You know what I like.'

Beth walked over to a table right at the back of the room - away from the windows and the eyes of potential authority figures - and Simon ordered.

'What can I get for you?' the woman behind the counter asked, but before Simon could answer, a voice in the corner of the room caught his attention.

'Is this another one of those magic plants?' a man said, his accent not a local one. Perhaps from Texas. He stood up, showing how tall and broad he was, and touched the leaf of a peace lily that wasn't too far away from where Beth was sitting. Beth glared at Simon before turning her attention to the man.

Simon stood still. All he found himself capable of was watching in horror as the man attempted to use a power that he had no right having access to.

A gush of wind suddenly blew through the place, sending serviettes and menus flying through the air.

'It is!' the man shouted with delight, seemingly to anyone who would listen. 'It's one of those magic plants!'

'They said it's kinetic energy on the news,' another man said, coming closer to examine the leaves.

'That's no kinetic energy,' a middle-aged woman said, striding forward with an obvious arrogance. 'It's plants all over the world. They're feeding off our emotions.'

'I reckon nature is fighting back,' another woman said, joining the now growing crowd around the plant.

'It's aliens,' someone else shouted out. 'Have you not seen *Little Shop of Horrors*?'

'Stand back, stand back,' the man who began the chaos

announced. 'It's my wife's turn next.' The arrogant woman edged forward and stroked the leaves with fascination.

Beth glared at Simon again, pleading for him to do something. He knew he had to do something. He couldn't just stand there and watch the abilities of his people become a fairground attraction to anyone who felt like it.

'May I have a look?' Simon said, pushing his way towards the plant.

'It's Rosie's turn next,' the man said, warning Simon off.

'Couldn't two people have a go at once?' Simon said.

'Can I have a go too, then?' a voice shouted.

'It was my idea and this man found the magic plant,' Simon asserted. 'It's only fair that his wife and I go next, and then the rest of you can have your turn.'

'Is that okay with you?' the first man asked his tall wife, a woman clearly not to be messed with.

'I like his accent. He seems nice and polite. He can go with me.' Her eyes became fixated on Simon, absorbing every inch of him. He was used to people staring, but not with such rabid hunger. It made him quite uncomfortable. 'I wonder if we'll feel a connection,' she said, and then she giggled with delight. Simon smiled through the churning of his stomach.

'Let's give it a go.'

He touched the leaf and quickly started to drain the power from the plant. He could feel her trying to draw the strength from it, but he wasn't going to let her get even the slightest drop of potency.

'Is it working?' the woman from behind the counter shouted.

'You're not doing it right!' a voice shouted.

'This plant isn't magic,' Simon said, pulling away as he felt the power from the plant swirl inside of him.

'It is! You saw what I did!' the first man insisted.

'You did nothing. The door must have opened at the same time and it blew a blast of wind through the place.'

'I came in when you were standing by the plant,' a voice said from the back of the onlookers.

'There you go then,' Simon said.

'I thought all plants were magic,' someone else said.

'It's kinetic energy!' a male voice shouted.

Simon took a moment to ensure that any other forces were drained from the place, just in case. It was a mere drop in the ocean compared to the world of problems they faced, but every little way he could stop someone believing that all plants had become magic, it was a small improvement on before.

'I swear it was magic,' the first man said, before his wife hit him on the arm.

Then she turned to Simon with sultry eyes. 'Maybe we could connect another time?'

'I'd better get to my wife,' he replied.

'Nice to meet you,' she said and Simon quickly grabbed Beth's hand. He squeezed it until the woman had walked away, and Beth held it firmly in return. When everyone had sat back down and the plant had been forgotten about, Simon headed back to the counter.

After a short wait, he finally got to order. Their drinks were prepared, with extra whipped cream on top, and then he took them to the table.

'Here you go,' Simon said, placing down the two mugs.

'Do you think scenes like that are going on everywhere?' Beth asked, her voice low.

'I guess so.'

'It makes you mad, doesn't it. Using our power like it's entertainment.'

'I know.'

'I take it you removed the power from the whole place, not just the plant?'

'Yes.'

'Although that's not fair, either, is it? Say a Malant comes in here and wants to cast a quick spell. The plant is useless now to anyone.'

'I don't think Malants generally use elements hanging around public places.'

'But still, it would be their right to.'

'Do you want me to put the magic back into the plant?'

'No! I'm just saying. This is all a disaster for everyone.'

'I know. But we can only fight one battle at a time. We need to get our daughter back first.'

'You're right.' Beth looked down at the mug in front of her. 'Did they not have food?'

'It's coming,' Simon replied. 'I ordered two grilled cheeses. I hope that's okay?'

'Is that cheese on toast?'

'Cheese in toast. Like a toastie.'

'Perfect. That's wonderful. Thank you. Right, to Letty. I've been thinking hard about this. We need to find a way to subtly get to her.'

'I've been thinking too. Damien is most probably out for the count. He'll be out for hours after teleporting three people. I say let's just go straight in, overpower Carly and take Letty back. We need to stop messing about and get this done.'

'Absolutely not.'

'What?'

'Carly is bound to be ready for us. She's going to know we're coming. If we just show up again, she'll have the upper hand. We won't know what we're walking into. And what if Damien used dark magic? He'll be fully on the ball.'

'He won't have used dark magic.'

'How do you know that?'

'Of all the things that Damien has ever told me, I've never believed anything more than him saying he didn't want to go back to prison. If he used dark magic, it would add to his sentence significantly. I can't see him taking the risk.'

'Whilst that sounds very plausible, we don't actually know it for sure.'

'I think we can be pretty certain. Without dark magic, he's still got more power than he's ever thought possible. He probably couldn't cope with anything more at the minute.'

'But we still don't know for sure. And we need to be certain. Especially after what happened last time.' Beth addressed Simon very directly. She was trying to look commanding, but Simon could detect the fear and panic. 'This is our daughter we're talking about. We can't possibly take the risk of anything going wrong a second time. I can't take the thought of this getting any worse.'

'Okay,' Simon said, holding Beth's hand. 'I hear what you're saying. Maybe I shouldn't have gone all guns blazing last time. I just thought Damien would be there and he'd think he'd blocked us. I thought he'd be all smug and I'd bring him down a peg or two. I was totally thrown by what actually happened.'

'Precisely. We can't make that same mistake again.'

'Okay. You're right. We need to be prepared for anything.'

'Actually, no. I think this time what we really need is... to go into some sort of stealth mode.'

'Stealth mode? Have you been reading those business books again?'

'Well yes, but in this instance it's a good idea. We have to secretly get in, secretly get Scarlett and secretly get out. It's the only thing that will work.'

'You don't think they'll be expecting something like that?'

'I would wager it's probably the only thing they won't be expecting. Mr Simon Bird may be a very private man, but at the same time everyone knows you. Your presence is undeniable and you've never had to creep around anyone. You're always the most powerful man in the room and so secret tactics have never had to be your thing. I'm right, aren't I?'

'I suppose. Creeping around has never really occurred

to me before.'

'And it hasn't in this instance either. So if it's not occurred to you, I doubt it will have occurred to them. If they're expecting Simon Bird, they'll be expecting all guns blazing. I love you, but that's what you do. And that's what they'll be preparing for. So let's creep in and creep out. By the time they've realised what's going on, we'll have Scarlett and we'll be home free.'

'Okay,' Simon said, sipping on his hot chocolate. It tasted terribly bitter. It wasn't particularly nice. 'So how do you suggest we enter into this stealth mode? They're going to be keeping a close eye on Scarlett. We wait until they're both asleep?'

'Two grilled cheeses,' the waitress said, placing down two plates in front of them.

'Thank you very much,' Beth said, immediately grabbing her food. She must have been very hungry. 'What did you say the time was?' she asked between mouthfuls of toast.

'Here or at home?' Simon asked as he picked at his snack, although he didn't feel remotely hungry.

'At home.'

Simon looked at his watch. 'Erm, ten to six.'

Beth shook her head. 'We can't wait until they're asleep. We'd have to wait until at least midnight - if not the early hours - just to be sure they were out of it. I don't know about you, but I can't wait around doing nothing while our baby girl is with those awful people.'

'No,' Simon said. 'I agree.'

Beth shoved the last mouthful of toast in her mouth, while Simon more humbly nibbled at his.

'I have one idea,' Beth said, as she took a sip of her drink. 'Ugh, this is horrible. Is this really chocolate? I miss tea.'

'I know. It's scary sometimes how similar we are.'

'Scary but sweet. Anyway, as I was saying, I have one idea. It might be completely nuts. And don't laugh at me if it is. I'm still learning about the potential of our magic. I have no clue if this is even possible, but if it is then it will give us just the solution we need. Probably in lots of ways. But you need to tell me if we can or can't do it. I have no clue. Please don't laugh at me.'

'Beth, just spit it out. At this moment, any idea is welcome. Nothing is off the table, no matter how ridiculous it may seem.'

'Okay.' Beth sat up straight. 'Can we make ourselves invisible?'

Simon stopped moving. He didn't know how to respond to that. That was the last thing he'd expected. 'Invisible?'

'Yes. Is there a spell we can cast to make ourselves invisible? If there was, then we could just sneak in, grab Scarlett, and sneak out. No one would know. They'd just see that Scarlett had disappeared and they'd never be able to work out where she'd gone. It would be perfect.'

'That certainly is stealth mode.'

'But is it possible?'

'I've never considered it before. I don't know.'

'You've had magical powers all your life and you've never considered whether you can turn invisible?'

'It's not like you just generally try things out, is it?' Simon reasoned. 'You're taught spells. You're taught how to use your ability. Even with our extra power, the principles are still the same as a normal Malant. And I've never heard of anyone turning invisible before.'

'So it's not possible?'

'I didn't say that. I just said I've never heard of it.' Simon sat back. 'Let's think about it. If we could do it, it would most likely take immense power. That could be why no one ever does it. I suppose it could be similar to a teleportation spell, in the sense that you're changing your body. But rather than moving it, we're making it disappear.'

'Teleportation is a huge spell.'

'Yes. And even if we did manage it, we'd still have to teleport as well. Think of the power we'd need just to attempt this.'

Beth's shoulders seemed to slump. 'The only feasible way to achieve this is with dark magic again, isn't it.'

'It might be feasible without dark magic, but it could take days. We'd have to cast each spell and then take time to recover between each one.'

'We can't do that. With every second that Scarlett is gone, the more danger she's in.'

Simon sat forward. 'And not just from Carly and Damien.'

'Who else?'

'Jane.'

Beth shook her head. 'She wouldn't really hold Letty to ransom, would she?'

'Jane will know that she can't keep us in prison. You can't lock up people with innate magical abilities. She physically can't stop us from doing anything.'

'So what are you saying?'

'The only option she has is to force us to choose to be arrested.'

'That's awful. Scarlett's her niece.'

'There's a reason why Jane rose up the ranks so quickly. She's very good at what she does.'

'But that's so heartless. She wouldn't do that, surely.'

'Did you think she'd ever put out arrest warrants for us?'

'No. But she's hurting at the minute. She's not being rational. It won't last.'

'We can't take the risk.'

Beth didn't say a word and Simon watched as she absorbed all the horror of was what happening. He wanted to be able to make it all right. He wanted to take away the pain and fear. He'd never felt so helpless.

'Do you think we could try invisibility?' she mumbled after a few moments.

Simon considered his response carefully. 'How comfortable are you with using dark magic again?'

'For our daughter, I'd do anything. And we only have to use the magic we need. We don't have to get sucked in completely.'

'No. And I wasn't before. You have to know that. I was on the edge, but I still felt like me inside. I could never give myself to it completely.'

'You know what, this is bigger than Jane and her Malancy rules. Life has just got very complicated and we need to bend the rules to keep our daughter safe. If there's one thing that the Malancy has taught me, it's that good and bad are not always distinct. As much as I hate to admit it.'

Simon squeezed his wife's hand. When they'd met, she'd looked at the world with such innocent and hopeful eyes. He hated that her life with him had made all that crumble. So many horrible things had happened to them. Despite all of them being completely out of their control, Simon had never been able to find peace with the idea that if Beth hadn't met him, she might still have her beautiful innocence.

'Jane would do exactly the same if the tables were turned,' Beth stated.

'As would Paul,' Simon agreed, and then he felt the stabs of pain again. He knew his uncle would have his back right now, and that notion tore away at him. How was he going to battle through life without his uncle? How would Simon cope without that immeasurable support that, until this moment, he'd always taken for granted?

The force of his grief once again grasped onto him and Simon took a few breaths as he tried to push it away. He couldn't deal with the hurt right now. He had to block it out.

'Are you okay?' Beth said.

'Absolutely. I think we need to try your plan.'

'You mean turn invisible?'

'We should at least give it a go.'

Simon expected Beth to look pleased, but she seemed to be even more concerned.

'What's the matter?'

'Can you try it first?' she said. 'You're much better at spells than me. If you can figure out how to do it, you can teach me.'

'Of course. But that's not what's bothering you, is it?'

Beth hesitated. 'No.'

'What is it?'

'If we do succeed, we won't get stuck in an invisible state, will we?'

Simon couldn't resist a smirk. It was actually a welcome relief. 'Are you serious?'

'It's just occurred to me.'

'Of course not. That's ridiculous. If we can find a way to turn invisible, we just cast the same spell in reverse. Turning back is the easy bit.'

'Do you promise?'

'This was your idea.'

'I know. But until you said let's give it a try, I didn't really think it through.'

'Beth, trust me. If by some miracle we manage this, it will be no issue turning back. There's not even a one percent chance there will be any problems.'

'You're sure?'

'Yes.'

'Okay then. Let's do it.'

'Good. But not here. Shit, we can't go back to the apartment. We can't take the risk. We need to find somewhere quiet. Not an easy task in New York City.'

'We could get a hotel room?' Beth suggested. 'If we pay in advance, it won't matter if we just disappear. It will also give us the time and space to practise and get this right.'

'Good idea. There's a hotel I know just a couple of blocks from here. It's a nice place. We won't be bothered there. Are you ready?'

'I am, but you're not. You've barely touched your food.'

'I'm not hungry.'

'You need fuelling up. Even with dark magic, we're about to cast some mighty spells. Eat your food.'

Simon smirked. He felt so loved around Beth. 'Yes dear.'

He forced down the remains of his toastie and they headed out of the coffee shop.

Simon had everything crossed that this would work. He couldn't see any sound reason why they couldn't make themselves disappear from sight, but this was new territory even for an experienced Malant like himself.

All he could hope was that this day wouldn't get any worse.

SIXTEEN

The check-in process couldn't have been smoother. They paid for a basic room and headed on up to the third floor.

It was a large, modern chain hotel, bustling with people. They exited the lift and Beth couldn't wait to get to the peace and quiet of their room. Ever since Beth had tapped into dark magic, everything had seemed far noisier. As one of the most powerful Malants, she was used to sensing other Malants around her, but this was most unprecedented. And it was becoming not only distracting, but highly irritating. It was as if her senses were constantly being tormented.

They reached their room and Simon opened the door. It was a clean, generally white room, and not particularly big. But it was perfect for their needs.

'Let's get straight to it, then,' Beth said, taking a seat on the bed. 'Do your magic.'

'You're going to watch me?' Simon asked, taking his jacket off and throwing it down next to her.

'Yes. What else am I going to do?'

'I don't know. Look out the window or something. Being watched adds a lot of extra pressure.'

'All right, how about I close my eyes?'

'Or you could look out the window.'

'I just want to sit here. I'll close my eyes. Look, they're closing now.'

'Okay.'

Beth heard Simon shuffle to the centre of the room. She gave it a few seconds and then she opened her eyes. She knew Simon would have to close his to cast the spell, and she wanted to see for herself what he was doing and if it would work.

As Simon concentrated, Beth saw the flecks of the dark magic scatter across his arms. Now in his t-shirt, she could see the darkness consume him, almost becoming like a bright red vine that was wrapping itself around his skin. It was quite a disturbing sight. For something that felt so good, it had an alarming physical presence.

Simon's body started to glow with a scarlet sheen and Beth knew the spell had started. She squinted her eyes, knowing what was to come, and, just as predicted, the crimson became brighter and brighter. It soaked the room with its rays and Beth snapped her eyes shut.

As quickly as it came, the red disappeared, and Beth opened her eyes again, desperate to see.

Simon was no longer standing in front of her.

'Simon?' she called out.

'I'm standing right here. I can't see me either. It's worked.'

'You've turned invisible?'

Beth stood up slowly and walked forward to where Simon had been standing. She held out her hand and suddenly it hit something she couldn't see. She flattened her palm and rested it on what she knew was her husband's chest. It was definitely Simon, but it looked like she was touching firm air.

'How did you do it?'

'Just like I said. I started to do a teleport spell, but instead of imagining where I wanted to go, I imagined myself disappearing. Like erasing myself.'

'That's amazing. How do you always know what to do?'

'Practice. I've probably cast more spells than any other Malant alive. Once you know the logic, you can apply it quite easily I suppose.'

'When this is all over, we should definitely experiment more. Being invisible could be fun. A whole new world of hide and seek.'

'Maybe not.'

'Why not?'

'It takes a lot of power, Beth. Without dark magic I'd be keeled over right now. Even with the dark magic, I feel like I've run a few blocks.'

'Oh. Maybe just for now then.'

'Are you going to have a go?'

'Yes. Okay.'

'Will you stop worrying,' Simon said, reading Beth's mind as always.

'We will be able to turn back, won't we?'

'Yes. I've told you. Don't worry about that. We're in total control. You can teleport back out of places, can't you?'

'Yes.'

'Well, there you go. It's the same spell. We'll just think of reappearing instead of disappearing.'

'Are you sure?'

'Yes. I've been doing this sort of thing for a long time. I'm absolutely positive. But don't make me prove it. I need to conserve my energy. We have a lot more spells to do in the imminent future.'

'Okay.'

'Good. Now make yourself invisible.'

'Okay.' Beth stood back. 'So, like a teleport spell, but imagine myself disappearing?'

'Yes. Like erasing yourself from sight.'

'And just tap into the dark magic I need.'

'You need quite a lot. Be careful. You really need to

control it.'

'How much is quite a lot?'

'Beth, you'll be fine. Just take it slowly. Be cautious and you'll be fine.'

Beth exhaled heavily before she closed her eyes and tried to relax. Bit by bit, she let herself fall away, stripping away at the barriers to the darkness just a little.

She could feel the spasms of enjoyment sparkle up her arm as the darkness crept in, but she fought against it so it didn't take hold. With the power that she needed now shooting through her veins, she built up the energy in her chest to begin the spell.

As the power intensified, she conjured up images of herself being erased from view. She rubbed herself out of sight in her mind and she could feel the spell begin to work. The power became greater and greater and her images became more vivid. Something was definitely working.

The whole room blew up with a red glow and then instantly it vanished. Beth immediately opened her eyes and looked down.

There was nothing. She couldn't see her body. She was invisible.

'Simon?' she said, calling out across the room. He could be anywhere.

'I'm here. I'm right in front of you. I think.'

'We did it.'

'Are you okay?'

'Yeah. Like you said, a little breathless, but generally not bad. That was quite a spell.'

'I can't believe we've done it. We must be the first Malants ever to do this. We'll have to share it with Ralph.'

'Hopefully one day,' Beth said, realising that Malancy HQ was now the last place they should go to.

'When this nightmare is all over with,' Simon said, with clear regret in his voice.

'It will be. Soon. So what's next? I suppose we need to

track down Carly and Damien?'

'Yes. But let's go home first. I doubt Damien would have left the country - that would be far too complicated - and it will be much easier tracking them down when we're close by.'

'Good thinking. I could only sense you very weakly when I was looking for you before.'

'But you still found me.'

'We always find each other.'

'Now we have to do the same for Damien.'

'Hang on, what if Jane's in our house?' Beth asked.

'You think she'd break into our house?'

'She wouldn't have to. She has a key. She knows the security combination. She's supposed to be family.'

'Well, if she is, now is the perfect time to find out. We're invisible. We'll see her and she won't even know we're there.'

Beth's heart began to pound. This all felt so enormous and dangerous.

'Can I hold your hand, please?' she said.

'Of course.'

Beth felt something brush against her arm.

'Is that you?' she asked.

'Yes. Is that your arm?'

'Yes.' She felt Simon run down the length of her forearm and reach her hand at the bottom. His fingers found their way through hers and they squeezed each other tightly.

She suddenly felt herself being stretched towards the bed and then she saw Simon's jacket lift up, as if all on its own accord.

'Can't forget that,' Simon said. His jacket seemed to flop in the air and Beth guessed that it was now lying across his arm. At least it meant she could locate him.

'Let's do this together,' he said as he felt across her body and down her other arm. His other hand grasped hers so they were locked together. 'Like always, you think of home and I'll cast the spell.'

'Just like always,' Beth agreed.

'Ready?' Simon asked.

Beth nodded before realising that her silent gesture wasn't very helpful. 'Yes,' she replied.

'Right. I'm starting the spell.'

Beth closed her eyes and imagined their bedroom at home. She focused intently, desperate to get back there. She wanted to be at home and for everything to go back to the way it was, before this awful day began.

She concentrated so much, she didn't even notice the red glow around them as the spell worked.

'Clear upstairs,' a voice said and Beth snapped her eyes open. They were home, back in their large, beautiful bedroom. But they weren't alone.

Simon squeezed her hand again and then whispered in her ear. 'You wait here. I'm going to deal with this.'

'What are you going to do?' Beth whispered back.

'Do you trust me?'

'Always.'

'Then wait here.'

Simon let go of her hand and his jacket fell to the floor. She no longer had any idea where he was.

Seconds later their bedroom door swung open as if by magic.

'Get out!' she heard Simon order from across the landing in his tempestuous tone that never failed to make an impact. How glad she was that he was on her side. 'I said get out!' His command was followed by shocked yells from male voices.

There was no way Beth could just wait around. She had to see what was going on.

She raced out the room where she saw two men flying through the air. They looked absolutely horrified.

They were pushed down the stairs by an unknown force, gliding them safely but urgently.

She followed them down the stairway that arched over

the reception area. Before she reached the bottom, the front door opened and the two men were thrust outside.

Three more men followed, being hurtled through the air from different directions. They were screaming with fear, before they landed with a gentle bump onto the paved driveway.

'How dare you come into my house,' Simon barked. The men looked around, searching for the owner of the voice, but the source was nowhere to be found. 'You tell Jane that none of you are welcome here. You will leave us alone or face the consequences. I am still in charge of the Malancy and I will not be threatened by anyone.'

Beth raced to the door, sure that Simon was standing somewhere on the drive.

The gates suddenly flew open and a gust of strong wind blew all the five men and their two cars straight through it. As soon as they were safely on the other side, the gates swiftly slammed shut.

'This house is now protected.'

Beth felt a warmth slowly cover all the air around them and then she noticed a faint red tinge spark over the entire house and all the land surrounding it.

She watched in awe. She could never have managed all that. She must have the power, but Simon could always think so quickly and execute everything with such command. She just didn't have that in her. She was so grateful for him.

Beth felt a smack against her and it knocked her back slightly.

'Beth?' Simon's voice asked.

'I'm here,' she said, realising she was blocking the entrance. 'I'm standing back.' She walked into the centre of the reception area.

'I told you to wait in the bedroom,' Simon said, coming into the house and closing the front door. 'You could have been hurt.'

'And miss all that? It was incredible.'

'I can't believe that just happened.'

'What were they going to do? Arrest us in our own house?'

'They were searching all the rooms, invading our privacy. No doubt they were told to look for clues as to our whereabouts. I suspect Jane was also making the point that she has all the power. She must have given them our security passwords and everything. I am not impressed. Paul won't be happy.'

Simon halted his words and Beth felt a sad silence fill the room.

As everything became very still, Beth lost where Simon was. Then she became lost herself. Did he need a hug? Comforting? Was he crying? Was he getting angry? She hated that she couldn't see him and couldn't tell what to do.

Beth wanted to reach out for him, but she didn't even know where to start. Panic rose in her and she began to feel quite overwhelmed.

The only thing surrounding her was empty space, but she knew her hurting husband was somewhere in the vicinity.

'Simon?' she blurted out. 'Simon, are you okay? I don't like this. Are you okay? Do you need me?'

There was a small pause where Beth began to panic even more, before Simon said, 'Can you hear Damien's heartbeat?'

Beth almost collapsed. Now Simon was clearly just hiding from his emotions. What she knew he'd been doing since they got to that coffee shop. They had to get Scarlett back just so they could start to deal with everything else.

'Hang on,' she said. 'There's a lot of noise.'

Beth focused through the din to find the heartbeat that had been so prominent in her ears just hours before.

There it was.

'Yes. I've got it. It's not close, but nowhere near as far as you were.'

'Maybe a hundred miles away? Two hundred?'

'Something like that.'

Everything went deathly silent again. Beth hated it. Most of the time she loved having a detached house set away from most things, with just a few neighbours further down the road. But suddenly this large house seemed so empty and so lacking in life. The stillness was quite unsettling.

'Are we just going to tap into it to find him?' she asked, pushing things along.

'We'll have to, I suppose.'

'What if we don't get it right, though? What if we teleport into a dangerous situation and we're in threat?'

'You mean like Paul did?'

'We have no clue where Damien is or what he's doing. All we have is his heartbeat.'

Things fell silent again and Beth became increasingly edgy.

'You said Ralph was very sure that Damien got his powers from an element tainted with my power,' Simon said. 'Is that correct?'

'Yes. You believe that now?'

'I believe that Ralph is never wrong. I don't know how it could be true, but let's assume that somehow it is. That would mean that Damien essentially has my power. So he must be connected to me.'

Beth quickly latched on to his thinking. 'So you should be able to find him as I found you, actually connecting to an image?'

'I knew you'd remember.'

'After a small panic.'

'We'll always be able to find each other. Know that.'

'So we should always be able to find Damien too.'

'It's worth a shot. There has to be one good thing come from him using me.'

'Give it a go.'

'I'm doing it now. Give me a few minutes.'

Beth felt the stillness close in on her and she willed Simon to think quickly. She unconsciously crossed her fingers as she waited for Simon to say something.

'I've got it,' he finally said. 'I don't know where they are. It's some hotel room again. Damien is asleep on the bed. As I suspected, he must be wiped out from teleporting. Carly is on the floor playing with Scarlett.'

'Is Letty okay?'

'Yes, she seems to be. She looks tired but fine. We need to get to her.'

'If Carly's playing with her, how can we take her?'

'I have a plan. I'll create a distraction. When Carly goes to check it out, you grab Scarlett and go. Don't wait for me. Just grab her and leave. Come back here. I'll meet you back here.'

'Will you be okay?'

'We're going to be fine. You can't fight something you can't see. They won't stand a chance. Even better with Damien asleep.'

'If you're sure.'

'I'm positive. Take my hand again.'

'Where are you?'

'I'll move right by the door. Head for the door. I'm standing just in front of it.'

Beth stepped slowly forward. She reached out her hand to feel where Simon was. She felt something soft just before the door and she placed her hand fully onto his t-shirt. She followed his stomach over to his arm, and then ran down his silky skin to reach his hand. There she fed her fingers through his, so they were once again fully as one.

'Are you ready?' he asked.

'Let's get this over with.'

'We need to swap this time. I'll tap into the image of where they are, you do the spell.'

'With dark magic?'

'Yes. But only use what you need. This is getting more

and more dangerous.'

'We'll get her back and then we'll stop using it. You didn't need dark magic to overpower those men, did you?'

'No. That was easy.'

'Good. We need to rid ourselves of it.'

'We'll get Scarlett back and then we'll end this.'

'Yes. Right, I'm closing my eyes now. I'll let go of your hand when we get there so you'll know. Create the distraction as soon as you can.'

'I will. Good luck.'

'You too.'

Beth closed her eyes and summoned up the power in her chest. She could feel the dark magic taunting her, but she fought as best as she could against it. She didn't need that much power.

She sensed the spell igniting in her and a red glow was obvious behind her eyelids.

The power became more and more intense as she linked her magic with Simon's. Together they were immense.

The glow increased, emitting dazzling beams around them. Then instantly they vanished.

Beth opened her eyes to see Carly and Scarlett on the floor next to them. But before she could do anything she was jolted backwards, as if something fierce was pushing against her, trying to force her out of the room.

Carly had heard the thud of two bodies being slammed against the wall. There was no mistaking that Simon was in the same position as Beth. She bit her lip to stop herself from making another sound, though.

Clearly curious, Carly picked up Scarlett to study her surroundings, but she wasn't yet suspicious.

Beth looked at Scarlett. She seemed tired but happy. Her new farmyard toys were all over the floor and she rested against Carly as if she didn't miss her mother at all.

Beth tried to combat the pain of her sadness when suddenly a bright red beam appeared next to her. She could see the silhouette of Simon casting a spell.

Carly gasped. She turned to the bed were Damien was tucked up fast asleep.

'Damien! They're here. You were right!' she screamed.

He stirred and Beth knew she needed to follow Simon's actions.

She went to close her eyes, but before she thought of home, she snuck in once last glance at her daughter who was now starting to cry. How Beth wanted to go over and comfort her. It was heartbreaking. But Carly was begging for Damien to wake up and he was becoming more coherent. Beth had to get out of there.

Beth closed her eyes and pictured the place she'd just left. As the image of it slowly built up in her mind, she knew she was glowing red herself.

'Look, it's Beth!' Carly shouted. 'Damien! Stop them!'

Beth closed her eyes tighter as she heard Scarlett start to scream. Beth's heart was in shatters, but there was nothing she could do.

She concentrated harder until the final red beams shone out.

Darkness.

Beth opened her eyes again and she saw she was home. Back in the reception area, just where they'd left.

'Beth?' Simon said.

'What was that?' Beth cried.

'Where are you?'

'I don't know. What the hell just happened?'

'Are you here?'

She felt an arm wrap around her. She closed her eyes to better sense where Simon was, and they hugged each other tightly.

'Why were we pinned against the wall?' she asked.

'Damien must have protected the room. His spell was trying to cast us out. If we'd been much longer, I think we probably would have been pushed through the wall completely. He definitely means business.'

'So there's no way for us to get Scarlett?' Beth wept.

'There is always a way. He won't win. Do you hear me? Damien will not win.'

SEVENTEEN

'Can we turn back now?' Beth said. 'I hate this stupid invisibility. What a crap idea.' She felt riddled with anger.

'It was a good idea,' Simon assured her. 'We managed to get in to see our girl, at least.'

'She looked okay, didn't she?'

'Yes. I hate to say it, but she seemed happy when we arrived. I don't think Carly means her any harm. I think she actually wants to be her mother.'

'I'm her mother!' Beth yelled, with more venom than she'd intended.

'I know. You are. Her only mother. But as long as Carly believes she can replace you, then we have to believe that Scarlett will be safe.'

'What about Damien?'

'I think he'd be too scared to try anything. Now he knows she's our daughter, I don't think he'll take any chances.'

'What are you talking about? This is Damien. Anything is possible!'

'Did you see his face?' Simon said. 'I think all Damien wants to do at the minute is get away. I believed him when he said he didn't want to go back to prison. He won't risk increasing his sentence. I'm sure of it. We need another plan and we need one fast, but for now keeping Scarlett safe is in both of their interests.'

'You'd better be right.'

A tense silence gripped the room.

'Come on, let's turn back,' Simon said softly. 'I'll do it first.'

Beth felt Simon step away. Not a sound could be heard and then his frame suddenly started to glow red in front of her. She was so relieved to once again see his outline. Something was working. She prayed it would work properly.

She closed her eyes as she prepared for the bright red beams. They shone out, drowning the reception area, and then everything went dark.

Beth opened her eyes nervously. She wanted to collapse when she saw her husband standing fully in front of her.

'See, I told you. Nothing to worry about,' he said.

'Thank God.'

'Now it's your turn.'

'Okay. All I have to do is the same as before, but this time imagine myself reappearing?'

'Yes. It's as easy as that. Although you'll have to factor in a little darkness.'

'The darkness isn't an issue,' Beth said. Ever since Simon had turned to dark magic, it had been tantalising her deep inside, trying to drag her down with it. It took more strength not to use it than use it.

Beth closed her eyes and began the spell.

It was easy to draw from her emotion. She was feeling particularly brimmed with emotion that day. She also easily tapped into the dark magic, and within a few seconds redness sparked across her body.

She conjured up images of herself and this time she focused on being there. With intense concentration, she imagined herself being brought back to life and she felt the spell take hold.

As the room lit up with the final illumination, she unconsciously crossed her fingers. How she hoped it would work.

Darkness fell and she opened her eyes. She instantly looked down and she couldn't have been more relieved to see her body.

'Welcome back,' Simon said.

They both stood staring at each other, an unusual frostiness between the couple when they were normally so close.

'I think we should try to eat something,' Beth said, thinking of a reason to escape. She had this urge to get away from him. 'We need to keep our strength up.'

'Okay,' Simon nodded. 'I'm just going to get out of these clothes. I need to get comfortable. Then we can take stock of everything and come up with another plan.'

'Good idea. I'll go and see what we've got in the fridge.'

They glared at each other one more time and then Simon headed upstairs while Beth made her way into the kitchen.

She opened the fridge to explore what was in there, but all she found herself doing was staring aimlessly. Her brain was whirling at a million miles an hour, and even choosing food was now more than she could handle.

She closed the fridge and took a seat at the breakfast bar, cradling her head in her hands. Before she knew it, tears were racing down her cheeks and she found herself sobbing quietly.

It was the first time she'd actually been able to absorb the reality of everything that had happened, but she couldn't be sure whether the tears were from sadness or pure rage.

Her head fell down to the counter as she cried and cried. She had never felt such loss.

She heard movement upstairs and she sat up straight. She wiped away her tears and took a few breaths. She had to get some control. She couldn't let Simon see her like this. See her so weak. He was always acting like the strong one. She wasn't going to let him think she was weak.

She stood up, deciding that she needed to rid the house of the painful silence.

She flicked the radio on, hoping that it would help to distract her. She then went back over to peruse the contents of the fridge once more, telling herself that this time she'd get a grip. She hadn't even noticed that it was just adverts on the radio.

She stood staring into the fridge, trying to get her mind to focus. She shook her head. She had to sort something for dinner.

'It's eight o'clock and we're heading straight for the news,' the DJ said.

Eight o'clock? How had it got to eight o'clock? Beth closed the fridge as she considered the twelve hours of madness they'd just endured.

Just twelve hours earlier she'd been having breakfast in this very kitchen, worrying about stupid work problems that seemed so vastly unimportant now.

'...I stopped it with just my hands. Whatever this energy is, it saved my life.' Beth tuned in as the words on the radio caught her attention.

'The bus driver told us that he hadn't seen Mr Berryman walking into the road, and the bus seemed to grind to a halt all of its own accord,' the newsreader said. 'Scientists are calling today a miracle day, but they still haven't been able to share with us what is causing these strange occurrences. Some people are calling it witchcraft, others are saying it's a sign that it's the end of the world. However, most are trying to find more logical, scientific explanations. Whatever the case, it's clear that we still don't yet know the full potential of this new energy. The police are urging people to be extra careful over the next few days whilst further research is conducted. In other news...'

Beth rested her head against the fridge. Paul, Jane, Damien and Carly - there was so much already to deal with without adding the new world of Malants into the mix.

She felt the huge weight of everything that had happened that day press on her shoulders. It was crushing. She both wanted to curl up in bed and not come out until it was all over with, whilst at the same time run around blasting her magic at everyone until they finally succumbed and her true power was appreciated.

With a determined grasp of her fists, she stood tall and opened the freezer. There was nothing they could feasibly do at that minute. They needed sustenance and rest so they could take stock of everything and then fight it in the right way. Charging into another battle at that moment would be vastly unwise.

The darkness was twitching inside of her, begging her to do something drastic, but her head was winning the struggle.

She quickly found a pizza in the freezer and decided that would do. At least that was one proactive thing sorted.

Some cheery eighties pop music filled up the room as the news ended, and she forced her brain to just focus on that and the pizza.

She turned the oven on, and whilst she waited for it to warm up, she prepared some salad to go with it.

A little job was exactly what she needed.

The pizza was cooked not twenty minutes later and Beth placed it on a plate on the kitchen side. There had still been no sign of Simon.

She headed up the stairs to let him know dinner was ready, but before she'd even reached their bedroom, she saw through the doorway that Simon was sitting on the cdgc of the bed in his pyjamas. He was staring out, seeming so distant and sad. She edged forward to see his eyes all red and blotchy. He'd clearly been crying.

'Simon,' Beth said, entering the room. Seeing him like this melted her, helping to push the darkness down. She sat down next to him on the bed and hugged him. Within seconds he was sobbing into her shoulder. He hadn't said a word. But he didn't need to.

She let him cry out for a few minutes, barely noticing that the darkness was losing its power over her. 'I'm so sorry,' she uttered. 'So so sorry. This day has been awful.'

She concentrated hard to control her own tears. She needed to be strong for Simon. She'd had her time crying, and she could cry again later when he was asleep. For now she just needed to be there for the man she loved.

'It's so unfair,' she said. 'I'm so sorry.'

Simon's tears finally began to ease and he moved his head to look at her. She knew he wanted to speak, but there were just no words that would have been right.

'Dinner's ready,' she said instead, filling the void. 'I've done pizza. Do you want some?'

Simon shrugged.

'Come on. Let's go downstairs. I'll get a bottle of wine open as well. I think we've earned a drink today.'

Beth took Simon's hand and she led him down the stairs. He seemed out of touch with everything, his grief now taking charge.

She sat him at the table and she served him pizza and salad, and then she poured him a large glass of red wine.

'Can we turn this racket off?' Simon said.

'Of course,' Beth replied. She went to stand up to turn the radio off, when Simon clicked his fingers and the room fell instantly silent.

That silence was all that remained throughout their entire meal.

After dinner, they moved to the living room with their wine and Beth turned the TV on. But Simon didn't say another word. He just sat, looking sad and beaten, his mind a million miles away. And Beth felt pretty much the same.

They didn't say another word for the rest of the night.

Beth woke up with a start the next morning. She'd had the most awful dreams about Scarlett being killed. She felt shaken to the core.

She turned over but Simon wasn't next to her.

Worried about him, she grabbed her dressing gown and left the bedroom on a search.

She found him in the kitchen, fully dressed in jeans and a shirt. He was sitting at the breakfast bar sipping on a cup of tea.

'Morning,' Beth said, kissing him on the cheek.

'Morning,' Simon said, his usual warmth not present.

'How did you sleep?'

'I don't think I did.'

'I had a horrible nightmare.'

'That's not surprising.'

Beth decided it was probably best not to share the details of her horrific dream of Scarlett dying. Instead she headed towards the kettle ready for her first cuppa of the day.

'Have you looked out the window yet?' Simon asked before she could take the kettle in her hand.

'No. Why?'

'There's a car parked just in front of the gate. Having realised they can't get in, it now seems they've turned their attention to stopping us getting out.'

'What?'

Beth stormed to the front window in the living room. Trying not to draw too much attention to herself, she peeked around the side of the curtain to see a black car parked firmly in front of the gate.

'The bastards.'

She marched back into the kitchen.

'No doubt this is all Jane's idea. As if we haven't been through enough. What are we going to do?'

'Nothing,' Simon replied quite calmly.

'Nothing?'

'What can we do? They can't get in so let's not worry

about it.'

'But what if we want to get out?'

'We managed it yesterday.'

'Yeah, using dark magic. We said we wouldn't do that anymore.'

'What choice do we have?' Simon slammed his mug down before giving Beth his full attention. 'Jane is forcing us to do things we don't want to do. We have to get out because there are bigger things happening here than her tantrums. She's just too dumb to see it. Yes, Paul has died. I can't believe it. I literally can't...' He took a sharp breath as the words became stuck inside. 'But there are things that we have to deal with before we can start to mourn my uncle. Like the fact that our daughter has been kidnapped. Her niece! And that's on top of the problems with the world having adopted magical abilities. Something that Jane will actually need our help to resolve, not that she seems to have considered that at all.'

'And there's Damien.'

'Who's using my power for his own selfish gain. That cannot be allowed to happen.'

'At least she's got an arrest warrant out for him and Carly. Maybe the Malant police will get to them first?'

'And do what exactly? Even if they do find him, he's got our power. Jane would never be able to control us, so how does she think she's going to control Damien?'

'Okay. What do we need to do then?'

'I don't know. I've been thinking about it all night. I really don't know. But we can't just sit around trapped in our own house. And we certainly can't let ourselves be arrested. How is that going to help anyone?'

'I agree.' Just as Beth was about to continue, the house phone rang. It caught both Beth and Simon by surprise as it rarely made a sound. Most people contacted them on their mobiles.

Beth raced into the living room to find the landline.

'Hello.'

'Bethany, where have you been?' It was her mother.

'Hi Mom.'

'What's going on? We've had the police here.'

'The police?'

'Yes. They're still outside. I've been trying to call you on your mobile. You normally have it with you everywhere you go.'

'Sorry. There's been a lot going on.'

'They said there's an arrest warrant out for you. What have you done?'

'Nothing, Mom. Nothing.'

'Are you to blame for all these Malant powers that people have suddenly got? Your dad sent a loaf of bread flying across the kitchen yesterday. It's horrible. How do you cope with it?'

'You get used to it. And that has got nothing to do with me. We don't know what's caused the sudden emergence of worldwide power yet. Although we have our suspicions of who might be to blame. You said the police are still outside?'

'Yes. Well, it's the Malant police. Aren't you supposed to be in charge of them?'

'You'd think. This has actually all come from Jane.'

'Jane?'

'I have some bad news, Mom.'

'Bad news. What sort of bad news? Worse than the whole world getting Malant powers?'

'Yes. Quite a lot of bad news, actually. For starters, Paul died yesterday.'

'What?' The shock in her mom's tone made Beth feel even sadder. 'Oh no. What happened?'

Beth hesitated. 'He was murdered.' She took a moment to gulp down her sorrow. 'Well, sort of. I don't know. It might have been an accident. Either way, Jane has taken it very badly.'

'Murdered? That's awful. Poor Jane. They've only just got married. She waited all that time to be with her soulmate. Who would want to hurt Paul?'

'Well, Jane's blaming Simon.'

'She thinks Simon killed his uncle? He would never hurt Paul. Would he?'

'Of course not. Of course he wouldn't. Jane's just looking for someone to blame and Simon couldn't save him. Now she's out for both of us.'

'Both of you? How can she blame you?'

'I've just got drawn into it. It's too hard to explain. But that's not the only problem. Scarlett's been kidnapped too.'

'What?' her mother shrieked.

'By Damien. And Carly. Our own nanny.'

'Why? What has Damien made her do?'

'Nothing. It would appear that it was all Carly's idea. She says she wants to be Scarlett's mother. She said I'm unfit to be Scarlett's mom. Is that true?'

'Of course it's not. What a load of rubbish. You're a fantastic mother. There's something wrong with her. I was always suspicious of her.'

Beth shook her head. Her mother had always loved Carly.

'How are you going to get Scarlett back? Is Jane helping with that?' her mom asked.

'We don't know. It's all such a mess. Look, can I call you back in a few days when we've had time to straighten it out.'

'Of course you can. But make sure you do. And let us know if there's any way we can help.'

'I will. Speak to you soon.'

Beth placed the phone down. She took a breath to calm herself before she returned to the kitchen. Simon was making a cup of tea for them both. Whenever they were in dire straits, Jim had always made them a cup of tea. It was now the thing they associated with calming their minds.

'It was my mom,' she told him.

'Calling the landline?'

'Yes. She said she'd been trying my mobile. I think I've

left it upstairs. I'd better go and check to see if anyone else has called.'

Beth's legs felt heavy as she plodded up to the bedroom where she found her bag. She dug out her phone and saw that she had seventeen missed calls.

What?

The battery was almost dead, so she swiftly plugged it in and then she started to scroll through her missed call list.

Just three were from her mom. The rest of the calls were from Gayle. What was her problem? Work really didn't matter right now. Surely Gayle was clever enough to figure that out?

Beth quickly looked at the text message she had from Gayle as well. All it said was: "Call me ASAP."

Fourteen calls and a text message. Something in Beth's head told her that she should listen to the voicemails. This wasn't normal from Gayle – even with the direst of work problems.

Beth hit the voicemail button.

'You have one new message,' the male voice told her. 'First new message...'

'Hi Beth, it's Gayle. Call me back as soon as you can. I've found something out. It's to do with Diane. I've just overheard her on a call. Apparently she's been performing magic for quite some time. We both know she's not a Malant, but it sounded like she's heavily involved in these weird things happening somewhere. I thought you'd need to know. Whatever's going on right now, I've got a feeling that it's started right in this office. In your husband's own building. Call me back and I'll tell you all.'

Beth hung up slowly as the shock of the message sunk in.

Diane? Her own employee?

She sat on the bed as a chill crept through her. If it ended up that anyone at Bird Consultants was involved, this could turn Jane against them even more.

She knew she had to tell Simon, but the very idea absolutely petrified her.

Just when she'd been thinking this couldn't get any worse, it now felt like it was only just beginning.

EIGHTEEN

Beth crept down the stairs. Simon was in an emotional enough state as it was. Learning that the emergence of non-Malant powers might be related to an employee of Bird Consultants could just be enough to send him over the edge.

He'd never been a big fan of Diane anyway. She'd always taken pleasure in stirring the pot and she'd be caught spreading more than a few rumours about Simon during her time at the company.

After Diane's knowledge about the Malancy had been escalated, it seemed to calm her down a bit. But perhaps her attention was now just pointing in a different direction. The awful rumours might have stopped, but it seemed Diane was still causing trouble.

Beth poked her head into the kitchen, but Simon wasn't there. She headed to the living room to find him sitting on the sofa, slumped over in clear anguish.

'Simon, are you okay?' Beth asked, sitting down next to him.

He sat back, his eyes red. He seemed exhausted. He seemed broken. But rather than it worry her, she felt instead inexplicably irritated.

'I've been thinking,' Simon said. 'Maybe we should pay Jane a visit. We can't go on like this. It's ridiculous. We need the full force of the Malancy government behind us if we're going to get Scarlett back.'

'She'll have us immediately arrested.'

'She can't arrest us. We'll just disappear. If she's too obstinate to talk to her own family then we'll just disappear. Just like you did last time. I saw the handcuffs on the floor in our bedroom. I'm so sorry. I can't believe she did that to you. It's madness. That's why we at least need to try to talk to her.'

'Maybe. But there's something you need to know first.'

'What?'

'I've just checked my messages. I had a message from Gayle.'

'I'm really not interested in work stuff right now.'

'It's not about work. Not directly.'

'What is it, then?'

'Gayle said that she'd overheard Diane talking on the phone. It would seem that... apparently... Diane has been able to perform magic for quite a while.'

Simon turned to face Beth with confusion. 'What are you talking about?'

'Diane isn't a Malant. Definitely not.'

'I know that.'

'But Gayle overheard her on the phone telling someone that she's been performing magic for quite a while. That's all I know for now, but Gayle did say she thinks that whatever is happening right now might have started in our very own company.'

'Bird Consultants? What the hell does Bird Consultants have to do with this?'

'I don't know. That's all I know.'

'You didn't call Gayle back?'

'I thought I should talk to you first.'

'For fuck's sake.' Simon stood up in a rage. 'How are we constantly at the centre of all these problems? I mean why is it that Damien's power is somehow inexplicably linked to my own? How can that possibly be? I know Ralph wouldn't have said it if he wasn't totally sure, but it doesn't seem real. And now one of our employees seems to be linked to this further? We can't keep being at the centre of everything. Jane is going to have a field day with this.'

'She can't know yet. Gayle wouldn't have told anyone else.'

'Ralph might have figured it out, though. We're out of the loop now. Who knows what developments there have been that they're keeping from us.'

'Do you want me to call Gayle back?'

Simon took a second. He paced around in deep thought, ending up at the window, looking out at the car still guarding the gate.

'We need more information,' he said. 'We need to know what we're dealing with. There are threats coming at us from every direction. Including from our own family.'

'Okay. I'll call Gayle back now.'

Simon turned to Beth. 'Don't ask her anything about Diane.'

'What?'

'We don't know who's listening. Call her but just to find out what's happening at Bird Consultants. Like have the police been there. Tell her not to mention anything else to you on the phone. Just find out whether anyone's been asking questions and if anything out of the ordinary has been going on.'

'You think Jane would send the police to our office?'

'Right about now, I think anything is possible.'

'Okay. I'll call her now.'

As Beth stood up to leave, Simon's phone vibrated from his pocket. He pulled it out to look at it and Beth held her breath. She couldn't take much more. She didn't know how she was coping as it was.

'It's just that bloody client,' he said. 'They can wait.'

'Okay. I'll be back in a second.'

Beth raced upstairs to find her phone, where it was still plugged in. She wasted no time in dialling Gayle's number.

'Where have you been?' Gayle quickly answered. 'I've been worried sick.'

'Are you in your office?'

'Yes.'

'Good. Close the door and don't let anyone know you're speaking to me.'

'Okay,' Gayle replied hesitantly.

Beth waited for a few seconds while Gayle closed her door.

'Right, I'm alone,' she said. 'What's going on? There are these weird police people everywhere. They say they're from some sort of special branch. They're asking lots of questions about you and Simon.'

'It's the Malancy police.'

'Malancy police? Is it about the fact that everyone has powers? Did you get my messages?'

'I can't talk now, Gayle. It's too complicated. Don't tell me anything and don't ask me any questions.'

After a short pause, Gayle said, 'Okay. This is all getting pretty serious, isn't it?'

'You have no idea.' Beth felt a spark of relief talking to her friend. 'Look, I'll just tell you these two things. I want you to know what we're dealing with. But I can't elaborate and you can't tell anyone. Okay?'

'Of course. I won't tell a soul.'

'Firstly... Paul Bird.'

'What about him?'

'He died yesterday.'

'What?'

Beth felt tears prick at her eyes as she said the words.

'Paul's dead?' Gayle seemed choked up herself. She'd worked with Paul for a long time. She was one of the original administrators for the company and she'd always enjoyed a good relationship with Paul. Not Simon. No one at the office liked Simon. But everyone loved Paul.

'I'm afraid so.'

'What happened?'

'It's a very long story. I can't say much more. But Jane has taken it very badly and she's blaming Simon.'

'She's blaming Simon? What are you talking about? What happened?'

'It's too long a story for now. I'll explain it all another time.'

'I can't believe this. And there's something else as well?'

'Yes. Scarlett's been kidnapped.'

'What? Who would do that?'

'I can't say any more. But at least you know why I've been distracted.'

'I'm so sorry, Beth.'

'You said the police are everywhere?'

'Yes. They've taken over the boardroom and they're questioning all the staff. I haven't been brought in yet, but it's only a matter of time.'

'I bet they're outside too?'

'There are cars and coppers everywhere.'

'Right. Sit tight. If they call you in, tell them you haven't heard a thing from me since yesterday. Please don't tell anyone anything about Diane. Or Paul or Scarlett. I just really wanted you to know.'

'Okay. Whatever you say. I'm here to help. Whatever you need.'

'Thanks Gayle.'

'I'm really sorry about everything.'

'So am I. Speak soon.'

Beth hung up with a huge sigh. She quickly got dressed in jeans and a t-shirt, throwing a light cardigan over the top, and then she darted back down to join Simon.

He was staring out the window again when she entered.

'How did it go with Gayle?' he said, turning around as she approached.

'She said the Malant police are all over the place.

They're questioning every member of staff.'

'Shit. This can't just be related to us. Jane must be curious about the source of the outbreak. Who knows what they've found out. Who knows what they're going to find out. They have no right questioning anyone at Bird Consultants without speaking to us first. I can't stand being treated this way.'

'What are we going to do?'

Simon looked back out at the car that guarded the gate.

'If Jane wants to play games, then that's what she's going to get,' he said. 'Let's make this world of power work in our favour. Something needs to work in our favour for a change.'

'What are you thinking?'

'Where's your phone?'

'Charging upstairs.'

Simon threw his mobile to Beth. 'Call Gayle.'

'Call her again?'

'Yes.'

'Now?'

'Now.'

Beth flicked through to Simon's contacts, when she stopped herself. There was no way that Simon would have Gayle's number. Instead she pressed the phone to her ear and summoned it to ring. She wondered how she'd ever managed without her powers.

'Hello, Mr Bi... Simon,' Gayle answered, cautiously. As much as Gayle had become a friend of the family, Beth still knew that Simon unnerved her a bit. All those rumours over the years were hard to wash away.

'It's Beth. I'm just using Simon's phone.'

'Oh. Hello. Is everything okay?'

'I don't know. Hang on.' Beth glanced at Simon for instruction.

'Tell her to go down to reception,' Simon said.

'Reception?' Beth checked.

'You want me to go down to reception?' Gayle asked as

Simon nodded.

'Yes,' Beth told Gayle.

'Now?'

'Yes, now.'

'Okay. I'm on my way.'

Beth listened as Gayle left her office and journeyed to the ground floor.

'Just in the lifts,' she said. A couple more minutes passed by before Gayle spoke again. 'Right, I'm here. What do I need to do?'

'What do you want her to do?' Beth asked Simon.

'Tell her to stand against the back wall, out of the way.'

'I heard that,' Gayle said. 'I'm moving over there now.'

'What next?' Beth asked.

'Tell her to report back what she sees.'

Simon closed his eyes and Beth knew he was starting a spell.

'What do you want me to look out for?' Gayle asked.

'I don't know. Bear with us.'

Beth watched as her husband starting glowing red. Whatever he was doing, it was taking some force, although she was quick to notice that the red flecks were nowhere in sight. This was all good magic.

He began glowing with flames and Beth heard screams down the phone.

'Are you okay?' Beth asked Gayle.

'They're flying out the door,' Gayle said. 'I mean literally. The police, they're flying out the door.'

'You're pushing them out?' Beth said to Simon. For a fleeting moment she felt awe, but this was suddenly replaced with the harsh strike of jealousy. How was he managing this? She wouldn't even know where to start. And it was all good magic. She must have this equal power, but at the same time it seemed so out of her reach.

'Get her to tell us when it stops,' he ordered. 'We don't know how many there are, so we need her to tell us.'

Beth didn't take her eyes off Simon. She felt the

darkness tease her as she tried to imagine how he was conducting such power.

'Beth, tell her!'

Still with her eyes glued onto Simon, Beth spoke down the phone. 'Tell us when it stops.'

'Okay,' Gayle replied. 'There's quite a gust blowing through here. Two more. Wow.'

Simon was burning bright red now as he concentrated his spell.

'I think that's it,' Gayle said about a minute later. 'It's all stopped.'

'That's it,' Beth told Simon.

He brought his hands together and the flaming intensified. Then he stretched out his arms.

'The building's glowing red,' Gayle said. 'Is that right?'

'Yes,' Beth replied bitterly. 'I know what he's doing. I don't think you'll be bothered by any more police today.'

Simon threw his hands in the air and the ruby blazed a final time before it vanished.

Simon's phone bleeped. Beth looked at it to see a few emails coming in. They were all out of offices.

'Anything else you want from Gayle?' Beth asked him.

'Yes. Let me speak to her.' Beth passed over the phone.

'Thank you, Gayle,' Simon said. 'We're so appreciative of your help, and your loyalty. Could I just ask one more thing of you. Please could you mention to the reception-'

'Margaret,' Beth interjected before rolling her eyes.

Simon nodded. 'Please could you somehow get Margaret to believe that the strange new kinetic energy that's appeared is to blame for the police being blown out of the office. I don't care what you say, but start with Margaret and then target some of the bigger gossipers in the building. Get them to believe that it was all caused by the new inexplicable powers, and the police uniforms, badges - whatever you can come up with – got caught up in the blast and dragged the police outside. Do you see what I'm getting at?'

Beth watched as Simon nodded with relief.

'Thank you, Gayle. I'm so grateful. We're so grateful. We'll be in touch soon.' Simon hung up.

'Gayle said the building began glowing red. You've made it so only Bird Consultants' employees can enter the building, haven't you?' Beth said.

'Yes. And I've just sent an email to all staff to tell them not to speak to anyone claiming to be from a special branch of the police. I've made it clear that anyone who does will have to answer to me.'

'I think they'll listen to that,' Beth said. No one would dare cross Simon. He had so much more power than her in every possible way. 'But what if people have got visitors today?' she added.

'I love that you miss nothing. Don't worry, I've said that we've got some security issues and so only verified staff members will be allowed in the building until further notice. Any legitimate meetings will need to either be rearranged or held off the premises.'

'That's going to cause quite a stir.'

'I'd wager not as much as this morning's police presence.'

'We'll have to do a lot of explaining after this.'

'No we won't. Let them think what they like. They'll never be able to understand what's happening. And as for the police, no doubt when they hear about Paul, they'll think it's all related. I'm not explaining myself any further.'

Beth paused. Simon might have run things day to day, but Paul was the heart and soul of Bird Consultants and always had been. The news of his death was going to have a huge impact. She doubted that people would be quite so upset if Simon had died. Maybe he wasn't so powerful after all.

'What's next then?' she said, noticing the fire in her husband's eyes for the first time that day. 'What plan has the almighty Simon Bird got tucked up his sleeve now?'

'Are you all right?' he asked her, his tone softer and his

eyes full of concern.

'Just tickety-boo. Now tell me.'

NINETEEN

Beth walked around to lean on the back of the middle settee, subconsciously putting a barrier between her and Simon. She had this undeniable urge to get far away from him, but she also knew that they needed to work together if they were going to get Scarlett back. It sickened her.

'What's wrong?' Simon asked, watching her suspiciously.

'Nothing. Are we going to go and see Jane? Is that your idea?'

Simon didn't move. His eyes studied Beth, analysing every inch of her.

'There's something else we need to do first,' he muttered.

'What's that?'

'We need facts. Before we even attempt to approach Jane, we need to know what has been happening. We need to understand it for ourselves so that we can have a proper conversation with her.'

'Where do you propose we begin?'

'That's easy. We have a lead. Let's find out more from Gayle. And any other members of staff too. If there's anything to be found from our office, Jane is already one step ahead. We need to catch up.'

'Bird Consultants it is then.'

'I want you to have something to eat first. You haven't eaten all day.'

'Neither of us have.'

'So let's grab a slice of toast or something and re-fuel before we plough ahead.'

'If you insist.'

Simon focused on Beth. 'It's getting to you, isn't it.'

'What?'

'The dark magic. You're enjoying it.'

'No.'

'Beth.'

'No!'

Simon stepped around the settee and took her in his arms. She immediately wanted to push him away, but instead she took a breath and stood very still.

'You have to tell me,' he said. 'I'm the only person who can understand. I know how hard it is to resist. Tell me.'

Beth thought for a second. She looked up into Simon's eyes. Those eyes that normally offered so much comfort. But now all she felt was irritation. None of this was right.

She sensed the darkness within herself swirling around with joy. 'I suppose it has started to feel quite good,' she mumbled.

Simon pulled off Beth's cardigan. Red streaks were worming up her arms, the flecks having now morphed into larger scrawling lines.

'Oh my God,' Beth said, panicking.

She looked at Simon's hands. There wasn't a speck in sight and she could barely remember seeing one for hours.

'You're getting sucked into it more,' Simon said.

'But it's good. It's soothing the anger that I'm feeling towards everything else.'

'No it's not. It's not soothing anything. It'll make everything worse, you just won't realise it until it's too late. Beth, you have to fight this.'

'Why is it not getting to you? How are you fighting it?'

'I've been fighting it all my life. You've only been conscious of it for a few days. You get used to the call and you get used to shutting it down.'

'How, though? It wants me to give into it. And I want that too. Imagine what we could do with all that power?'

'No, Beth. No. It will ruin you.'

'It could make us.'

'It's not moral!'

That single sentence slapped Beth around the face. He was right. It wasn't moral. She grasped a hold of that thought as she searched for a new wave of inner strength.

'I'll do the teleporting for the next few hours,' Simon said, calmly. 'Let's wean you off it a bit.'

'We have to keep teleporting?'

'We have no choice. We can't confront Jane until we've learnt more. If she has any further reason to blame us for anything, I want to know well before I stand in a room with her. I'm not going to be on the back foot when someone is trying to arrest me.'

'You're right.'

'Let's get some food in us and then we'll get over to the office. I don't want anyone to know about Paul, though. Not yet.'

'I told Gayle.'

'What? Why?'

Beth opened her mouth to justify her reasoning but nothing came out.

'Beth, why?'

'I needed to talk to someone. She's my friend. This is my loss too. You can't stop me talking to a friend!'

'Okay,' Simon said as he hugged his wife. 'I don't want to talk about it with her, though. I don't want to talk about it with anyone. I want to pretend it hasn't happened. I can't deal with it at the minute. Not until all of this is over with.'

'I know. It's too much.'

Beth hugged her husband tightly, as if it might be the last time they would ever be able to do it. As her love for him battled through, the darkness started to fade.

'Right, let's get you some food,' Simon said.

'Toast sounds good. What do you want on it?' Beth asked, trying to keep her composure as she headed to the kitchen.

'What have we got?' Simon asked, following her.

Beth opened the fridge and they both scoured the contents.

'Strawberry jam?' she suggested.

'Perfect.'

Toast eaten and soothing cups of tea drunk, the Bird couple stood in their living room and got ready to teleport once again.

'I'm doing all the work this time,' Simon said.

'But won't that take more energy? You'll need to tap into more of the dark magic to do that.'

'It's only to give you a break. As soon as we see the specks start to disappear, we'll swap. Agreed?'

'Proper teamwork.'

'It's how we operate best.'

'Okay. I'm ready when you are.'

Beth closed her eyes while Simon took charge of the spell. She tried to relax, to let him have the control, but she was too edgy to really give in. She tried to clear her brain so she wouldn't interfere, but too many dark thoughts were taunting her. So much had happened. So many horrible things.

Simon let go of her hands and Beth opened her eyes. They were there. That had been so quick.

They were standing in the middle of their office, at the far end of the Executive Floor.

Simon turned to the door and reached out his hand. It promptly unlocked and swung open.

Beth followed him across the Executive Floor, passed

all the shocked faces of the fellow directors. As much as they were used to weird things happening with their beloved CEO, appearing from a locked office that he never entered must be up there with the weirdest.

'Don't ask,' Simon said, putting up his hand. Everyone complied, as always, just as Simon's office door slammed shut and locked itself.

'Simon,' Eric bravely muttered, 'could you confirm that it was you who blew all of the police out of here?'

'Yes,' Simon replied, without turning around. 'And the building is now open to staff only, as per my email. Did any of you talk to the police?'

There was a nervous silence and Simon turned to face his colleagues. 'Did you talk to them?'

'We had too. We all did,' Eric said. 'They started off on this floor. It was the police. We had no choice.'

'What did they ask?'

'If we've seen you. If we know where you are.'

'None of us said anything,' Nathan, the Finance Director, confirmed. 'We didn't know where you were and we haven't seen you since after the staff all adopted Malant powers yesterday. We couldn't tell them anything.'

'Do they think you're to blame for the spread of power?' Eric asked. 'Do you know what's happened?'

'I think it's best that I don't answer any questions,' Simon replied. 'The less you know the less you'll get caught up in any of this.'

Simon then turned around and opened the glass door before him. Beth swiftly followed behind. They entered the lift and Simon pressed for the ninth floor. It took just seconds to reach the floor below and the lift doors opened once again. Stepping out, they both headed through the glass doors leading into the admin office.

As soon as Simon appeared, an eerie silence washed over the entire room. This was the usual reaction Simon got as he walked around the building, and it never failed to make Beth sad.

Simon ignored the change in atmosphere – just as he always did – and Beth followed him directly into Gayle's office.

'Hello,' Gayle said, seeming both shocked and relieved at the same time.

'Could you spare us a few minutes?' Simon asked, although Beth knew Gayle would never say no and Simon would never accept that answer.

'Of course. Do you want to talk in here?' Gayle said.

'Yes.'

Beth turned to shut the door and they both sat down facing Gayle at her desk.

'We need to know what you know about Diane,' Simon said.

'Yes, erm... Things started to calm down a bit by lunchtime yesterday when the strange magic powers seemed to stop working. I headed out for a sandwich, and then, when I came back, Diane was in my office. This isn't unusual. She thinks I don't know, but she's often sneaking in here to make phone calls.'

'Do you not lock your office?' Simon asked, as if it were utter madness to leave an office unlocked.

'No. Sometimes the team needs files from in here. I don't have anything particularly secret. Anything secure, we keep in your office, so I've never felt the need to lock it.'

'And Diane just thinks she can use it as a private space for herself?'

Simon was clearly displeased with this behaviour. Beth knew he'd bring it up at a later point. To him, secrets and privacy were what kept the business running. No doubt he'd be questioning this lapse in office security. This would come back to bite her.

He could be such a moaning bastard at times.

'I don't condone it,' Gayle confirmed. 'Whenever I've spotted her, I've kicked her out instantly.'

'We'll come back to this,' Simon said and Beth resisted

a roll of her eyes. 'For now, Diane was in your office on the phone. Please continue.'

'I saw her straight away, but she didn't see me. I was all ready to open the door and tell her to do one, when I noticed she looked quite distressed. Diane distressed is not good. She's difficult enough as it is without having to deal with actual issues. So I thought I'd listen in. See what might be coming my way as her manager. I don't normally listen to people's private conversations-'

'I think you were quite entitled to on this occasion,' Simon said. 'She was in your office without permission.'

'What did you hear?' Beth asked, pushing the story along.

'I don't know who she was talking to. I never caught that. But she was asking how everyone has these powers. Whoever she was speaking to clearly knew something about how it had spread. Or at least she believed they might do.'

'And you have no inkling at all who it was?' Beth asked.

'I'm sorry, I really don't know. She never gave even the slightest hint.'

'What else was said?' Simon asked.

'She stated how they've been doing it for months without any issue at all, and then asked what could have changed. She seemed quite concerned.'

'You believe that her statement "doing it for months" relates to her having powers?' Simon asked.

'Yes. It definitely does, because she then said how she wanted it to go back to just her having the magic powers and not everyone else. She said they needed to find a way to stop it as soon as possible. It was as if she recognised the danger of everyone having the ability to cast spells, but somehow she excused herself from the problem. Even though she isn't a Malant. I could tell that.'

'She definitely isn't a Malant,' Simon confirmed.

'So the next step is to find out who Diane was talking to,' Beth said.

'There's only one simple way to do that,' Simon replied.
'What's that?'
'Let's ask her.'

TWENTY

'Just ask her, just like that?' Beth queried.

'We don't have time for games. We'll make her tell us.'

'All right,' Beth nodded. She knew Simon would get his answers. A small smile tickled her lips.

'Call her in here,' Simon instructed Gayle.

Gayle hesitantly picked up her phone and Beth turned around. Diane was seated on a desk just the other side of the glass. She was typing away, seemingly not a care in the world. Beth watched as she answered the call.

'It's Gayle. Could you come into my office, please?'

Beth didn't hear the reply, but Diane turned around cautiously, knowing that Mr and Mrs Bird were waiting for her.

'Yes, now Diane. Please. No it can't wait. Thank you.'

'She tried to put you off?' Simon asked.

'She said she's in the middle of something,' Gayle replied, carefully placing down the phone.

Simon shook his head but said nothing. No doubt another nugget that was being filed away to later grill Beth about.

God, he was irritating. Well, Beth had a few things she wanted to grill him about in return. Scaring people and demanding things from them was not acceptable in a twenty-first century business.

'Hello,' Diane said, opening the door. Simon stood up and headed for the table in the middle of the large office, where there was more room for them all to sit. Gayle and Beth joined him, and he stared at Diane until she also took a seat.

'Is everything okay?' Diane asked. She was sitting tall, trying to appear nonchalant, but Beth knew she must be terrified. How that thought made Beth want to smirk.

'You were chatting on the phone yesterday in this office,' Simon said. Diane glanced over at Gayle quickly before turning back to Simon.

'Yes.'

'Who were you chatting to and what was it about?'

Diane hesitated. She cast her eyes across the faces before her. 'It was my husband. Just having a catch up.'

'Don't lie to me,' Simon said.

'I'm not.'

'Let's make this easier. We know you were talking to someone about the powers that non-Malant people have mysteriously adopted, and we know this is something you've been personally experiencing for quite some time. Please explain how that's possible whilst also confirming who you were talking to.'

Diane opened her mouth but no words came out.

'We don't have time for this, Diane,' Simon said, his voice still measured. 'There is a great deal at stake here and you have information that we need to know. Information that could prove vital. So I'll ask you one more time.'

'I don't know what you're talking about,' Diane said. Beth would have almost believed her, had her eyes not been so full of panic. Lovely, joyful panic.

'If you won't do it the easy way, then we'll have to do it the hard way,' Simon said.

No one knew what to say as Simon stared fiercely at Diane.

Suddenly she gasped.

'What are you doing?' she asked breathlessly.

Her body seemed to tense up, like she was clenching all her muscles instantaneously. Her arms squeezed in around her torso and her face seemed to squirm in agony.

'You're hurting me,' she said, her voice full of fright. 'What are you doing?'

Beth watched as her husband squeezed Diane's frame; torturing her for information. There was a small niggle at the back of Beth's mind that told her it was wrong. It was signalling for her to say something. But the words never reached her mouth.

Instead she sat back and let it happen. She sat back and enjoyed it.

The red specks tingled up her arms as Beth felt pleasure from watching this torment. Diane had been the source of a great deal of frustration for Beth on several occasions. She might be good at her job, but she was also difficult, deceitful and dishonest. She liked to bend the rules to her own agenda and she never seemed to care about who got hurt. It was time someone showed her how that felt.

'Beth,' Gayle whispered, pleading for her to do something. But Beth just read the horror on Gayle's face as agreement on how difficult Diane was being. That was all Beth was willing to think about.

'Please, it really hurts,' Diane yelped, tears now swelling in her eyes. She was too scared to scream. Wisely so. She must have realised how far Simon could go. In the blink of an eye he could crush her.

Oh, that would feel so good.

That signal in Beth's brain poked her.

'Don't go too far,' Beth blurted out, but something about this outburst didn't feel right. 'She still needs to be able to speak,' she added, trying to rationalise her mixed emotions.

Simon suddenly turned to his wife with shock, freeing

Diane from his excruciating hold.

Diane sat back, breathlessly. 'Okay, okay. I'll tell you. Please don't hurt me again.' Tears rolled down her cheeks as she took gasps of air.

Simon still hadn't taken his eyes off Beth, and Beth read that as him wanting her to take charge of the questioning now. She was feeling more powerful than ever. Maybe he was recognising that and rewarding it.

It was about bloody time.

'Who were you speaking to and how have you had these powers before?' Beth asked, piercing her eyes into Diane's soul.

'I was speaking to Linda,' Diane replied, urgently.

'Linda? Who's Linda?' Simon asked, turning to Diane.

'Linda Malant.'

'As in George's wife?' Simon asked, astonished.

'George Malant?' Beth added, equally as surprised.

'Yes,' Diane nodded.

'What has Mrs Malant got to do with any of this?' Simon asked.

'I don't know. She doesn't know. Nothing. We haven't done anything.'

'She's been giving you powers, though?' Beth pushed.

'No, not her. How could she give me powers?'

'How could any Malant give you powers?' Simon asked.

'She's not a Malant,' Diane replied, confused.

There was a moment of puzzled silence before Simon asked, 'Mrs Malant isn't a Malant?'

'No. Surely you know that?'

'No,' Simon confirmed. 'But I've never met her. I've only met George once. Did you know?' Simon asked Beth.

'No. How could she not be a Malant?' Beth replied.

'I don't know. George and her go back a long way.'

'I suppose George wouldn't have to marry a Malant,' Beth noted. 'Just because he's a direct descendent from the original Malant family, it doesn't mean he only knows Malants. You can't help who you love.'

Beth turned to Simon as a streak of hatred ran through her.

Simon studied Beth's glower before focusing back fully on Diane.

'If it's not Mrs Malant then, who has been giving you powers?' he asked.

Diane's breathing was erratic and nervy.

'Tell us, Diane,' Beth said. 'It's easier if you just tell us. You know we'll get it out of you one way or another.'

Diane glared at Beth, the fear so strong in her eyes. It was all Beth could do not to laugh.

'It's George,' Diane whimpered. 'George Malant. He's been casting spells so Linda and I get temporary powers. We just wanted to see what it was like.'

'Temporary powers?' Simon asked, his face now clearly calculating something. 'How could George Malant possibly do that?'

'I don't know. He said it was a secret spell.'

'No, forget about the spell a minute - although I have a million questions about that. I mean how can George be casting anything? He's in prison!'

Diane's lips were quavering as she spoke. 'I sometimes go with Linda to visit him. We're friends.'

'He's been casting spells in prison?!' Simon boomed, his voice rocking the table. He turned his fierce glare towards Beth. 'This is scarily starting to add up.'

TWENTY-ONE

Simon turned back towards Diane. His head was churning through a million thoughts, not least that his wife had clearly enjoyed the agony that he now fully regretted putting Diane through. His need for answers and the taunting of the dark magic had momentarily got the better of him. But he should not have done that. Beth seemed far less remorseful though, which deeply concerned him.

However, that had to wait. It was another issue to add to the ever stacking pile of problems that he had to deal with in the imminent future. But for now Diane was before him and she had to be his priority.

'Are you telling us that you went to visit George Malant in prison with his wife where he cast a spell that gave you temporary magic powers?' Simon asked.

Diane nodded before muttering, 'Yes.'

Simon had never heard of such a spell. How could it exist? And how was it that George knew about it? Since Simon and Beth had taken over running the Malancy government - after George had been found guilty of treason - they and the team had been through every resource. There were hundreds of Malant books detailing everything about the history of the Malancy, including spells that were long forgotten about. But not once had anyone come across a spell that could give a non-Malant power.

This opened up a whole new stream of things for Simon to be concerned about. What else did George know that Simon wasn't privy to?

'Do you know anything about this spell?' Simon asked Diane, clutching at straws.

Diane shook her head. 'The only thing he told us was that it was highly secret and no one could know about it. That's what I was calling Linda about. Our highly secret magic is now out of the bag once and for all.'

Simon caught a look in Diane's eye. He'd always been exceptionally canny when it came to reading people. 'Tell me,' he ordered.

'What?' she fearfully answered.

'You were going to say something else. What is it?'

'You might as well tell him,' Beth said, a rancour to her voice that Simon didn't recognise.

He glanced over at her and he could see the black swirls of the dark magic dripping through her eyes. Gayle and Diane must have seen it too, but they wouldn't know to be concerned. Strange occurrences often accompanied Beth and Simon. They must be used to not questioning it.

But Simon knew that the darkness was getting a solid hold of her. He knew he'd have to do something soon. If only he knew what to do.

'Mr Bird can be very persuasive if you won't speak,' Beth said, and Simon heard a small giggle.

'Don't hurt me again,' Diane gasped. Simon had absolutely no intention of causing anyone further pain. He hated that he'd done it at all.

Although it was giving them results.

'What else were you going to say?' Simon pushed.

'I was just going to ask if you're trying to stop all these people from having magical powers,' she said, bravely.

'No one should have Malancy power if they are not a

Malant,' Simon replied. 'It's a gift that is passed down from generation to generation, and all Malants are ultimately linked somewhere down the line to the original Malant family. It's sacred and should not be passed on like a prize.'

'Linda is George's wife,' Diane justified. 'Her name is Malant.'

'By marriage only,' Simon asserted.

Diane looked down. He sensed her lack of response as an admission that he was correct. Even though he had no doubt that given the opportunity again, she'd grasp the power with both hands. But then, who wouldn't. It truly was a gift. That was why it needed protecting.

'There's something else, isn't there,' Simon said, interpreting Diane's twitchiness as withholding.

Diane looked up at him, but this time she seemed more eager to share. 'When George cast the spell before, it only lasted for twenty-four hours. That's all we got. Magic for a day. But this... new thing. It's been over a day now and people are still able to perform spells.'

'It was only temporary before?' he asked, trying to get his head around everything.

'Yes. But it isn't now. I tried it out over lunch. I can still do stuff.'

'How many times has George performed this spell on you?'

Diane shrugged.

'How many times?' Simon asked with more force.

'About seven or eight.'

'Seven or eight?' Simon shook his head but he retained his fury. 'And when did he last do it?'

Diane hesitated.

'Diane!' Simon urged.

'On Sunday evening. It was just a normal visit at five o'clock. We were all there in the room, with all the other prisoners and their visitors. There was nothing unusual about it at all. He performed the spell as always and we left. I noticed nothing out of the ordinary.'

Diane's words clicked something in Simon's head.

'Do you know Damien Rock?' he asked.

Diane nodded.

'Was he there?'

Diane nodded again.

'He was there, in the visitors' room?'

'Yes. I often see him. He was there with his parents, I think.'

Simon sat back. Things were slotting into place. He didn't like any of it, but the answers were starting to form.

'How did George cast the spell?' Simon asked. 'There are no natural elements in the prison at all. It's deliberately designed to prevent anyone from casting spells.'

'The prison is, yes. But you can take stuff into the visitor room. Linda takes a flower with her. They don't check the visitors, they just check the prisoners before they return to their cells.'

Simon turned to Beth. 'Visitors can bring in elements?'

'What difference does it make?' Beth shrugged. 'Not all of us need elements.' Simon could tell he wasn't going to get much sense out of her. She was engulfed with darkness.

Simon quickly reasoned that maybe it had just never been a concern. Spells tended to emit red glows, so a prisoner casting anything would be easily spotted. As long as they weren't allowed to bring elements back into the prison, it had probably been deemed as an unnecessary use of resources to confiscate them from visitors. Most Malant people would carry a few elements around with them. It was the source of their magic. Why would they leave home without a way of casting spells? It was their birthright.

He didn't agree with this line of thinking, but at least there was some sense to it.

The question then of how George had managed such a spell without sparking off red beams passed through Simon's mind. But he'd have to learn more about the spell to understand that.

'So you entered the visitor area, George cast the spell using his wife's flower, and then you left,' Simon clarified.

'Same as every other time,' Diane confirmed. 'I promise, we didn't do this. Or at least not knowingly. I don't want any of this. I hate that everyone's got powers.'

'Then you can appreciate how I feel. Myself and all the other Malants.'

Diane nodded and Simon knew his point was sinking in.

'One more question,' he said. 'Did you talk to the police yesterday?'

Diane shook her head.

'Did you?' he asked.

'No. They never got around to this department.'

'They started with the directors and then went through the contracts team,' Gayle added. 'I guess we would have been high on the list, being that we work directly with Beth, but you literally sent them flying out the building before they could ask any more questions.'

Beth laughed at this, but Simon decided to carry on as if it hadn't happened.

'Has anyone approached you since?' he asked Diane.

'Yes,' she replied, shakily. 'But not just me. They're outside the building. When anyone goes out they ask them if they'll be willing to talk. But I know no one has. We got your email, Mr Bird.'

'So, to your knowledge, no one has spoken to the police?'

'Not since they left here yesterday,' Diane responded.

'I really don't think anyone has,' Gayle agreed. 'People listen when you give them instructions.'

'Very well. Thank you, Diane. We're not the enemy here. I'm sorry for hurting you but this is a desperate situation. You have given us very valuable information and I'm grateful. I urge you to please be more forward with it in the future. It will help us all.'

'Okay,' Diane mumbled.

'So if you think of anything else that might be useful, you'll let us know?'

Diane nodded.

'Is there anything else?'

'No,' she mumbled.

'Right, you're free to leave.' Simon spotted the tears filling up in her eyes and he felt a pang of guilt. 'When we've left, I encourage you to please speak with Gayle about going home early. I think you've earnt a rest today.'

Simon turned to Gayle who nodded her understanding. He then glanced at his wife who seemed charged up with venom.

'Come on, Beth. We need to go.'

She stood up with great energy. He could see the flecks sparking across her hands and he suspected that her cardigan was hiding a hideous sight. She was riddled with darkness and he had to tackle that next.

If only he knew what to do.

He grabbed Beth's hand and led her to the lifts.

'There was me thinking Diane had balls,' Beth said with a snort as they waited for the lift to arrive.

'What?' Simon asked.

'One little squeeze and she was putty in your hands.' Beth giggled again and Simon was horrified.

The lift doors pinged open and he pulled her inside.

'You need to calm down,' he said as he pressed for the tenth floor.

'Why?' she snapped. 'Why are you being so serious? We're on a roll! We need to be thinking about what's next. We need to be using this fantastic momentum. We should break George out of prison and properly interrogate him. What could we do to him? Oh, this could be so good.'

'We're not breaking anyone out of prison,' Simon replied as the lift stopped on their floor. He grabbed Beth's hand and led her back through the glass doors and across the Executive Floor.

He threw his free hand out in front of him and his office door unlocked and opened. He then bundled Beth inside. With a click of his fingers, the door shut, locked itself and all the windows to his office darkened, leaving them properly alone.

'Beth, you have to take control,' he said, placing his arms around her. 'The dark magic is taking over. Don't let it.'

'Oh stop moaning,' she said, pushing him away. 'It's fine. I feel brilliant. Nothing that feels this good can be bad. The only problem I've got is your constant whinging and controlling.'

'These things you're saying, they're not you. You would never let me hurt Diane like that. You know you wouldn't.'

'It was the only option we had.'

'It wasn't. We would have found another way.'

'You got results. She deserved it.'

'No she didn't. It was completely immoral and wrong.'

He saw the darkness flicker in her eyes. She was still in there somewhere but he was losing her fast.

His uncle had told him stories about those who truly gave in to dark magic. Once you surrendered yourself to it, it was extremely hard to come back. Mostly because a person wouldn't want to. It felt good. It oozed through the body like an addictive drug. Whenever spells were cast, it rewarded the user with a heady delight, encouraging them to do it again. It would open up a world of possibilities and it would feel fantastic at the same time. But it also cost a user their inhibitions, sense of decency and, often as a result, their life as they knew it. Hence why it was illegal.

Most Malants steered well clear of it. Some from the sheer fear of what it would do to them, others from the fear of imprisonment. For Simon, it had always been the fear of what would happen. A fear that was now playing out right in front of him.

He rubbed his forehead as he berated himself. He was totally to blame. She wouldn't have even put a toe in the water if he hadn't turned to dark magic himself. He'd been sure he could control it. Positive in fact. He'd just never factored in for one minute that Beth would be pulled down with him.

He knew he needed help. He needed his uncle. Paul would know what to do.

He sat down on the sofa that rested against the back wall of his office and he put his head in his hands.

If this was the mess he got into without Paul for one day, how was he going to survive without Paul forever? He wasn't ready to lose Paul yet. Not yet. It was too soon. He'd already lost one father. He couldn't even contemplate losing another.

Just as Simon felt the prickle of tears at his eyes, Beth bounced on the sofa next to him. 'Don't get all depressing. If I'm going to be stuck with you, at least we could have some fun together. Let's go and cause havoc at the prison. We could sack Jane! That might make you smile. She's been letting prisoners get a hold of elements. That's surely a sackable offence. Hell, we're in charge. We could sack her for making a bad cup of tea. Not that I think she's ever made tea for me. You people and your bloody servants. How hard is it to make a cup of tea? Bloody snobs. Scarlett won't be ruined like that. She'll be cooking for herself and learning to be independent. She won't be useless like you.'

'Thank you,' Simon said, although he wasn't letting Beth's words pierce him.

'So come on. Let's go and sack Jane. It will be the end to all our problems. We could throw her in prison!' Beth rolled back on the sofa with delight. 'I bet she wouldn't like being handcuffed!'

Simon sat up straight and took Beth by the hands. 'We are not going to sack Jane.'

'But it would end all our problems.'

'And no doubt cause a thousand more. She's well liked and respected, and we don't actually know if she's done anything wrong. The last thing we want is a revolt within our own government.'

'What can they do? Nobody can overpower us. Especially not now.'

'Having power does not mean you always have to use it. We have both always believed in doing what's right, not just what we're capable of. You're the best person I know. You don't mean any of this.'

'You taught me that the world isn't black and white,' Beth said and Simon's heart broke. He hated it when she blamed him for the destruction of her innocence. 'Life sucks and Jane deserves to be thrown in prison.'

'The world isn't black and white. That's why we need to tread carefully and always make sound decisions.'

'We can make any decisions we want. Don't you see? We can literally do whatever we want. Why is this only just occurring to me? We're completely unstoppable!'

'That's why we must stop ourselves! We must have self-control.'

Beth rolled her eyes. 'Yawn! You're so boring and strait-laced. How have I married such a dull man? We're in a big pile of shit and we have a very easy way of getting out of it. Why are you being so difficult?'

Simon stood up. He had to think. He had to get help. He was struggling with what to do, but he couldn't let her sink like this. There had to be a way to pull her back.

Without Paul and Jane, he didn't know who else he could turn to. They had always been his rock.

That was when he realised what to do. He pulled Beth to her feet.

'We're going to see Jim,' he said.

'Jim? Oh yes! I like Jim. What's he done? Are we throwing him in prison?'

'No. Nobody is going to prison. I'm hoping he'll be a voice of reason and he'll help us.'

'What if he calls up Jane? Those two are too close for comfort sometimes.'

'No, he's been too loyal to us over the years to suddenly stab us in the back. I'm sure he'll help us. We have to at least try. Worst case scenario, he'll just send us away.'

'I suppose we can't just sit around here getting bored. Let's get teleporting again. Are we going to try his house?'

'No!' Simon insisted.

'Where else would he be?' Beth's face lit up with delight. 'We're going to Malancy HQ?'

'No, we're not teleporting. It's too dangerous. We need to use as little power as possible, and steer well clear of dark magic. We can't risk you slipping into it any more.'

'I can easily just tap into it for a few seconds. I'm in total control.'

Simon shook his head. She seemed to really believe that.

'No, we're doing this old school,' Simon said, adamantly.

'What does that mean?'

Simon paced around as he considered all his options.

'There is very little chance that Jim will have the police watching his house. Not just because no one would suspect we'd go there, but also because he'd insist that he be left alone. He'd ban anyone from watching him. So if we can get to his house, we'll probably have a good chance of talking to him unnoticed. We just need to get there. Public transport is out of the question. We'd have to take about six buses. It's too complicated. Driving is our only viable option.'

'We could fly! I bet we could fly. I bet I have the power now to make us fly. If we can turn invisible-'

'No! No more dark magic.'

'It's helping us out!'

'It's ruining you!'

'Do you really want to start an argument with me?' Beth said, squaring up to him.

Simon thrust out his hand and pinned her to the sofa.

He didn't want to hurt her, but he was hoping the shock might make her back off a bit.

'We might have equal power on paper, Beth,' Simon warned, 'but you don't know how to use it as well as I do. Don't start down that road with me. You'll never win.'

Simon lifted his hold of her and she remained still. She didn't look happy, but thankfully she didn't respond. Simon had to think quickly.

He could summon up one of his cars to the office. That was a simple spell that required very little power. But Jane knew all of his cars and number plates. They'd be followed before they left Heaningford.

He needed a car that no one would be looking for, and one he could honestly and easily get a hold of.

'Paul!' Simon blurted out.

Beth looked at him. 'He's dead.'

Simon breathed through the pain that struck him.

'We could use one of his cars,' he said. 'No one is going to be looking for Paul's cars. Anyone would believe they're safely at home and not going to be used. I'll summon one of his cars here and we can drive that to Jim's, totally unnoticed. It has to work.'

'What, you're going to summon it into this office? We might have trouble getting it in the lift.' Beth chuckled. 'I still think we should give flying a go. Do you think we could really do that? How amazing would that be!'

'No,' Simon said, terrified of the idea of them even trying. 'Being invisible is one thing, anti-gravity is something completely different. I don't think it's possible.'

'But we could-'

'No, Beth. Leave it there. We're driving.'

'I'm going to give it a go.'

Simon studied her as Beth closed her eyes, ready to perform a spell. 'Do you even know where to begin?' he asked. 'Let's say that flying was possible – which I highly doubt – you're not experienced enough to create new spells. Let it go, Beth. We're going to drive. You like cars.'

'I can create new spells. I have equal power to you.'

'But not equal knowledge.'

'I fucking hate you. I'm going to create a spell that makes people permanently yawn around you, so the whole world will feel just as I do in your presence. Then we'll see who can't create spells.'

'You do that, Beth. But in the meantime, let's drive over to Jim's.'

The animosity was alive in her eyes as she stood tall glaring at him, but Simon refused to be jarred by her. He just looked back at her coolly.

'What car are we taking?' she demanded to know. 'The Aston Martin?'

'Paul doesn't have an Aston Martin.'

'No, but he's got a Ferrari! I've never been in his Ferrari.'

'We're trying to get around unnoticed. A Ferrari will bring too much unwanted attention. I'm going to summon his BMW.'

'That's so boring! Trust you to pick the world's most boring car.'

Simon sighed. This was getting exhausting. 'We need to blend in. I will summon it into my space in the car park. We haven't brought a car today so the space will be empty. Well, it better be. We'll summon it, get in and drive straight over to Jim's. I know where the keys are in Paul's house. It will be easy, honest and straightforward. Are you ready?'

Beth pulled a face. 'I guess I have to be.'

'Let's get you out of here.'

Simon clicked his fingers so that the windows were transparent once more, and then the door popped open. He grabbed Beth's hand again and led her out of the office.

Simon had everything crossed that Jim could help. Because if Jim couldn't, he didn't know what other options were left.

TWENTY-TWO

They left the office and headed down to the ground floor, but rather than heading out the front doors, Simon pulled Beth to the back of the building.

'The Malant police are outside,' he said. 'We need another exit.'

'Are we going to teleport through the wall?' Beth asked with excited eyes.

'No.'

They reached the fire door at the end of the corridor. Simon placed his hand onto it to sense if anyone was on the other side. He couldn't feel anything so was pretty confident that they were safe. He pushed open the door, pulled Beth through, and swiftly closed it again.

'Don't you just think of everything,' Beth said with a snarl.

'I wish.'

Simon took Beth's hand again and led her down the small path to his space in the car park. Sure enough it was empty. Simon looked around. There wasn't another person in sight.

He quickly closed his eyes and summoned up the image of Paul's BMW, which he knew would be locked in one of

Paul's garages. Then he thought of the keys that would be in the drawer in Paul's study and he focused on the images intently.

Within a few seconds, the keys appeared in his hand, and the car magically appeared out of thin air right into the space before them.

Simon sighed with relief. Step one was easily over with.

He clicked the button and the doors opened.

'Get in,' he said to Beth. She reluctantly complied and sat in the passenger seat.

The journey to Jim's was relatively easy. Traffic was heavy, but they weren't bothered by anyone and they made it to Jim's house in twenty-five minutes.

Simon parked just down the road. He stopped the engine before checking the surroundings.

'Do you see anything suspicious?' he asked Beth.

'No. I bet I could do a spell to scan for people in the area.'

'Or we could just use our eyes.'

'It won't be as thorough.'

'But it will be safer.'

'Maybe not. Not if someone's lurking behind a bush or something.'

'Why would someone be lurking behind a bush? As we speak, the Malant police are sitting outside our house and the office. They're not being covert. It wouldn't benefit them to be convert.'

'I say we cast a spell.'

'I say I'm going to knock on Jim's door and see if he's at home. You wait here, and if you see something suspicious-'

'Batter them!'

'What? Beth!'

'What? We can't have people after us.'

'You don't condone violence. You know you don't.'

'Not on innocent people.'

'Not at all. If you are concerned about anything, lock

the door and wait for me.'

'Lock the door? Are you serious?'

'Yes. Don't push me.'

Beth sat back in a huff. Simon prepared himself for a further argument, but she remained quiet. Moody but quiet. That would have to do.

He stepped out of the car and slowly walked down the pavement to Jim's front door. He tried to seem as casual as he could.

As soon as he reached the drive, he saw his Jaguar sitting there from where he'd left it the day before. He'd completely forgotten about that. He also remembered that he'd left his Aston Martin at Malancy HQ. They had been doing far too much teleporting lately. It really wasn't good.

He quickly checked that no one was watching and then he cast a spell to send his car back home. It swiftly vanished. He then did the same and cast a spell to move his Aston Martin safely back to his driveway. Moments later, it was all completed. Then he continued on to Jim's front door.

He pressed the bell but there was no answer. He also couldn't sense Jim inside. It was only mid-afternoon, though. Jim would still be at Malancy HQ.

Simon returned to Paul's car.

'He's not at home.'

'That leaves only one option,' Beth said.

'What's that?'

'We'll have to bust in to Malancy HQ and have it out with him and Jane.'

'Or we could just wait. I think it would be best to speak to Jim at home.'

'But he could be hours.'

'Or he could be five minutes.'

'I'm bored already.'

'What a surprise,' Simon mumbled under his breath.

'We can at least do something to pass the time, can't we?'

'Like what?'

'I don't know. We could have sex.'

'What?'

'Come on. I feel so turned on right now. I've honestly never felt this good.'

Simon studied her. He loved her with all his heart, but the woman in front of him was not the woman he married.

'You want to have sex in this car in the middle of the street?'

'Yes. I mean we can blacken the windows if you're going to be all uptight about it.'

Simon stared ahead, refusing to respond.

'Come on! I know it's Paul's car, but it's not like he'll ever know.'

Her words stung bitterly, but she didn't even seem to acknowledge how cruel they were.

'We're in the middle of a major crisis right now,' Simon stated. 'Forgive me for being all uptight, but I'm not really in the mood for intimacy.'

'Ooh, intimacy! Don't worry about that. I wasn't planning on being intimate. I just want to fuck.'

'Beth!'

'Come on. It'll loosen you up. Make you feel *so* much better.'

'You're not thinking straight. We need to focus on Jim's house and be ready for when he gets home.'

'Even if we miss him getting home, it's not like he'll be going out again. He's as boring as you are. Especially now Carly's dumped in.'

'Beth, listen to yourself. This isn't you.'

'You mean wanting to have sex outdoors?'

'No, being so cruel.'

'Saying it like it is isn't cruel. I'm just being honest. You know I value honesty. I'm not the one with the problem.'

Simon was losing his strength. He willed Jim to come home soon.

Beth grabbed Simon's knee. She caressed it gently

before slowly working her way up his thigh.

'Leave me alone,' he said.

'No.'

'I'm warning you. I'm not doing this right now.'

'I'm not your biggest fan right now either, but you're still hot. We can still have sex.'

'Remove your hands.'

'No.'

'I'm warning you.'

'What are you going to do, Mr Boring?' she sneered, and it was this that made Simon finally snap.

He grabbed her wrist tightly and moved it away from his leg.

'I am not having sex with you,' he growled. His voice was so deep and threatening it made the car vibrate.

He kept a hold of her wrist as they glared at each other angrily. Simon was too fired up to give in, and he held Beth's eyes until she cracked.

'Fine,' she said, shaking away his grip. 'I don't want to have sex anyway. You've become so irritating. God knows what I used to see in you. It must have been a powerful spell that made me want to marry you.'

She sat back in a huff and Simon tried not to let her words wound him. They'd said many a nasty thing to each other in the heat of an argument, but this ran deeper. He actually felt as if she meant the horrible things that were coming out of her mouth.

It's just the dark magic, he told himself, but he was shaken with fear that he was losing her. Jim needed to come home soon.

'Am I at least allowed to get some food and drink?' she barked.

'Of course,' he replied as calmly as he could. 'I can summon up some food. What do you fancy?'

There was a pause before Beth answered, 'A McDonalds.'

Simon sighed. 'Beth, I'd have to steal that to summon it

here. I can't exactly pay for it long distance.'

'So? It's like a billion dollar company. I'm sure they can afford to lose a couple of burgers.'

'It's not right. It's not moral.'

'Okay. What can we summon up then?'

'I was thinking more like snacks from our own cupboard at home.'

'Is that all?'

'Do you want something or not?'

'I suppose that'll have to do. It's not like I could ask you to cook something. Do you even know how to turn the oven on?'

'Beth!'

'All right. I'll have some chocolate. And crisps. And a can of coke. Can we play I-Spy then?'

'You want to play I-Spy?' Simon asked with surprise.

'It's the only game I can think of where I know you won't be able to cheat.'

This wasn't meant to be humorous, but it made Simon smirk. 'When do I cheat at games?'

'When we played that card game a couple of weeks ago. I swear there were six Aces in that pack by the end of the night.'

Simon laughed. 'I thought we both bent the rules to our advantage?'

'As I said before, some of us are honest.'

Simon addressed her fully. 'You have all the same powers as me. I thought we were both having extra fun with the game. In the way that only we can. Like how we said we'd play golf. I thought you were doing it too.'

'Well I wasn't.'

'Never?'

'Never.'

'Oh. Well I won't do it either, then. I thought we were the same.'

'We are so far from the same.'

An uncomfortable silence settled in the car. A silence

that was now nothing to do with the dark magic.

'So are you getting me this chocolate or not?' Beth demanded, jolting Simon from his contemplation.

'Getting it for you now.'

Two hours later, when lots of junk food had been eaten and everything in sight had been guessed at in their drawn out game of I-Spy, Jim arrived home.

The Bird pair watched as he pulled up onto the drive and then got out of the car. They waited for him to enter the house before moving.

Simon took Beth's hand as they walked up to Jim's front door. It didn't take long for him to answer.

'What are you doing here?' Jim asked, his face full of shock.

'If you feel uncomfortable, we'll leave,' Simon said. 'But we really need your help.'

'Hi Jim!' Beth laughed. Jim took one look at her eyes then stood back to let them in. He glanced up and down the street before closing the door.

He led them into his living room and they all sat down.

'I wanted to get in touch,' Jim said. 'I don't approve of Jane's actions. She's got every resource possible looking for you. She's labelled you as highly dangerous and everyone's got a bit fired up about it. It's become a nightmare.'

'Dangerous?' Simon asked before he noticed Jim glance at Beth. 'You mean the dark magic?'

'It's not dangerous. It's amazing!' Beth added.

'You never should have used it,' Jim said.

'I know,' Simon replied. 'But there are bigger things happening right now. Like where are Damien and Carly with our daughter and why has the world adopted Malancy powers?'

'We're working on that as well. Ralph hasn't left the lab and I've taken charge of research.' Jim paused. 'I need to tell you about it, but I don't know how you're going to react.'

'I know that Damien used an element apparently laden with my power. Although I don't know how that's possible.'

'I do,' Jim said and Simon fell silent. He waited with trepidation for Jim to continue.

'It was a stone that we found in Damien's cell,' Jim explained. 'It had your magic in it.'

'Beth told me that. But how?'

'I did! I knew all about that!' Beth said.

'It slotted all together for me straight away,' Jim continued with a look of regret.

'What did?'

'One day a few weeks ago Carly started asking a lot of questions about the stones in your garden. She seemed fascinated. I assumed at the time it was because she'd never considered that you and Beth would ever need to use elements. Now I'm thinking differently.'

'You think the stone Damien had was from my garden?'

'I know it was. It was confirmed the second I saw it. Do you remember that large stone you found on the beach years ago? The shiny one?'

Simon's heart thudded with anger. That was his favourite stone. The stone he hadn't been able to find when he'd been looking in his garden earlier in the week. Now it made perfect sense why. 'She stole a stone from my garden?'

'And she chose well. She must have been trying different ones; sensing the potency in them. I'm guessing you used that stone the most, and every time you did, a little piece of your magic must have got sucked into it making it very potent indeed. I didn't know that was even possible, but Ralph confirmed it. It's become incredibly powerful over the years.'

'She took it to Damien?'

'You don't need a stone when you've got dark magic,'

Beth boasted. 'It's the most incredible thing in the world!'

'I'm guessing Damien's parents dropping by your house on the day of Scarlett's birthday wasn't a coincidence,' Jim said, ignoring Beth's outburst.

'But they just stood at the front door,' Simon argued.

Jim sat back. He seemed broken. 'Carly saw them out.'

'No. That makes no sense. If they were going to steal a stone, they'd do it when we were out of the house. Why be so obvious and do it on the day of our daughter's birthday party?'

'Probably because they couldn't take the risk of you missing it. If you'd spotted the stone missing, you would have been suspicious. They had to wait until the very day they were seeing Damien and putting their plan into action.'

Simon felt winded. 'This was all so pre-meditated. So evil. I'm sorry, Jim. None of us could have known how deceitful she'd end up being.'

'None of you were as close to her as I was. I should have seen it.'

'If it's any consolation, I think she genuinely cared for you before Damien got into her head. He's good at that.'

'Maybe.' Jim seemed lost for a few moments before he turned back to Simon and said, 'Anyway, you came here because you said you need my help. What can I do?'

'I didn't know where else to go,' Simon told him.

Jim looked at Beth, as if he understood.

'We've had no choice but to use dark magic to survive the threats from Jane,' Simon explained. 'I've managed to keep it under control. But as you can see…'

'Beth's been struggling,' Jim finished. 'I was afraid of this.'

'I haven't been struggling,' Beth argued. 'I've never felt better.'

'I can't lose her completely,' Simon pleaded. 'She's still in there. I've seen her come back to me. Just flickers of her, but she's there. What can I do? It hasn't been such an issue for me, but I guess I've had more experience with keeping the darkness at bay. It's always been calling to me. Beth's only known about her powers for a few years.'

'That can't be relevant. You're both equally strong in will power, and that's the key element to keeping the darkness at bay. There must be something else that's causing the difference between you. Tell me about what you've been up to. What have you both been doing since you first tapped into the darkness? Let's break it down.'

'I've been doing magic!' Beth said. 'Teleporting. And then Simon made Diane's bones crush. It was fabulous!'

'You did what?'

'She's fine,' Simon said. 'I didn't crush her bones, although I do deeply regret the hurt I did cause.'

'We even turned invisible,' Beth finished.

'Invisible?' Jim asked with shock.

'I need to talk to Ralph about that,' Simon said. 'When this is over with. It was quite a spell.'

'I didn't know our power could do that.'

'I have a feeling we could do just about anything.'

'I want to fly,' Beth announced.

'You can fly?' Jim asked.

'No. And we won't be trying,' Simon stated. 'To answer your question, when I left here yesterday, I tracked down Damien. It wasn't what I expected.' Simon hesitated. He was cautious about mentioning Carly to Jim. 'As I think you know, Beth got stabbed.'

'I saw the blood.'

'Then, Paul...' Simon's voice choked up.

'I know.'

'I couldn't save him. I could only save Beth.'

'You couldn't have saved him anyway,' Jim said. 'We found out he... It was immediate. There was nothing you could have done.'

'There is always something I could have done. I have unlimited power.'

'And you used that to save your wife.'

Simon looked down to the floor as Jim's words settled in. Why had he been given such a cruel choice?

He squeezed Beth's knee. He couldn't go through all this and lose her too.

She smacked his hand away and he looked back up to Jim.

'I went to New York then,' he continued. 'I had to use dark magic for that. But I didn't care. I just needed to get away. Although it wasn't the dark magic that made me not care. It was the grief. The dark magic didn't really get to me. Why was that?'

'This was straight after you'd healed Beth?' Jim asked.

'Pretty much.'

'What other good magic have you been using?'

Simon thought back. 'I suppose quite a bit. Removing all of the Malant police from the buildings I own for starters. I didn't need dark magic for that.'

'Imagine if you had used it, though,' Beth said, her eyes aglow with wonder. 'You could have got them to leave and never come back.'

'We have to help her, Jim. Yes, I've used good magic. But I've used lots of dark magic too. But only when we've had to. I promise, we've not used it for recreation. As much as Beth is now desperate to.'

'I think I might be able to help,' Jim said, giving Simon some well needed hope. 'Since I've been in charge of the Malancy, I've done a lot of research into dark magic and how we can overcome it. Will power is up there, of course, but good magic also counteracts it. And something like a healing spell will heavily draw the darkness away. It seems to me that you've not been affected so much because you've been counterbalancing it. I bet Beth hasn't.'

'Of course. Yes. Beth has only been using dark magic. I've been doing everything else. I thought I was helping.'

'Then let's get her doing some good spells.'

Without thinking about it, Simon headed into Jim's kitchen. He knew Beth loved him. Above everything else,

Beth loved him. Dark magic couldn't possibly stop someone loving. It was drastic action, but a moment as desperate as this required drastic action.

He grabbed a sharp knife from a drawer and headed back into the living room.

'Beth,' he said. She turned to him, still with that unrecognisable smile. 'I love you. Don't let me down.'

He took a breath and thought no more about it. He stabbed himself right in the stomach.

TWENTY-THREE

Beth glanced over at her husband as he dropped to the floor in agony. She actually felt relief. He was finally quiet.

'Beth!' Jim shouted, kneeling down to help Simon. 'Do something!'

'Like what?'

'Heal him!'

'He can heal himself.'

'No he can't! Look at him, Beth. He's bleeding. He's going to die.'

'What an idiot. What did he do that for?'

'I can't imagine,' Jim said. 'Please help him!'

Beth rolled her eyes.

'Do you want to lose him?' Jim challenged.

Beth couldn't answer the question. She found herself actually not caring at all.

'Do you want Scarlett to lose her father?' Jim added.

These words struck her. She couldn't have that. Scarlett needed her daddy. For all Simon's faults, he was a good father.

'Okay,' Beth said. She calmly walked over. She knelt down, the blood instantly soaking into her jeans.

'Oh bloody hell. I really like these jeans. You'd better

come up with a good cleaning spell after this,' she said, before finally placing her hands on Simon's wound.

She pushed him onto his back as he groaned against the pain.

'Stop moaning. I'm here aren't I?' she said to him.

She pressed firmly against the wound and her hands became quickly drenched. It was far from pleasant and she couldn't resist using more force than necessary, causing him extra pain to serve him right. He whimpered and she smirked.

She'd never healed anyone else before, but she used the logic that Simon always insisted on. When she needed to self-heal, she channelled her energy on whatever part of her body was injured. So for Simon it made sense that she would just channel that same magical energy, but down her hands and onto the slice across his belly.

She began the spell, only needing to use good magic. The power slowly grew within her, and as it did she could feel the blood slow between her fingers. The wound tightened below her hands as it sealed itself, but she barely noticed. All she could feel was deep sadness.

The spell completed and tears instantly pooled in her eyes.

Simon sat up, the shock and relief evident on his face.

'Why did you do that?' she screamed at him, shaking.

'Beth?' he muttered. 'Are you okay?'

'Am I okay? No! Of course I'm not. My husband just stabbed himself.'

'I'm sorry,' he whispered. 'But I had to.'

'No you didn't. You never have to do things like that.'

Simon took her cheek in his hand and looked at her face.

'I was losing you,' he said before curling her hair behind her ear.

'What does that mean?'

'You were so sucked into the dark magic. You weren't you.'

Beth's tears halted as she considered what Simon was saying.

She acknowledged how different she had felt five minutes before. How could she have let herself be so drawn in like that?

'Jim said that good magic counterbalances bad,' Simon explained. 'I thought a mega healing spell and a shock to your system might be just the medicine. I'm so glad I was right.'

'I nearly lost you, you bastard!' She hit him on the arm.

'Ow! I have just been stabbed you know.'

'Yes, by your own hand, you idiot. Never do that again. I don't care how bad things get, never risk your own life like that.'

Beth kissed him before snuggling against him for a cuddle. She needed it.

'I needed to take drastic action. I knew you still loved me somewhere deep inside.'

Beth felt the guilt sicken her as she realised that her love for him just hadn't been there. It was her love for Scarlett that had made her take action. She couldn't tell him that, though. How could she admit that?

'You're back now, but the darkness is still going to taunt you,' Simon warned. 'We need a plan. I can't have you getting sucked in like that again.'

'It felt so good,' Beth said. 'It was like I couldn't think straight, but it didn't matter.' Beth looked into Simon's eyes. 'We hurt Diane. We should never have done that.'

'I know.'

'I need to apologise. I was laughing.' Beth was unbearably ashamed. It had seemed delightful at the time, but now she felt wretched.

'I already apologised,' Simon said. 'Let's leave it there. Diane has too many important contacts for us to seem weak. We don't need anyone else realising how vulnerable we almost became.'

'I felt far from vulnerable. I was stronger than ever. I

literally think anything could have been possible. Even flying.'

'Do you still want to do that?' Simon asked with concern.

'No,' Beth smiled. 'It seems ludicrous now. I was a wreck being invisible. Imagine if I actually left the earth? No, I love our power just as it is, and that's enough for me.'

'I couldn't agree more. We need to steer clear of dark magic as much as we can.'

'We need to steer clear of it completely.'

'Now you're back with us, Beth,' Jim interrupted, 'could we try to tackle some of these other issues?'

'Of course,' Beth said. 'Thank you so much, Jim. I dread to think what would have happened if you'd not been here.'

'It's my pleasure. I'd do anything for you two. And I'm glad to see you're back to yourself. Dark magic is very dangerous. We need to find a way to rid you of it completely.'

'I feel better now,' she said.

'Simon's right,' Jim replied. 'The darkness has got a grasp. A grasp of you both. You've let it in and it's going to be very difficult to rid yourselves of it now.'

'We can't think about that at the minute,' Simon said. 'We need to focus on getting Scarlett back. Then we can worry about the darkness. For now we just need to control it.'

Beth kissed Simon on the cheek before rising to her feet. 'I agree. I'm just going to pop to your bathroom, if that's okay?' she said to Jim, putting out her bloody hands as if to signal she wanted to wash them. Jim nodded and she made her way to the toilet near the hallway.

She shut the door behind her, closed the toilet lid and sat down. She needed a minute. Her whole body felt a jumbled mix of electrifying energy and shaky fear. It was most disconcerting.

She had a little weep as she let the emotions of the past couple of days seep out. It was all too much. Too much had happened in such a short space of time and they weren't even through it yet. Beth took a breath as she considered whether she could even go on. She wanted to disappear back to her bedroom, hide under the covers and not come out for a few weeks. Maybe it would all be over in a few weeks.

Then she glanced at her blood soaked hands and she realised she was needed. As much as she needed Simon, he needed her too. They could only combat this together. They had always made a terrific team. It was time for them to put their synergy into action.

Beth stood up and turned the taps on. She watched the blood wash away down the sink and she told herself that was her weak moment done with. She'd step outside this bathroom and get her head into gear. There would be no more dark magic and no more distractions. They needed to get these problems resolved so they could properly mourn the loss of Paul and start a new phase of their lives without him.

As sharp tug pulled at Beth inside. Paul was their rock. They both relied on him for so much. Life was going to be very different now. It was going to lack something so important. Things would never be the same again.

Another tear rolled down Beth's cheek. She wiped it away and took another breath.

Enough! No more weakness.

She dried her hands and turned around. She could cry when this was all over with, but for now she had to be strong.

She walked back into the living room to find Simon sitting next to a pile of neatly folded clothes.

'I summoned up a change of clothes for us,' he said. Beth looked down to see the blood stains across her jeans and t-shirt.

'Two days of bloody clothes. This can't be a good

omen,' she said, glancing at the jeans and t-shirt replacement Simon had chosen for her. The t-shirt was pink. He always loved her in pink.

She then turned her attention to Jim's floor. The blood from the carpet was gone. Simon really did know a good cleaning spell. They could have just removed the stains from their clothes too, but it wouldn't have felt right. It was good to change.

'Now you're back, I think we need to tell Jim about what we learned today,' Simon said.

'You've not told him yet?' Beth asked, sitting down next to Simon on the settee.

'We're a team. I was waiting for you.'

'What have you found out?' Jim asked, sitting forward on the adjacent armchair.

'You're not going to like this,' Simon said.

'That doesn't come as a surprise. I've not really liked anything that's happened lately,' Jim replied.

'And it just keeps coming. It seems your brother is involved in some of what's been happening over the past couple of days.'

'George? How can George be involved? He's in prison.'

'Did you know that visitors can take elements into the prison with them? Only in the visitors' room. Prisoners get checked before they enter their cells again. But that room is open to anyone casting a spell.'

'That doesn't make any sense,' Jim said.

'So you didn't know about this?'

Jim considered his response. 'I suppose I've never been checked to see if I'm carrying an element when I've visited George, but I've always assumed it wouldn't be allowed. Are you sure?'

'Yes. Definitely.'

'Okay. As strange as that seems, I have no reason not to believe you. It's Jane who's in charge of the prison and that side of things.'

'I knew Jane would be involved!' Beth said, feeling bitter towards the woman who had them on the run. 'She's such a hypocrite.'

'We don't know anything yet,' Simon replied.

'What has this got to do with George?' Jim asked.

'I take it you know who Linda Malant is?' Simon said.

'Yes. My sister in law. Why?'

'She and a woman from our office, Diane, have been visiting George. And during those visits he's been casting a spell on them. A spell that gives them temporary Malant powers.'

'What?' Jim said, shaking his head. 'That definitely can't be right. No such spell exists. I would know. I've been through every file, every book, every piece of information we've got. I've learnt about hundreds of spells, but I've come across nothing that would even so much as suggest that making non-Malants powerful is possible.'

'Did you know that Malants could turn invisible?' Simon countered.

Jim leant backwards. 'That's different.'

'How?'

'It doesn't affect our whole way of life.'

'But still. It shows that we have far more power than we're aware of.'

'Power that we're not aware of, but George is?'

'It certainly appears that way.'

Jim contemplated all that he'd been told for a few minutes, before he said, 'We need to know for sure.'

'I completely agree,' Simon said. 'And the only way to be sure is to ask him.'

'Are you suggesting that George is to blame for the whole world becoming magic?' Jim asked.

'I don't think-'

'He wanted to end the Malancy!' Jim argued before Simon could respond. 'That's why he's in prison. Giving the entire population our abilities is the whole other extreme. It makes no sense.'

'If George did do this, I certainly don't believe he meant to,' Simon said. 'From everything Diane has told us and what you've said today, I think I have an idea of what may have happened. But we need George to confirm it.'

'Confirm what?'

'What I presume happened is that Linda and Diane went to visit George on Sunday night at the same time as Damien's parents were also there visiting Damien. With the stone from my garden. I'm guessing that as George cast the spell onto Linda and Diane, Damien used his new stone to intervene it. It would have to be a powerful spell if it gives someone magical abilities. Imagine if that was mixed in with my power. My potency. It must have had a huge knock on effect that echoed across the world. With magic that strong, it only makes sense that the man holding the stone would adopt the core of it. Hence why Damien's abilities now mirror my own.' Simon turned to Beth. 'Ours.'

'Whilst that's plausible,' Jim said, 'there is one huge problem with your story. A spell that powerful would give off terrific red beams. How could nobody notice? The guards would have said something.'

'I thought that too. Perhaps that's even why elements aren't banned for visitors. There are very few spells that don't render a glow so it's hard to not notice when someone's using an element. So that begs the question, how did George manage it?'

'I can't see George being overly willing to help,' Jim said.

'He certainly won't help Beth and myself.'

Jim nodded. 'I see.'

'I was hoping you could go with us. He might be more willing to open up to you.'

'You want us all to go together?'

'Strength in numbers.'

'I hate to say it, but the second you appear anywhere near that prison, you'll have the police all over you.'

'I know. We also have to consider that if George is going to talk at all, he certainly won't be doing it with a bunch of guards keeping an eye on him.'

'So what are you saying? You want to break him out?'

'No. I want us to break in. Or at least teleport.'

'Simon, no,' Beth said. Fear crept up her spine. 'That would mean using dark magic again.'

'I think we have to,' Simon said, turning to his wife. 'It's just once.'

'That's what we keep saying! But it's not just once. It'll get a hold of me again.'

'No it won't. I'll do the spell.'

'You'll need a hell of a lot of power to transport three people.'

'Yes, but when we get back I'll do some good magic to counterbalance it.'

'I'm not stabbing myself,' Beth said. 'Or you.'

'No, I wasn't thinking anything that dramatic again. We'll just move a few things around the house. Perhaps redecorate. We've been saying for ages that we need to spruce up the bedroom.'

'You want to redecorate?' Beth asked, bewildered. 'The world is falling apart around us and you want to redecorate?'

'Only to help us counterbalance the darkness. What else do you suggest? Moving three thousand pencils around a room?'

Beth sat back. She saw his point. Redecorating would both be a positive use of their magic and have a practical purpose. It just felt so wildly insignificant at that moment.

'Okay. Whatever. But I'm not in the frame of mind to spend ages thinking about a colour scheme. We'll do whatever and we'll worry about the state of it when all this is over with.'

Simon smirked. 'Agreed.' He then turned to Jim. 'Do you know what time everyone has to be back in their cells? We'd need George to be alone.'

'Nine o'clock. Then lights go out at eleven.'

'Then we need to do it between nine and eleven.' Simon looked at his watch. 'We've got two hours to wait.'

'I'll cook us something to eat, shall I?' Jim offered, standing up. This was the Jim Beth knew and loved. Whenever things got tense, he'd always make a cup of tea or cook up something to eat.

The only problem was that Beth and Simon had stuffed themselves with a lot of junk whilst waiting for Jim to get home. She wasn't feeling remotely hungry. But she didn't want to admit that.

'Sounds wonderful, Jim,' she replied. Then she turned to Simon to stop him arguing. 'You haven't cooked for us in so long. I've missed your scrumptious dishes.'

'It won't be fancy. I was going to have an omelette.'

'Perfect,' Simon said, before glancing at Beth with a look that told her it was anything but perfect. She flashed him a shut up stare and he sat back defeated.

Just before Jim entered the kitchen, he hesitated.

'There's something you need to know,' he said, turning around to face Beth and Simon. 'I hate that I'm the one to tell you this. I completely disagree with it and I've told Jane just that. She has no right to do this. Yet she is.'

'Do what?' Simon asked. Beth could hear her heartbeat pound in her ears as she awaited Jim's response. This sounded very bad. How much more was going to be thrown their way?

'I don't know what's going on in her head. I've never seen Jane like this.'

'Just say it, Jim,' Simon urged. 'What is it?'

He took a breath. 'Jane is going to hold Paul's funeral to ransom.'

'What does that mean?' Beth asked, nervously. Of course she knew. Simon had suspected that Jane would do something like this. But Beth just needed to double check in the hope she'd misunderstood.

'Unless you both give yourselves up, she won't tell you

when or where the funeral is going to be,' Jim replied. 'She will literally go ahead with it and you'll never know.'

'She can't do that!' Simon said, snapping to his feet. 'She can't do that! He's my family. He's my blood relative. I'm his only blood relative. She barely knows him in comparison. I have every right to be there. Hell, I should be arranging it. She can't do this.'

'I know. I agree,' Jim said, edging away from Simon. Simon's anger could rattle just about anyone.

'What about everyone else?' Simon asked. 'Paul knew a lot of people. Surely someone else could just let me know the details? She can't not invite anyone at all to Paul's funeral.'

Jim regarded Simon regretfully. 'She's going to make everyone sign non-disclosure agreements. Spell-bound agreements. She's had them drawn up today. They're locked tight. Guests will only be able to find out about the funeral plans after they've signed.'

'What the hell? What on earth? What are people going to say to that?'

'Paul's a very wealthy and powerful man. It will be easy for her to convince people that she wants to protect the day. Keep out the press, control the numbers and all that.'

'People won't buy that.'

'Why wouldn't they? It's too crazy to believe anything else.'

'Damn right it is.'

'So unless we give ourselves up, we'll miss Paul's funeral?' Beth asked. Tears threated to fall again as she waited for clarification that she was really understanding this right. It was such a horrific notion.

'I'm afraid so.'

'No,' Simon said, pacing up and down the living room. 'No. She's not doing this. He's my uncle. My only living relative. I have every right to have a say on the funeral, and more than every right to go. She can't do this. This goes against everything Paul believes in. She's stripping away at her family when it meant absolutely everything to her husband. She's not doing this!'

'No, she's not,' Beth said, standing up so she could address Simon directly. 'She won't get away with this. You'll find a way around this. Or you'll make her see sense.'

'I've lost enough,' he said. Beth could tell he was on the brink of breaking down. He seemed to tense himself, trying to keep desperate control. 'I've lost too much. Why is she making it so much worse?'

Beth stood before him. 'This isn't over. We have this information now and we'll use it wisely. She won't get away with this.'

'No,' Simon said. 'She can't stop me saying goodbye to my uncle. I have to be able to say goodbye to him. I can't not say goodbye to him.' Simon's body was shaking and a small tear appeared in the corner of his eye.

'You are definitely going to say goodbye to him. She won't win. None of us will let her.'

'Have you signed the non-disclosure agreement?' Simon asked Jim.

'No. I refused to. I told her exactly what I thought. So, like you, I don't know the details of the funeral.'

'But we're going to find out,' Beth said.

'I'll never forgive her for this,' Simon said, taking deep breaths to keep his composure. Beth didn't know how he was doing it. His face seemed so strained and devastated, as if he were mere millimetres from complete rock bottom, yet he still stood strong. 'And Paul would never forgive her either,' Simon finished. 'She must know that.'

'I will never forgive her. And neither will Jim. How on earth is she going to explain you not being at the funeral? People will be infuriated. She'll see sense. She has to. She's just hurting. It's all still so raw.'

'Not just for her.'

'Maybe if we get to George and get all the answers, we can go and see her and have a proper conversation,' Beth suggested. 'If we solve all of the other problems, she'll have to see sense. She'll surely calm down a bit if she has less to worry about.'

'Yes, that's a good idea,' Jim said. 'She's got a huge amount on her plate at the minute. I think if you take away some of her stresses, it will definitely help. Absolutely.'

Simon breathed slowly and Beth could tell he was calculating everything in his head.

'Let's go and see George,' he said. 'Perhaps we'll go just after nine. Then we'll pay Jane a visit and end this nonsense.'

'Sounds like a good plan,' Jim said. 'I'll get the dinner on so we're ready to go.'

Jim walked into the kitchen and Beth turned to Simon.

'Nothing beats us Birds,' she said, taking his cheeks in her hands. 'Nothing. We're in this together all the way and we will come out triumphant. Do you trust me?'

'Always,' Simon replied and then she kissed him.

'I love you so much. I won't let her hurt you like this.'

Simon smiled slightly. 'You're going to look after me?'

'Always.'

TWENTY-FOUR

By eight o'clock, the food was finished. While Jim tidied up in the kitchen, Beth and Simon hopped through channels on the television, although they weren't really interested in anything.

The next hour dragged by, with barely a word being said between any of them. The tension was mounting as they were forced to wait. If only they could speed up time.

When nine o'clock eventually came around, they were all jittery with anticipation. Deciding it was perhaps still a little too early to leave, they found things to do to get ready, such as taking it in turns to go to the toilet, running through the very simple plan over and over, triple checking their shoes were tied up properly; anything to fill up a few more minutes. They knew the longer they left it, the more likely it would be that George would be safely locked up in his cell for the night alone. Although it was right to wait, it was becoming agonising.

It was around quarter past nine when they stood together in Jim's living room and they decided it was time to leave.

'Are we all ready?' Simon asked, taking Beth and Jim's hands.

'Yes,' Jim replied.

'Let's get this over with,' Beth said.

Simon closed his eyes and Beth watched as he tapped back into the dark magic. She kept her mind as blank as possible, but she couldn't help little worries sneaking in. Would this be okay? Would George even speak to them, let alone give them the answers they needed? Would the amount of power needed to transport all three of them push Simon over the edge?

She tried to blank it all out, but the stakes were too high for her not to worry.

Simon's frame glowed red as the spell took hold. Within seconds they were standing in the middle of George's cell.

George, who had been sitting on the bed with a book, jumped up with a yelp. When he saw who it was, he bent over and sighed.

'I assumed I'd be getting a visit from the government,' he said. 'Although I did expect it to be a bit more official. What are you doing?'

'Hello George,' Jim said.

Beth had forgotten just how alike Jim and his twin brother were. It was only the fact that George had a few extra pounds around the waist that anyone could tell the difference.

'I take it this isn't a social visit?' George said.

Beth glanced around the cell, eager to know what a Malant prison was like. She was ultimately in charge of all of this, yet she'd never even considered it before. It was very white and clean. The room was small, but George was lucky enough to have a radio, a small TV, quite a comfortable looking single bed, a little wardrobe and desk, and, off to the side, a small en suite. It was far more luxurious than any cells she'd seen in mainstream prisons (well, on the telly). Malants were treated very well indeed. Damien really couldn't have had things that bad. Especially considering what he deserved. Beth couldn't decide if this was fair or not. Should someone serving a prison sentence suffer more? Or was having your freedom taken away punishment enough?

She made a mental note to add it to the agenda for the next Malancy HQ meeting, before quickly realising how that might not be possible. Maybe never again. Maybe things were going to change forever.

She shuddered at that thought. She had been so happy. Life hadn't been perfect, but it had been fairly close. Yet now it all felt shattered, all in the space of a few hours.

She focused again on George. He had to help them. With Paul gone, things could never be the same. But they needed to salvage whatever they had left.

'We're not here for enjoyment,' Simon stated, quite coldly. 'We're here because we need answers.'

'I thought as much,' George replied. 'Although I had expected Jim to just visit me as normal. I never anticipated such a dramatic entrance. I'm honoured.'

'You know we need to speak to you in private,' Jim said. 'You might be locked up in here, but let's not pretend you're not fully up to speed with everything that's been happening on the outside.'

George sat back on the bed. 'Which part? The whole world adopting Malant powers? Or the fact that the infallible Bird couple are now wanted for arrest? Is it right that it's in relation to Paul Bird's murder?' George asked, with genuine curiosity.

Simon glared at him. 'No.'

'But Paul is dead?'

'George,' Jim warned. 'We're not here to discuss that.'

'But it's really true?'

'We have other more pressing matters to discuss,' Simon replied.

'If you're not wanted for Paul's murder - as I was led to believe - why else would the ever vigilant Mrs Parker want you arrested?'

'It's Mrs Bird now. Jane Bird. And I couldn't tell you

why she wants us arrested,' Simon said, a fierce undertone seeping into his voice. 'I haven't had the chance to talk to her about it.'

'There's conflict in the family,' George said, and Beth spotted faint pleasure in his expression.

'There's conflict just about everywhere,' Jim said to his brother. 'And we have reason to believe you know exactly how it all started.'

George studied the three faces in front of him.

'I do,' he said. 'I actually have a lot of the answers you might be looking for. I know exactly how the whole world has managed to adopt Malant powers. I didn't expect it, but I know what caused it.'

'We know it relates to the spell you cast on your wife and Diane from our office,' Simon said, taking George by surprise. 'We also know that Damien had a very powerful element in his possession at the same time. What we want to know is how you know about this spell and how you hid it from the guards.'

This seemed to totally throw George.

'You have been doing your homework,' he said. 'But there are still a few gaps in your knowledge. Gaps I'd be happy to fill.'

'Really?' Jim said.

'For a price.'

'What do you want?' Simon asked.

'Fifty percent off my sentence.'

'What?'

'I won't negotiate.'

'You want to serve just fifteen years for the awful things you did? You tried to end the Malancy.'

'You must think it's terribly ironic that I'm now responsible for the whole world having powers. But surely that shows you I've changed my ways.'

'You could never change,' Jim said. 'The story might be different, but your self-serving agenda always runs through the heart of everything you do. If it benefits you, you'll do it.'

'That's true of anyone who has power,' George stated.

'Don't be so cynical,' Beth snapped.

'It's not cynical,' George replied. 'Look at Jane. Arresting you helps no one but herself. Whatever her reason for wanting you arrested, it has to be self-serving. If anyone actually cared about the Malancy and its importance, they'd never turn on the two strongest Malants. That was the mistake I made and look where it got me.'

'That's a terrible example,' Beth replied. 'I don't agree with Jane's actions, but she's in a state of grieving. She's not thinking straight. Besides, Simon and I are powerful and we're not self-serving.'

George shook his head.

'What?'

'You might have incredible magical abilities,' he said, 'but you don't have the power where it matters. Jane has the real power. She's the one that people listen to. That's why she's able to so easily back you into a corner. If you were really powerful, you wouldn't have to sneak into my cell after hours.'

Beth wanted to argue, but George's words had struck her in a way she didn't like. They were meant to be more powerful than Jane, yet Jane was overruling them on everything. How had that happened?

'All that matters at the minute, George, is whether the answers you can provide are worth fifteen years off a jail sentence,' Simon said, getting the conversation back on track. 'Jim, what are your thoughts?'

Jim studied George for a moment. 'They could be.'

'Why don't we make the action decide for itself,' Simon said.

'What does that mean?' George asked.

'If the answers you give really do help us to resolve some of the issues we're currently facing, you'll get fifteen years removed from your sentence. That will leave you just thirteen more years to serve.'

'Nice try. I'm not falling for that. You want me to tell you before you'll give me the reduction? That's not happening.'

Simon stood back. Beth watched as he held out his hands before him and closed his eyes. His flesh became fiery red, and balls of heat seemed to bounce over his fingers.

A couple of minutes went by and then an A4 document appeared in Simon's hands.

'Here,' he said, handing the document to George. 'A contract. If what you tell us is actually useful, then fifteen years will automatically disappear off your sentence. If what you have to say is useless, nothing happens.'

George regarded Simon with confusion for a second before he read through the contract before him.

'When did you write this?' he asked, seemingly quite alarmed.

'Just now.'

'You wrote this now? In your head? With magic?'

'Yes.'

'But you couldn't... You'd only be able to do that with dark magic. That's far too powerful a spell, even for you. To put something this complex together in such a short space of time. You couldn't.'

Beth noticed George's eyes scan Simon's hands. The red flecks were there. He'd used dark magic again. She wanted to slap him for being so irresponsible, but she kept her composure. She'd tell him off later. After they'd done some good spells.

'You're using dark magic now?' George asked, a little fearfully.

'I'm doing whatever I need to do to secure the future of my family.'

George seemed to contemplate this for quite some time. He was staring at Simon, as if he wanted to say something else. But he didn't. Instead he smiled and said,

'Let me read through it properly. A contract this important needs to be thoroughly absorbed.'

'Of course.'

Simon, Jim and Beth all watched George as he pored over every word in the small contract.

'Do we have the power to reduce his sentence?' Beth muttered in Simon's ear. 'Doesn't that need to be decided by a judge?'

'Theoretically,' Simon replied. 'But we have the power to override anything. We can do whatever we like. If George signs this contract and meets the terms, all of the paperwork surrounding his conviction will automatically get updated. No one can stop us.'

'Jane won't like that.'

'And I don't like her actions right now. I guess life is tough like that.'

'I can live with these terms,' George said as he closed the contract. 'I'm very confident I'll give you what you need.' He stood up and selected a pen from his little desk. He signed his name and dated the document, and then it instantly sealed itself with a golden glow.

George handed the document to Simon. He took it, clicked his fingers and it disappeared. Beth was dying to know what Simon had done with it. Yet again she was in awe of how smooth he was with his magic. At least she knew it was good magic he'd just used.

George sat back on the bed. 'You'd better make yourself comfortable. You're going to find this very interesting.'

TWENTY-FIVE

Simon clicked his fingers and three chairs appeared. He, Jim and Beth all grabbed one and they sat down opposite George, ready for him to reveal all.

'You know what happened,' he began, 'but you don't know how. I never imagined for a second that I'd be sharing this with you. But fifteen less years spent in this room is worthy of anything.'

'I hope so,' Simon said.

'I did cast a spell on Linda and Diane that gave them temporary powers. I've been doing it to Linda for years. She was always curious about what it was like to have magical powers, so I gave her a little try every now and then. Then when she became good friends with Diane, she convinced me to gift Diane with the ability as well.'

'Why would you do that?' Beth said. 'I get helping your wife, but Diane?'

'She served us well when we were trying to take down the Malancy. As I believe you well know. She proved herself trustworthy. It's good to keep her on side.'

Beth scoffed. 'At least she's trustworthy to someone.'

'Please continue,' Simon said. 'We know all about what you did, as you've already pointed out. Please tell us how you did it. How can such a spell exist?'

'There is a lot that exists that you don't know about. Spells that my old self would have detested you knowing about. I would have feared it greatly. However, it seems now, other than a bit of satisfaction, I have nothing to lose.'

'How do you know about these spells?'

'It's not just spells. There's an entire Malant world you don't know about. Very amusingly, it's been right below you the whole time.'

Beth looked down before realising he couldn't mean literally below them at that moment. Could he?

'In the basement of Malancy HQ,' he clarified.

'Malancy HQ doesn't have a basement,' Simon replied.

'Oh yes it does. A very well hidden one. It's so secret, you need a spell to access it. No one could just come across it. It's hidden by magic and only those in the know ever get to visit its wonders.'

'What are these wonders?' Simon asked.

'I suppose it's like a library. Five hundred years of information about the Malancy. Starting off with all the ideas from the original Malants, right through to spells people invented and curses that have been cast.'

'Who knows about this?'

'Only the direct descendants from the original Malant family. It was our grandfather who built the basement when the premises first opened, and it was he that made it secure. Before that, the archives had been kept at the home of whoever was currently in charge. The head of the family at that time. But, as you can imagine, that took up quite a lot of space.'

'You said curses,' Beth noted. 'Malants don't put curses on people.'

This made George laugh. 'Look who's talking. What do you think your own husband does?'

'What?'

'The success of Bird Consultants is reliant on casting

spells that benefit businesses. Granted, mostly it's good, but I know for a fact that your respectable husband has added in a dark side to many a contract. And he's not the first to do that sort of thing. Paul Bird just came up with a modern day twist. You didn't think you were unique, did you?'

'Does anyone currently at Malancy HQ know about this secret basement?' Simon asked before Beth could dwell too much on George's words.

'No.'

'I'm a direct descendant,' Jim stated. 'Why didn't I know about it?'

'You were never in charge. Besides, dad felt he couldn't always trust you. Probably for the best, since you swapped allegiances for the Bird family.'

'My allegiance was and always will be for the Malancy,' Jim replied.

'And my allegiance has always been to protect our family. Our birth right.'

'Your allegiance is to protect yourself.'

'How do we access it?' Simon asked, his patience clearly diminishing. 'What is the spell?'

'It's very simple really. It's just uncloaking. There's a button in all the lifts that takes you to the basement. There's also a hidden staircase to the right hand side of reception. Just cast a spell to uncloak any magic around you and you'll see the access points reveal themselves.'

'That's it?' Simon asked.

'That's not an easy spell for your average Malant to cast,' Jim noted. 'To uncover existing magic takes a lot of power.'

'It does,' George said. 'Although you do improve with practise. I'm sure our almighty Mr Bird won't find it too difficult, though, will you? Although a word of warning: you may want to limit who knows about it. The power that can be found down there will be surprising, even for you.'

'That's for us to worry about now,' Simon stated. 'I'm

assuming we'll also find a spell that allows a Malant to hide the red glow that magic emits.'

George smirked. 'I did that a long time ago. Thankfully. It meant I could easily cast the spell for Linda without anyone ever knowing.'

'Why on earth are elements allowed in the visitor room?' Jim asked.

'Because it plays to my advantage,' George replied. 'I once made all the rules. Luckily, no one ever thought to change them.'

Beth felt a spasm of anger at this, but she decided to say nothing. The oversight needed rectifying quite urgently, but part of her feared that they may never attend a Malancy meeting again to discuss it.

Instead, she asked, 'Why would there be a spell to give non-Malant powers? Who would invent that?'

'Why do you find greed so hard to contemplate?' George asked in reply. 'I don't know who invented it, but I would guarantee that it served their purpose once upon a time. Even if it was just to keep their wife quiet. As I used it for.'

Beth suddenly felt like the only Malant ever to have lived that hadn't at some point abused what was hers. Even Simon had.

'Will the special secret library also tell us how to stop all the Malants having power?' she asked. 'And can we find a way to stop Damien?'

George snorted a laugh. He turned to Simon. 'Delightfully naïve or a complete idiot?'

Beth saw Simon clench his fists. 'Perfect just as she is,' he replied, glowering at George. 'Not dragged down by the horrors of life like we are. We would all be better off if we were a bit more like Beth.'

Beth wanted to feel flattered by his defence of her, but she was feeling more and more like an idiot with each passing second.

She felt her characteristic gusto shrivel up as she

slumped her shoulders. Life had given her too many knocks lately and she was starting to get the message that maybe she deserved them.

Simon turned to her. 'We can stop all the non-Malants having power and cut Damien's new ability in one go by severing the spell.'

'Severing the spell?' Beth asked. She knew what that meant. Technically, the only way to sever a spell was to end the life of the person who cast it. However, there was a loophole. If you stopped the person's heart for a few moments it could be just enough to end the spell and not enough to kill them. It was a delicate operation where nothing could go wrong.

Something in Beth told her it couldn't be that simple, though. 'We have to stop your heart?' she asked Simon, fearfully.

'No. George's.'

'Why George's? I know he cast the spell, but it was your magic in the stone that sent it off around the world and gave Damien his strength.'

'My power was just a catalyst,' Simon replied. 'The spell still originated from George. So we need to stop his heart in order to end it.'

'And he's okay with that?' Beth asked, still waiting to hear what obstacles were inevitably going to be thrown their way. She turned her head to find George smiling.

'It was in the contract he just signed,' Simon explained.

'You're going to willingly let us stop your heart?' Beth asked George.

George shrugged. 'Let's lock you up for thirty years and see what you won't do to be free. Besides, I know Simon has done this before. I'd trust him more than anyone. Again, a sentence I never thought I'd say.'

Beth sat back in disbelief. After all they'd been through could this really be sorted out so easily?

'Shall we get this over with?' Simon asked.

'If you do this, Damien won't be hidden anymore, will

he?' Beth checked.

'She catches on quickly, doesn't she,' George smirked sarcastically.

'No. All the non-Malants will instantly lose their power, as will Damien,' Simon said to Beth, ignoring George. If only Beth could do the same. George's words were slicing through her like a blade. 'He'll go back to how he was the moment before the spell was cast. With no magic at all. We'll be able to perform a simple location spell, rescue Scarlett and arrest him.'

'We can do that,' Jim said to Simon. 'You sever the spell and then Beth and I will locate Damien. I want you to go and see Jane and tell her what we've done. What we're doing.'

'I think we both need to talk to Jane,' Beth said. Something in her brain signalled to her that she was putting more emphasis on confronting Jane than saving her own daughter. In fact she'd felt like that all day. Why was that?

'We don't have the time,' Jim said, cutting through Beth's thoughts and making her instantly forget her moment of doubt. The darkness was in control far more than she was realising.

'We need to get to Scarlett now and I need one of you to help me arrest Damien,' Jim continued. 'I don't have your power. I'd need a hundred elements to do the location spell alone. But you can't delay speaking to Jane either. At least one of you has to speak to her imminently. You need to sort this out. And I think it needs to be Simon. Paul was... is his uncle.'

'What's Jane up to?' George asked.

'None of your business,' Simon said. 'This will be easier if you lie down.'

'There are plenty more ways I can help,' George whispered to Simon. Beth only just made it out. She watched to see if Simon would respond, but he didn't.

'Are you ready?' Simon simply asked instead.

'Look after my brother,' Jim said. 'He's a bastard, but he's still family.'

'I won't hurt him. I know what I'm doing.'

Beth watched as Simon placed his hand across the left side of George's chest. He clenched his fingers and George gasped.

She turned away. She couldn't bear to see it. She heard quiet moans from George as Simon applied his power. It seemed ironic that this was a good spell. She assumed it was the same power as a healing spell, just applied differently. That was all about manipulation of the body and it certainly wasn't hard. Well, not for her and Simon anyway.

She heard the last moans and everything went silent. Nobody moved for what felt like an age. Far too long. Was George okay?

Just as she turned around, Simon stood up straight and George gasped for breath. He clasped his chest and he seemed to relax.

'Is it done?' Beth asked.

'I stopped his heart,' Simon said. He glanced down at George. 'He's still with us, so that's good news. Sort of. Now we need to see if it's had the desired effect. Beth, do you want to locate Damien?'

Beth nodded. For a short moment she didn't know where to start, but she took a deep breath and composed herself. Things were moving too fast again and she was losing the ability to keep up. She just wanted to sit down and take stock, but it was like a never ending battle that wouldn't cease, even when the problems had seemingly been solved.

She closed her eyes, tapped into her emotion, and conjured up images of Damien. She felt the red beams soak up the room around her as the spell took charge. She summoned more and more power as the images intensified, and then she had it.

She flicked open her eyes. 'I've got him. I've got him!'

'He's not hidden anymore?' Simon asked, the smallest of smiles grasping his lips. 'How's Scarlett?'

'She was asleep. She looked okay, but we have the best luck in the world! It's unbelievable. They were just arriving at a hotel. A hotel I know very well. It's in Staffordshire, just a few miles from my parents. It's a bit fancy, but very quiet and secluded.'

'That's where we need to go then,' Jim said.

'Do you know what you need to do?' Simon asked Beth.

'I'm too afraid to teleport,' she said.

'That's good. You shouldn't,' Jim replied. 'Simon can teleport us back to mine and then we'll drive up there.'

'But driving is so slow,' Beth said.

'I'm sure we've got a bit of time before Damien realises his powers have gone,' Jim stated. 'It should only take a couple of hours to get to Staffordshire.'

'When you find him, you need to freeze him,' Simon told Beth. 'And Carly. Use your magic to overpower them. Don't hesitate. Then Jim can arrest them and you can take Scarlett. If you give them even a second to think about it, they could get the better of you.'

'I know what I'm doing!' Beth snapped, feeling wounded by Simon's patronising words.

'I thought *I* did!' he snapped back. 'But, as you pointed out, it's best to take nothing for granted. Get control the second you can. You have the power, you're just not used to using it.'

'You'll have the whole journey up there to practise,' Jim said, joining in with the carving of Beth's dignity.

'I know how to use my power!' she blustered back. Although, truthfully, she wasn't quite as confident as she sounded. 'You'd better make sure you don't let Jane walk all over you,' she retorted, glaring at Simon.

'I have no intention of doing any such thing,' Simon replied.

Beth caught a small grin across George's face.

'Can we go? Have we got all we need from him?' she asked.

'I think so,' Simon said. He turned to George. 'Assuming everything is as we believe it is, your sentence should now be reduced.'

'Good,' George said, still rubbing his chest. 'It was great to see you. Please stop by again soon.'

'I'll come and see you as soon as I can,' Jim said to him. 'I'm really looking forward to it.'

Beth hated the sarcasm in George's voice. He was lucky Jim was bothering at all. She didn't know if she'd be quite so inclined if her brother was just as vile as George.

'Can we leave now?' she asked.

Simon took her hand and then Jim's. 'Back to your place?' he asked Jim.

'Yes. Then we'll part ways and get this all over with.'

'Or get the next part of this nightmare well on its way,' Beth muttered. Simon flashed her a dirty look before he closed his eyes. She stared at him while he cast the spell to move them. She watched as the red flecks danced across his skin. The dark magic toying with him, but never taking hold. Not like it did to her.

She loved Simon to pieces, but she suddenly felt incredibly envious. How could she be his equal and be so inferior at the same time?

As the red began to spark, she closed her eyes. The bitterness was rising in her and she was actually looking forward to a break from him to get some space to think.

TWENTY-SIX

'We're back,' Simon said, letting go of Beth and Jim's hands. They were in the middle of Jim's living room, exactly where they'd left not an hour before. 'Are you sure you're going to be all right to drive?' he asked Jim. 'It is late.'

'We have to,' Jim said. 'We need to get Scarlett back as soon as possible.'

'Is it a bit late for you to be dropping in on Jane?' Beth asked. There was an uncharacteristic bitterness to her tone that Simon couldn't understand. There were no signs of dark magic being involved. This was all Beth. She was upset about something and not being forthcoming about it. Which was most unusual.

'What's the matter?' he asked her.

'Nothing. What could possibly be wrong?' she replied.

'What aren't you telling me? You always tell me everything.'

'If I always tell you everything, then there can't be anything to tell, can there. Perhaps I'm just a bit overwhelmed. This has been more than a rollercoaster. The last couple of days have been like a never ending nightmare that we just don't seem to be able to wake up from. I mean, how can George be right?'

Simon sighed. He knew it.

He saw Jim scurry off into the kitchen. Probably a wise decision.

'How was George right?' Simon asked.

'How can we be the most powerful Malants, yet have no power? How has Jane managed to get the better of us? It should be her heart we're stopping. And not just to sever a spell. To serve her right. We're supposed to be in charge, not her!'

'Calm down,' Simon said. He moved over to take Beth in his arms.

'No!' she said, backing away. 'I don't need comforting like some baby. I need us to sort this out. We always seem to end up the victims. How can we be so strong and yet so weak at the same time?'

'We're not weak. We're guided by our ethics and therefore there are limitations to what we're willing to do. But I think that makes us strong not weak.'

Beth scoffed. Simon couldn't believe they were having this conversation. It was the last thing he needed at that moment. He was already full of dread at the idea of having to confront Jane. This pointless argument was just making him feel even worse.

'Go and get Scarlett,' he said. 'I'll go and see Jane, and when this nightmare is over with we can talk about this some more.'

'But we might not get a chance before the next nightmare begins. It seems clear to me that until we exercise our authority, events like this will keep happening to us.'

'Exercise our authority? What are you talking about?'

'I'm sick of being walked all over.'

'How are you ever walked all over?'

'I'm supposed to be one of the most powerful people in the world, but I'm still nothing.'

'You're not nothing. Look at what you've got. You've

got unlimited power, millions of pounds in the bank, control over a global business, a beautiful, loving family, and you live in a mansion. How is that nothing?'

'That's the point. I don't have that. Most of that is yours. I'm just tagging along for the ride. Can't you see that?'

Simon didn't know what to say. It seemed preposterous. She had everything anybody could ever want. Yes, much of it might have been his first, but now it was all hers rightfully and fairly too. He could see she was too angry to listen to reason though, and he just didn't have the strength to engage any more in this crazy argument.

'Let's talk later,' he said. 'Let's get these things over with, and then we'll talk at home. Is that okay?'

'I guess it will have to be.'

Simon exhaled, trying to calm his frustration.

'Jim, are you ready?' he asked, moving into the kitchen.

'Just packing some bits for the journey,' Jim said, tightening the lid on a flask. 'We'll need to stay alert.'

'Do you need anything from me?' Simon asked.

'No. Beth has it all in hand.'

'I do,' Beth stated adamantly.

'I'll get going then,' Simon said. He headed towards the hallway to leave the house.

'Don't take any crap from her,' Beth said, following him.

'I wasn't going to.'

'Good.'

'I'll see you back at home. Yeah?'

'Yes. Keep in touch.'

'You too.'

'You're going to drive there, right?' Beth asked.

'Of course. The car's outside.'

'Good. Don't use dark magic. Promise me.'

'What reason do I have to use dark magic?'

'Precisely.'

'Don't worry. Just go and get Scarlett and arrest Damien and Carly before they do any more harm.'

'We're on the case,' Jim stated, appearing next to them. He placed down his bag of refreshments and reached for his jacket from the cupboard under the stairs.

Simon kissed Beth goodbye before he hesitated. He studied the anguish on her face. She seemed so distressed. 'We'll talk later. Okay?' he said, trying to reassure her.

'Okay.'

Their eyes remained locked for a few moments as Simon contemplated whether he should say anything else. He hated leaving her when she seemed so upset. But he had no choice.

'Take care of her, Jim,' he said. 'See you both soon.'

Simon spotted Beth's lips frown. He knew the words "I can take care of myself" were about to leave her mouth. Too exhausted for any more conflict, he quickly turned around and left Jim's house.

He walked down the street to his car. It was dark and extremely quiet, and the cool air helped to clear his head a little.

Getting in the driver's seat, he started the engine and drove on for just a few minutes, before stopping the car at the end of a quiet road.

There was no way he could drive to Jane's house. She'd have a full security team outside protecting her. Even though he could overpower them, it was too messy. He needed to speak to Jane properly. If he was to have any chance of resolving this ludicrous situation, he needed to encounter as few obstacles as possible.

He looked around to check that he was completely alone, and then he stepped out of the car. He locked it up and then closed his eyes, immediately imagining Paul and Jane's house. He'd have to use dark magic, but it was the only realistic way. Anything else would be too dangerous and difficult.

But this was the final step now. This was the last time

he'd have to turn to dark magic. Then they could finally be free from the burden.

The spell took hold and within a few seconds he was in Jane's living room.

She was sitting on an armchair reading a book with her back to him. Next to her was a glass of whiskey. Paul's favourite end of the night tipple. How alike they were.

'Good evening,' Simon said.

Jane jumped in shock. 'What are you doing?' she snapped as he walked around to sit on the settee near her. 'You shouldn't creep up on people like that.'

'You left me no choice.' She was wrapped up in her red satin dressing gown, all ready for bed. But she looked far from relaxed.

'I suppose dark magic was involved in getting you here so covertly.' Her eyes glanced down at the specks of red dancing across Simon's hands.

'Again, you left me with no choice,' he replied as he folded his arms to hide his flesh.

'Don't you dare blame me. This is all your own doing.'

'I think it's time we talked. Don't you?'

'I do, yes.'

'You're not going to get your army in here to try to arrest me or anything, are you?'

Jane closed her book and placed it on the coffee table next to her. 'What would be the point? We both know no one can arrest you.'

'No, instead you're holding Paul's funeral hostage to get me to give myself up.'

Jane shook her head. 'How you simplify everything. It must be so glorious walking in your shoes where actions have no consequences and you can just do what the hell you like. Well, you know what, I believe actions should have consequences.'

'So the consequence of my action is to not get a chance to say goodbye to my uncle? He was my uncle. My blood.'

'I don't want to stop you from being able to say

goodbye to Paul, but how else can I get your attention?'

'Oh I see. I'm not playing by your rules so you're having a tantrum.'

'My rules? You think these are my rules? My special little rules that I've made up to mess with you? Well, they're not. They're *the* rules. The same rules that everyone has to abide by. The same rules that have been in place for a very long time.'

'Don't give me that law and order bullshit. You're pissed off because of Paul and you're blaming me.'

'Damn right I'm pissed off. I'm absolutely... I can't even begin to tell you about the size of the hole that has opened up in my world right now. I don't know what I'm going to do with myself. It was too soon. He was taken from us too soon.'

'You don't have to tell me. But it's not my fault.'

Jane sat back in her chair. Tears were forming in her eyes and she was clearly battling to keep them at bay. It was rare to see her so broken; so human.

'This isn't about a blame game,' she muttered.

'You want to arrest me for Paul's death. I'd say you're blaming me for that.'

Jane sat forward, calmly. She looked Simon directly in the eyes. 'I hate to say it, but you are ultimately responsible. You might not have stabbed him, but if you hadn't turned to dark magic, he'd still be alive. Tell me he wouldn't.'

Simon took a moment to catch his breath as her words stung. 'I've done many things I'm not proud of. Believe me, if I could go back and change that moment when I let the darkness in, I would. But I can't.' Simon felt the tears prickle at his own eyes. 'I couldn't heal him, Jane. You know I couldn't. I was still healing Beth.'

'You couldn't have healed him anyway. The knife went straight into his heart. It was pretty instant.' She paused. 'He had such a big heart.' A few tears escaped and trickled down her face.

Simon let her words sink in. He couldn't have saved Paul. That confirmation soothed his guilt just a little.

'Don't blame me for this, Jane,' he said. 'We're supposed to be a family. This is tearing us apart.'

'Is that what you think I'm doing? Trying to tear us apart?'

'You're trying to punish me because you're angry. I get it. But we need to stick together right now. It's what Paul would want.'

She shook her head. 'You have totally misread this situation. I'm not punishing you because I'm a bit emotional. I'm doing the job that you asked me to do. I'm the only one doing the right thing.'

'How is any of this the right thing?'

Jane stood up, as if to assert her authority. 'Is dark magic illegal?'

Simon remained silent.

'Is dark magic illegal?' Jane pushed.

'Essentially, yes.'

'So when you turned to dark magic, you essentially broke the law. Right?'

'The circumstances were-'

'Don't give me that bullshit, Simon. You broke the law. Do you think you're above the law?'

'I think this very unique situation required-'

'So you think you're above the law?'

'I think complex matters-'

'Answer the question. Yes or no. Do you think you're above the law?'

'It's more complicated than that.'

'Only because you want it to be. But the reality is we can beat Damien without dark magic. We can beat anything together. How could one man be more powerful than all of us combined? We have such incredible resources.'

'Scarlett could have been hurt.'

'Paul *was* hurt. You say I'm making emotional

decisions, but I'm the only one who isn't. You turned to dark magic because you feared for your daughter. That's totally understandable. But if we arrested another Malant for doing the same thing, would you be willing to let them get away with it?'

Simon didn't say a word.

'I love you, Simon. You're my family. I tried to cover things up for you at first. I told Beth that if she could get Scarlett back to safety without anyone ever knowing that you'd turned to dark magic, I'd let it go. But now you've been all over the world flaunting your new powers off.'

'Over the world?'

'We know you were in New York. Albeit not for long. CCTV shows that Beth was overcome with the red flecks. How am I supposed to spin that? New tattoos she was trying out? Questions will get asked about you and Beth. You know they will. You're the famous leaders of the Malancy and you've clearly turned to dark magic. And at the same time, the whole world has miraculously been gifted with our special power. I have no doubt that there are rumours going around the Malancy community right now that these strange events are somehow related to you.'

'Who's been spreading rumours?'

'I don't know. I'm just saying it's inevitable. It only needs a few people to have noticed the change in you and we've got a massive problem.'

'We can sort it out.'

'You mean lie to the people we represent? That's not what we stand for. We have a code of ethics.'

'I know, but-'

'Besides, even if you've had a complete personality transplant and you no longer believe that you need to pay for your actions, if I don't prosecute you for breaking the law, we could have a rebellion on our hands.'

'Don't be ridiculous,' Simon said.

'The leaders doing whatever they like with no consequence - that was the government George ran. We always said we wanted to be better.'

'We are better,' Simon insisted. 'I've ended the problem of non-Malants having power. If that helps.'

This seemed to surprise Jane and her firm stance relaxed. 'How?'

'It was George who cast the spell. It's a long story, but I've stopped his heart and now non-Malants no longer have abilities, and, as we speak, Jim and Beth are on their way to arrest Damien and Carly, and finally get Scarlett back.'

Jane took a moment to process this. 'Thank you. No doubt there's a lot to unravel in everything that's happened, but I'm glad we're out of the danger zone. So thank you.' She sat back down. Despite her words of gratitude, she seemed irritated. 'You would have used dark magic, I suppose, to get to George unseen.'

'It was the only way.'

'Was it?' she challenged, glaring into his eyes.

'It was the only way because my team was fighting against me.'

'Answer me this. If we'd been working together, would dark magic have made any difference to finding a solution?'

'It's not my fault we weren't working together,' Simon bit back.

'You really think you're an innocent victim in all of this, don't you?' Jane said with bile in her tone. But it wasn't her tone that sent a chill through Simon. It was that word: victim. The same word Beth had used. *We always seem to end up the victims.*

'You're implying that I've backed you into a corner,' Jane continued. 'But it's actually the other way around. If I say, "It's okay, Simon Bird can do what he likes as he's super powerful and special and we're just going to turn a blind eye, no matter what he does," what do you think will happen to me? To our government? You want to be in charge and uphold our rules, but you want to be able to bend them to suit you at the same time. Well, which is it going to be, Simon? Are you guilty or not?'

Simon sat very still as Beth's words spun round and round his head. He had more power than Jane, and he was technically supposed to be in charge of the Malancy, yet something about this exchange was making him feel weaker in every way.

'What is it you want, Jane? An apology?' Simon said, deciding that he needed to be exceptionally careful with every move he now made.

'I want you to give yourself up. Face the sentence for your crimes. Do what you'd expect of any other Malant.'

'You're talking about prison?' Simon asked, feeling his strength dwindling every time Jane opened her mouth. 'You want me to go to prison?'

Jane looked at him. 'I'm afraid you'll have to.'.

TWENTY-SEVEN

'Dark magic always carries a custodial sentence,' Jane explained. It seemed like there was regret in her eyes, but Simon chose to ignore it. He was now far too cautious to believe anything he saw. 'To not give you one would be the only ever exception.'

'Well, that would make sense. In terms of the Malancy, I am an exception. I think that puts a different slant on things.'

'You can't have a different slant on right and wrong. It's black and white. You're either guilty or you're not.'

'And the people who decided that using dark magic was wrong, did they see that there was a clear choice between using it and not using it?'

'There is a clear choice.'

'Not for me and Beth, there isn't.'

'I don't-'

'You want to punish me for breaking a law that assumes we're all the same. But we're not all the same. You can't ask me and Beth to abide by a rule that doesn't take into account our very different circumstances. It's not reasonable.'

'I understand that the dark magic calls on you.'

'I don't think you really do. Most Malants choose to turn to dark magic for some - usually selfish - reason. For me and Beth, though, the dark magic taunts us. It always has done. We have magic within us in a way that no other Malant could ever understand. Dark magic as well as good.'

'That may be the case, but you still have the same choice as to whether you use it or not.'

'No we don't. And it's unreasonable to think that we do. For other Malants the darkness is a way of achieving more. It's a conscious decision made out of greed or desperation. For us, the darkness actually burdens us. Inside. It tries to get us to sink into it. And the second I did, it felt extremely good.'

'That's just giving in to temptation. It can't be excused by law.'

'But the law doesn't apply to our circumstances. If we face different obstacles to other people, the law must take that into consideration.'

'And it will,' Jane said, showing the first signs of frustration. 'The normal minimum sentence for dark magic is ten years. I propose that you serve much less. If you plead guilty now, I'll recommend to the judge that you serve just two years. I'll put forward a very convincing case that your sentence should be reduced.'

'Does that make you feel better?' Simon asked. 'You get to blame me, get me to plead guilty and get to punish me, but you can walk away with a nice clear conscience that you made it all fair with a vastly reduced sentence. Is that what you'll tell Paul when you stand at his grave?'

'How dare you. I'm just trying to uphold the law that you put me in charge of.'

'You're trying to punish me for Paul's death.'

'I'm trying to punish you for a crime you're guilty of.'

'I'm not guilty of anything.'

'Then how come you feel guilty about Paul? I know you do.'

Simon paused. Whatever he may or may not feel, she was not going to get to see it. 'I didn't throw that knife,' was all he said.

'The events that led up to Paul's death all started the second you turned to dark magic.'

'They started the second Scarlett was kidnapped. All of this is pointing to Damien, not me.'

'And Damien will be punished for his part in this as well.'

'Who else is getting punished for your grief? Jim? Ralph? The hotel staff? Who else can you pin something on? My parents? Perhaps if they'd never had me, Paul would still be alive.'

'Don't mock me. I know you didn't mean to cause anyone harm, but you turned to an illegal force and it led to his death. You must face the consequences.'

Simon stood up. He was now feeling weary with Jane's blinkered perspective.

'I was hoping we could have a reasonable discussion about this, but it's clear you're still far too emotional. Perhaps I need to give you some more time before you're ready to be rational.'

Jane scoffed. 'All I'm asking is for you to face up to a crime you committed. You literally committed a crime. You turned to dark magic and that is totally forbidden by law. But you're twisting it this way and that to excuse yourself. Acting like the victim. Yet somehow I'm being irrational.'

'Trying to make me guilty of a law that in no way takes my personal circumstances into account is utterly irrational.'

'Right, I didn't want to have to do this. You're leaving me no choice.'

'Don't even think about withholding the details of Paul's funeral. I'll bring down a world of power on anyone I have to. I will be there to bury my uncle.'

Jane took a breath. She sat back, calmly. 'Yes, I feared

you might. He's in a Malant funeral home, surrounded by Malant people. You could easily overpower any one of them. I saw that the minute I told Jim all about it.'

Simon stood very still. He could tell she was on the cusp of revealing all and he didn't want to interrupt her flow.

'Paul's funeral is next Friday,' she said. 'In Clapham. Where he grew up.'

'At the Malancy hall?'

'Of course.'

'You are burying him, yes? It's what he wanted.'

'I know. I'm burying him next to your parents. Reunite the family, just as he'd want.'

Simon took a second to reply. 'Perfect. Thank you.'

'Of course you're welcome. Even though you'll be in prison, I'll arrange it so you can attend the funeral. I have the authority to do that.'

Simon shook his head. He knew it was time to leave. He'd got the funeral details. That was a win for now. Everything else could wait until Jane was being more reasonable.

'I'll speak to you soon,' he said, turning for the door.

'If you don't plead guilty, I'll have Scarlett put into care.'

Simon stopped in his tracks.

'Excuse me?' He very slowly turned around to look at her. 'You leave my daughter out of this.'

'I've already made a few enquiries,' Jane said. 'One call and I can get social services very interested in your family. You're never there. You work all hours. She was kidnapped due to your neglect.'

'How can you say that?'

'I used to be in the police force. I have an excellent relationship with social services. If I say I have concerns, Scarlett will be taken from you.'

'There is no way that will happen. Just as you can't have me arrested, I won't let you take my daughter.'

'What are you going to do? Put a spell on your house to stop anyone getting in?'

'If I have to.'

'And how will that look to the regular social services? These aren't Malants. We don't have Malant social services. These are just regular people who aren't aware of the power we have. I don't only know Malants. You don't get to my position without having good contacts in all areas.'

'What are you saying?'

'I can just see it now. I alert social services to a problem. They send someone over to check out your house to find your daughter being strangely locked inside. It will certainly seem sinister. They won't understand, and they will have to remove Scarlett while they investigate. I'll make sure of it.'

'You'd do this to your own niece?'

'This is all on you. You're being stubborn and refusing to admit to a crime you have committed. A dangerous crime, I'd like to add. By being so selfish, you are putting me in an impossible situation. It has to be seen that I am doing everything in my power to bring you in.'

'This is an abuse of power.'

'No it's not.'

'You would never do this to anyone else. If you were to threaten another Malant's daughter... you'd lose your job.'

Jane smirked. 'You said it yourself. You're an exception.'

'You leave Scarlett out of this.'

'Plead guilty and I will.'

'Don't do this.'

'I wonder what Beth will say when she sees Scarlett taken away and there's nothing you can do about it. You won't be able to use your magic as it will only make you seem more like unfit parents.'

We always seem to end up the victims. Beth's words once again echoed through Simon's mind. They were the people with all the power, yet had no power at all.

He wanted to fight this. But at that moment he couldn't see a way to win. He had no idea what Jane was going to say to her contacts at social services, but he had every reason to believe she was going to say anything to get her way.

Simon was well respected across the business world. He knew all the top people at all of the FTSE 100 companies. He had incredible contacts with an abundance of wealth and influence. But not one of them could help him fight Jane at this moment. He could manipulate business. Jane was about to get him right where it really hurt.

This had just become very personal.

Simon's brain quickly flicked through all of his options. He considered a multitude of scenarios, but the same thing happened in every one of them: if he didn't meet Jane's wishes, Beth would bring Scarlett home only for there to be a knock at the door tomorrow and for Scarlett to be taken away all over again.

He might have the ability to fight it eventually, but as soon as Scarlett was in the system, he could see things becoming very tricky. And very bleak.

He wanted to find a solution. He was desperate to find the loophole in Jane's evil plan. But panic was rising in his chest. The sting of how personal things had become - and from his very own family - was stopping his brain from functioning clearly.

Simon saw only one option that would protect his daughter, and that was to plead guilty. He didn't want to give in. He didn't believe that he deserved to be punished. But if he pleaded guilty, it kept his family out of it. And when he knew they were safe, then he could process how to protect himself.

He had to put his family first right now.

His eyes were glaring fiercely at Jane's face. He swore there was smugness in her expression.

'Beth had no choice,' he said. 'When I turned to dark magic, she got dragged down with me.'

Jane crossed her legs delicately. She seemed utterly relaxed. 'Are you going to plead guilty?'

'If you leave Beth and Scarlett alone, I'll do as you wish.'

'Very well. We can easily excuse Beth from blame if you're willing to be accountable.'

'I don't think willing is the word. Perhaps blackmail is more accurate.'

'Whatever helps you sleep at night. Either way, now you're seeing sense, I'll just have to get you to sign the contract. I'd show it to you now but the team is still finalising it. It will be ready by tomorrow.'

Jane stood up to refill her glass of whiskey from the enormous oak drinks cabinet at the back of the room. It opened up like a wardrobe and was always fully stocked.

'Contract?' Simon asked.

'Can I get you anything?' she asked, pointing to the array of bottles.

'What contract?' Simon repeated, impatiently.

Jane filled her glass halfway and closed the cabinet once again.

'A necessary contract, I think,' she said, moving over to address Simon directly. 'As we both know, I have very little power to keep you behind bars. You might be pleading guilty now, but I know the first chance you get to escape, you will. As soon as I'm looking elsewhere, you'll find a way out of prison. A contract is the only power I have to ensure you serve your sentence.'

'Do you mean like a Bird Consultants contract?'

'Yes.'

'You want to use my own way of working to ensure I'm doomed?'

'You're so dramatic. And it isn't your way of working. It was Paul's. It was his idea.'

'Even worse. You know Paul would be disgusted with

what you're doing.'

'That's the problem when someone dies. They don't know what you do anymore.'

'You really do blame me, don't you.'

'This is not a blame game. This is about me upholding the law.'

'If you say it enough, I'm sure you'll start believing it. So, go one, what are the terms of this twisted contract? What will happen if I break it?'

Jane took a long sip of her drink. She couldn't look at him. 'I had to make it real. It has to be a real threat.'

'What does that mean?'

Jane hesitated. 'If you break the contract, you'll never see Scarlett again.'

'What? You're going to bring in social services again?'

'No. Something different. A Bird Consultants contract is magic after all.'

It was rare that Simon felt scared, but fear was now snaking through him. 'What are you going to do?'

'If you break the terms of the contract - that is if you use magic of any kind, or if anyone uses magic for your benefit, such as Beth thinking she can magic you out of there - then you'll never see Scarlett again. She will simply disappear from your view. You could be in the same room as her, but you won't see or hear her. She'll be non-existent to you.'

The anger began exploding inside of Simon. 'Jane, that's evil. That's despicable!'

'Do you think I want to do this?' she said, the anger rising in her own tone. 'I know this is awful. But it has to be something so drastic to make you abide by it. You'll have the ability to escape at any time. You must agree, it has to be a big enough consequence to make you want to stay.'

Simon turned away from her as he let her cruel idea sink in.

'There's one more thing you need to know,' she said.

Simon felt sick. He couldn't say a word. He couldn't see how things could get any worse, but he felt a lot worse was just around the corner.

'I also had to consider the structure of the contract,' she continued, hesitantly. 'If I'm going to do my job correctly, it has to be related to something concrete.'

'What do you mean, concrete?'

'You're the great Mr Simon Bird. If I don't relate it to something concrete I know you'll find a loophole. You always do. You're a master of manipulating contracts. It's your job. It's how you've made your millions. I can't have you breaking this one and then nipping off to see Beth and Scarlett for breakfast one day. It'll make us both look like fools.'

Simon shook his head. This whole thing already made them look like fools.

'You don't trust me?' he asked, turning to look at her.

'I wouldn't trust anyone after six months of being kept away from their family. Especially if they knew they had the power to see them.'

'What concrete thing are you using?'

Jane took a deep breath before she downed the rest of her whiskey. 'I've related it to Paul's death.'

'What?' Simon shouted.

'I had to. The content has to be solid throughout. If I just said something vague like you used dark magic, I know you'll find a loophole. It has to be more definite. As much as it's horrific to even think about it for one second, Paul is dead. It isn't changing. It's a concrete fact that none of us can do anything about, and that means it's the best I've got.'

'You want it to be on record that I killed Paul? That's the best you've got?' Simon was shaking with rage now.

'It doesn't say you killed him. It's worded to say that actions relating to the death of Paul Bird mean you're facing a prison sentence. Whatever sentence the judge deems as necessary.'

'What? No way. You want me to sign a contract to agree to a sentence before I'm sentenced?'

'That is usually what happens. People don't usually get a choice in the sentence they face.'

'You'll push for twenty years. I know it.'

'Now you don't trust me?'

'Exactly what are you giving me to trust?'

'I don't want this. I don't want Scarlett to grow up without a father. I don't want any of this. I give you my word I will talk to your lawyer and the judge and push for a lenient sentence.'

'Why are you doing this?' Simon had never felt more like crying. His whole body was throbbing with distress and dismay.

'Tell me what options I have, Simon? It's the most rational action. Anyone in my position would do this. It might be personal but that's not the issue. I can't excuse what you did, no matter how much I'd like to. As awful as it is. As much as I wish none of this was happening, it is. And whether you like it or not, it started with you.'

'I did not kill my uncle,' he stated. 'How can you twist it to make it look like I did.'

'That's not what I'm doing.'

'We both know you are.'

'Now you're just twisting things. You have two simple options. Plead guilty, sign the contract and take whatever comes your way. Or walk away now and face social services. Face Scarlett being taken away from you.'

An image of Scarlett being carried away burst into Simon's mind. He couldn't let that happen. Pleading guilty was his best shot at resolving this. Despite Jane's attempts, he had to hold onto the hope that he'd find a loophole. He did not want to have a criminal record. He didn't want to serve any sort of sentence. There had to be a loophole, and he would just have to play along until he found it.

'Do I come back tomorrow to sign the contract?' he asked.

'No. We arrest you now and take you to the Malancy prison. We'll bring the contract to you tomorrow where you can read and sign it. But until your signature is on that document, my finger will be ready to dial my contact at social services. One way or another you will pay for your actions. What's it going to be?'

Simon wanted to smack Jane around the face. He felt such contempt towards her. A woman just a week ago he totally admired and respected. Now he couldn't hate her more.

'I want it added into the contract that when I sign it you are no longer able to threaten my family with social services. If that isn't included, you won't get my signature.'

Jane paused. She considered her response carefully. 'Okay. I can agree to that.'

'You know I'll read every word. It must be fair.'

'I know you will.'

'I'm not signing any contract I'm not happy with. And it better not say that I killed Paul.'

'It won't. You're not pleading guilty to Paul's death. Damien will be punished for that. You're pleading guilty to using dark magic.'

'You're a bitch.'

'I'm just doing my job.'

'This isn't your job. I should know. I wrote the job description. You're abusing your power and I hope you get your comeuppance.'

'I've lost the only man I've ever loved. Nothing could be worse for me now.'

'You know punishing me for it won't give you the peace you desire.'

Jane's eyes pierced into Simon before she picked up her phone from the coffee table and dialled a number.

'He's in my living room,' she said. 'He's willing to work with us now. See you in a second.'

TWENTY-EIGHT

It was well past midnight when Jim and Beth arrived at the hotel. It was a grand building seemingly in the middle of nowhere, buried in the Staffordshire countryside.

Beth had spent the journey growing progressively angrier about the things George had said. His words were spinning around her mind like a warped merry-go-round. The more she thought about it, the more she realised he was right. She didn't have the power where it mattered. Jim and Jane were running the Malancy, and she'd even become a slave to admin in her role as Administration Director. She could barely remember the last time she'd actually directed anything. In fact, it felt like the more power she'd gained, the weaker she'd become. She was nowhere near as strong now as the Beth who first moved to London. The Beth who was completely alone with barely a penny in her pocket, but she'd had unquestionable grit and a fierce desire to succeed. What had happened to her?

Beth's frustrations built up so much that by the time they were parked up and she set foot on the gravel, she was ready to explode with determination.

'Have you considered what we're going to say to

reception?' Jim whispered, trying not to be too conspicuous considering the absolute silence around them.

'We're not talking to anyone,' Beth stated in return. Her heart pounded. She had never felt so fired up.

'How will we know what room he's in?'

'I have power. Let's use it.'

'Location spell?'

'That will tell me what his room looks like, not where he is.'

'Then how...?'

'Watch and learn, Jim. Simon's not the only one who can be creative.'

Beth had witnessed Simon utilise his magic hundreds of times as if he were merely breathing. It was utterly effortless for him. She knew she had equal power to him, so the only thing getting in her way was her mind. That had to stop. She decided it was time to cease her overthinking and just let her power do the talking.

She marched on and Jim quickly followed. She approached the automatic glass doors of the hotel and they swooped open with ease, instantly annoying her. It was too simple and she had something to prove.

She walked up to the reception and immediately spotted the computer.

'Can I help you?' a young man asked in a smart blue uniform, as he appeared from a door in the back.

'I don't think so,' Beth said. She threw out her hand and pinned him to the spot. 'Don't move and it won't hurt.'

'Beth, what are you doing?' Jim asked with an edge of panic.

She placed her other hand on top of the computer monitor and channelled the surge of emotion she was feeling into it.

'What name can you see on screen?' she said to the man who was frozen to the spot from the power of just her fingertips. Beth couldn't deny how good it felt. She nudged her knuckle so he could speak.

He didn't move, now frozen with fear.

'Tell me what name you can see on screen,' she demanded.

'Damon Rockwell.'

She turned to Jim. 'At least he was bright enough not to use his own name.' She looked at the frozen man again. 'What room is he in?'

'I...'

'Don't argue. Just tell me.'

'Room seventeen.'

'Good boy. Now I'm going to leave you like this just until we've sorted out our little problem. Mr Rockwell is a criminal and we're here to arrest him. I know we don't look like the police. Let's just say we're a special branch. So you stay here and behave and it will all be over soon.'

'Why did you do that?' Jim challenged as Beth turned around to find directions to the rooms. 'We could have just said we were the police. You could have magicked up an ID.'

Beth glared at Jim. 'I was making it up as I went along.' She looked around again and spotted a sign to the bedrooms. 'Come on. This way.'

Within a minute, they were standing in front of room seventeen. Beth placed her hand on the handle and willed it to open. Sure enough there was a small click and the door was free.

She stepped in and snapped her fingers. The room lit up and Beth fizzled with delight. That felt so good. She'd never done the finger snapping thing before. It was effortlessly brilliant! No wonder Simon did it so often.

Carly and Damien shrieked from under the large, comfy duvet, but Beth gave them no time to react. She pinned them to the bed.

She heard Scarlett whimper from the little cot placed in the corner of the enormous room. The whole place exuded a vintage warmth, but Beth had no interest in the décor. 'Hello Letty. Mommy's here,' she called over. 'Don't worry. Everything's okay now. Jim, will you take Scarlett to the car, please.'

'I don't want to leave you alone.'

'Jim, do as you're told.'

'What are you going to do?' Jim asked.

'Nothing easy,' Beth said. She kept her face straight, just as Simon always did, but delight was dancing through her. 'Now take Scarlett before she screams the place down.'

Scarlett was starting to cry as Jim picked her up and swiftly carried her out.

The second he was gone, Beth nodded her head and the door slammed shut.

She felt utterly liberated.

'Hello, you two,' Beth said, still keeping them very much in her magical grasp. 'How have you been? Noticed any changes?'

Beth glared at Damien and his frightened eyes stared back. She flicked her knuckle so he could answer.

'How did you find us?' he muttered.

'You don't know yet, do you,' she said with a grin. She moved her arm to the left, sending a pyjama clad Carly zooming across the room. Beth pinned Carly against the wall before re-focusing her attention on Damien.

'Fancy a little magic fight?' she said, easing her grip of him.

'What do you want?'

'Show me what you've got.'

'No. Anything I do, you'll try to use against me. I'm not falling for it.'

'What can I possibly use against you? As long as you don't use dark magic, then what's the problem? You could teleport?'

Damien's expression turned to confusion. 'What have you done?'

'Go on. Give it a try.'

'What have you done?'

'Try to teleport. I'll even let you take Carly with you.'

Beth stood back and put her hands behind her. 'See, I'm not getting involved.'

Damien sat up cautiously. He took a few moments to assess the situation. He was clearly very suspicious.

Finally he closed his eyes, but within seconds they were wide open again.

'Where's my magic?' he shouted.

Beth laughed. 'Good, isn't it! You can thank George for that. He didn't mean to give you power in the first place. It was only right he take it away.'

Damien looked so small and terrified sitting in that giant bed.

'This is the police.' The knock at the door made Beth jump. She could sense immediately that it was the Malant police and her heart pumped harder with vexation.

She had the urge to do more. She wanted to cause harm. She wanted to make Damien suffer. Showing him up was only phase one of her plan.

'Open up!' the male voice shouted through.

Seeing she had no choice, Beth twisted her hand and the door popped open. She prepared herself to teleport. Dark magic or not, she'd really stopped caring. She just needed to get out of there.

Just as she closed her eyes, a voice cut through. 'Well done on capturing these criminals, Mrs Bird. We can take it from here if you like.'

Beth halted the spell and opened her eyes. She turned to see the kind face of a policeman.

'Well done?' she queried.

'We couldn't have done this without you. We know that.'

She saw two police officers approach Damien. As he reluctantly stepped out of bed, they handcuffed him.

'Who told you to come here?' Beth asked.

'Mrs Bird – Jane Bird, that is - asked us in the Midlands

branch to support you. She explained everything.'

Beth could only deduce that Simon had managed to get Jane to talk and they'd found some sort of peace. Beth knew she should be grateful, but her husband's excellence at everything was just plain irritating.

'Would you mind, Mrs Bird?' a female officer asked from beside them. Beth turned to see her pointing towards Carly who was still pinned awkwardly to the wall.

'Right. Of course.' With all of the excitement gone, Beth had to remember how to work her magic. It took her a few seconds, but she eventually flicked her fingers and Carly slipped carefully down the wall and into the clutches of the officer.

'Thank you, Mrs Bird.'

'So you're not going to arrest me as well?' Beth asked the policewoman as she placed handcuffs on Carly.

'No, the arrest warrant for you has been dropped. We're only here to support you.'

The relief almost floored her.

'And Simon's back at Malancy HQ?' Beth asked.

The officer glanced at her colleague uncomfortably.

'What is it?'

'The arrest warrant for you was dropped, Mrs Bird,' the man who appeared to be in charge said.

'Are you saying you still want to arrest Simon?'

Again the officers glanced at one another.

'Don't look at her,' Beth ordered. 'Tell me.'

'We thought you knew.'

'Knew what?'

'Mr Bird. He's not at Malancy HQ.'

'Well, where is he?'

'Everyone's talking about it. This sort of news travels fast.'

'Is he okay?'

'Yes. As far as I know.'

'Then what's the matter? What's travelling?'

'The news.'

'What news?'

'Erm...'

'Tell me!'

'Mr Bird has been arrested for the murder of Paul Bird.'

'What!' The rage in Beth began blasting through her like rockets. 'What did you do to him?'

'Nothing, Mrs Bird. No one did anything. Apparently he pleaded guilty.'

TWENTY-NINE

Beth raced out of the room, through the dimly lit corridors and into the cool night air. She almost threw up as her feet hit the gravel. She took a few breaths as she struggled to make sense of what she'd just been told. Why on earth would Simon plead guilty to Paul's murder? What had Jane done?

She ran towards the car park to see Jim placing Scarlett in her car seat.

'He's been arrested!' she shouted as she approached him. Her terrified voice was the only sound, and it seemed to make her words all the more poignant against the silent dark night.

'I saw the police arrive,' Jim said, backing out from where he'd just strapped Scarlett in. She was still crying, but Beth couldn't deal with that now. 'Shall we get out of here?'

'He's been arrested!'

'I know. But the important thing is you haven't been. I really wasn't sure what was going to happen. Let them deal with Damien and Carly and we can get back down south.'

'No. Not Damien and Carly. Simon. Simon's been arrested.'

'What?'

'They just told me. He's been arrested for Paul's murder.'

'How could Simon get arrested? That can't be right. He's probably back home now with a protection spell all over the house.'

'No. No he's not.' Tears were choking Beth now as the reality set in.

'No one can arrest Simon if he doesn't want them to.'

'I know. That's the point.' Her sobs were coming thick and fast. 'He pleaded guilty. He willingly let them take him away.'

'What?' The sobering look on Jim's face told Beth that he was just as alarmed as she was.

'Jane must have done something,' she said. 'She's tricked him or something. I have to get to her. I have to find out what's going on.'

'Right. Come on. Let's get moving.'

'I'm teleporting, Jim.'

'You can't.'

'Please look after Scarlett. Please. Take her to your home or take her to ours. Whatever is best for you. Just text me where you are and I'll come and find you as soon as I've sorted this out. I can't let Jane get away with this. Simon did not kill his uncle!'

'I know. Of course he didn't. All right, do what you have to. Just pretend I don't know.

'Thank you, Jim. I don't know what we'd do without you.'

Jim just shook his head.

'I'll see you soon.'

With that, Beth closed her eyes and summoned up an image of Jane's house. At this time in the morning, she assumed Jane would be in bed, sleeping happily now that she'd got her way and Simon was behind bars.

Beth was about to change all that.

Within seconds Beth appeared in Jane's bedroom. As

Beth suspected, Jane was curled up under the silk sheets.

'You bitch!' Beth shouted. Beth clicked her fingers to flick on the light, and then she flung Jane out of bed and against the wall with just her hand.

'Beth,' Jane gasped, squinting against the sudden light. 'I'm guessing you've heard the news.'

'Simon did not kill Paul!'

'I know that. Not directly.'

'Then why have you arrested him for it?'

'I haven't.'

Beth relaxed her grip slightly. Jane slid down to her feet. She was still pinned in place, but at least she wasn't hanging anymore.

'The police told me Simon had been arrested.'

'He has. But not for Paul's murder. It's funny how these rumours get started.'

Beth pinched her stare. Funny indeed.

'Then what has Simon been arrested for?'

'This evening Simon pleaded guilty for using dark magic, and he was arrested accordingly. Just as any Malant would be.'

'How could you?'

'As I told Simon, I'm just trying to do my job.'

'Arresting innocent people is not your job.'

'Is using dark magic illegal?'

'Are you kidding me?' Beth spat back.

'Well, is it?'

'How can you make it so black and white?'

'Because it is.'

'No it's not.'

'The law is the law.'

'Malants don't have the ability to render magic without an element.' Beth twisted her hand and Jane was forced to her knees. 'So how come I can? Not everything is black and white.'

'All of us in the government are in a position of authority,' Jane said. 'It's more important for us than anyone to abide by the law that we set. We can't be seen to be above it.'

'What about to the side? How does that factor?'

'Simon knows that if he doesn't face the consequences for the law he broke, our government will crumble. At best. There could be a revolution.'

'What a load of nonsense. Simon would never spout such crap. What did you do to him?'

'We have CCTV footage of you clearly under the influence of dark magic.'

'So?'

'People know that you've both turned. How can I let Simon get away with illegal activity and still be taken seriously? He has to face the punishment for his actions.'

'Punishment? Who the hell do you think you are?'

'The woman you put in charge of the Malancy government. The woman ultimately responsible for our law and order.'

'Think about what Simon's been through.'

'I'm well aware.'

'No you're not! I can barely understand it. He has spent most of his life cast out. He's too weird for normal society. People fear the magical essence that oozes from him because of his special innate ability. Imagine that as a teenager? Imagine that as a young adult when you're trying to start out in life? And he's an outcast in the Malant world as well because he's different there too. People fear what they don't understand, and no one understands Simon. He only had us that he could rely on. And now you've turned your back on him.'

'We all believe in being good, moral people-'

'That's a joke!'

'Simon broke the law. I have to treat him the same as I would with anyone who broke the law.'

'And what punishment do you think this so-called crime deserves?'

Jane took a breath. It made Beth's heart stop.

'Dark magic always comes with a custodial sentence.'
'What!' Beth screeched. 'No!'
'It always does.'
'Absolutely no way. He's done nothing wrong.'
'He broke the law.'
'What did he do?'
'He used dark magic.'
'And to what result? He stopped actual criminals. And in the process he lost the man closest to him. What more do you want?'
'It's not what I want.'
'He is not going to jail.'
'I've promised Simon that I'll help his lawyer put a good case forward for a reduced sentence. Vastly reduced. Dark magic normally carries a ten year minimum sentence.'
'What!'
'I'm confident we can get Simon just a two year sentence.'
'Aren't you all bloody heart. Do you want me to thank you? You're trying to take away my husband. My daughter's father. It's not happening. That's the end of it.'
'This is Simon's choice.'
'Simon would never choose this. What have you got over him?'
Jane paused as she considered her words. 'He's signing a contract tomorrow.'
'A contract? As in like a Bird Consultants contract? I don't think so.'
'It's already been written. Simon is aware of the terms.'
'Simon finds loopholes in the most intricate of contracts. It's what he does. Do you really think you can beat him?'
'On this occasion, I'm afraid so.'
'What does that mean?'
'We've given it a great deal of consideration. There was only one option.'
'What option was that?'

'Unfortunately... I've had to relate the contract to Paul's death. I needed a concrete event that even the all power Simon Bird couldn't change.'

Beth felt on the verge of taking off as the anger was now charging through her so violently.

'How dare you! Simon didn't do anything to Paul! You know as well as I do, he isn't to blame for this. He couldn't have saved him.'

'I know. Paul died instantly. There's nothing anyone could have done.'

'Then why are you blaming Simon?'

'I'm not. It's not about blame. I just know that Simon is a master when it comes to breaking contracts. Paul's death was the only concrete thing that I could think to tie it to. It's just wording.'

'Very convenient wording. I'm guessing there are consequences too, if Simon breaks the terms of the contract?'

After a small hesitation, Jane said, 'Yes.'

'And they are?'

'He'll never see Scarlett again.'

The silence that followed was almost crippling. Beth was now glowing red, trembling with anger.

'You will not tear this family apart,' she seethed. 'We've lost Paul. I am not losing anyone else.'

'I'm sorry, Beth, but it's not your choice. Simon is guilty and that's all there is to it. He will serve a prison sentence and that's final.'

'You'll pay for this.'

'Simon is the one who's paying for his crimes.'

'You let him free.'

'I can't do that.'

'Let him free now.'

'I can't do that.'

'Let him free!'

The fury in Beth suddenly peaked, taking control of her. Without any thoughts at all, she picked up her arm and she let the dark magic in. It felt so good, and she needed that sensation so badly against the pain and hurt that was decaying her insides like acid.

She blasted Jane across the room, sending her crashing into a Chesterfield armchair that sat innocently in the corner.

'Let him free!'

She yanked Jane to her feet with just the power of her fingers, and then slapped her fiercely across the face.

'Beth, do this and I'll have no choice but to arrest you too.'

'Stop it! Stop abusing the power you have!'

With a smack, Jane was thrust against the wall again and Beth opened her arms wide. She stretched Jane hard, expanding every limb, pushing them further and further from her torso. Jane screamed in agony, but this only delighted Beth even more.

'You want it to stop?' Beth asked, almost a giggle in her tone now. 'Simply let Simon go.'

'Who's abusing their power now?' Jane gasped before she screamed again. This time it was so shrill and striking, it hit Beth right in the heart. Instantly Beth halted her actions and Jane fell straight to the carpet.

Panting, Beth stared at the crumpled woman on the floor before her. Jane was crying. Weeping desperately through sadness and obvious pain, and Beth knew she'd gone too far.

Her goodness was fighting back. Jane's shriek had woken it up and Beth was so relieved.

She stepped over and placed a hand on Jane's shoulder.

'Get off me!' Jane yelled with terror.

'Let me heal you.'

'I don't need you.'

'And I don't need you and all the problems you're causing me. Life's shit like that. I'm going to heal you and then I never want to see you again.'

Jane didn't fight this time as Beth placed her hand

down and began the healing spell. Within seconds Jane had recovered, and Beth knew she had to leave.

She stepped back, closed her eyes, and thought of home.

Like a flash, Beth appeared in her bedroom. She raced straight for her bed and buried her head in her pillow. She didn't stop crying for hours.

THIRTY

The next week couldn't have been more tense. Beth hadn't been allowed to see Simon. She wanted so desperately to find out what was going through his mind and why he'd allowed this to happen, but Jane was clever enough to stop them talking.

Jane had also been clever enough to give Beth a copy of the contract that Simon had signed. She'd certainly enjoyed dropping that round. There was no mistaking Simon's signature, and the terms were shocking. Beth also saw quite clearly that if she tried to intervene on Simon's behalf, the contract would come into play and Simon would never see Scarlett again. Quite literally.

Even worse was the fact that the first day Beth was going to see Simon was on the day of Paul's funeral. How could she talk to him then? He needed to grieve not battle with her.

And on top of all that, there was the matter of the office. The emails and calls seemed relentless, and Beth knew she had to deal with things. She couldn't leave everyone in the dark, and the staff needed help from the CEO. Not doing anything was just delaying the inevitable, and would undoubtedly just make it worse in the long run.

Simon was yet to be given his sentence, but Beth knew he was going to prison for years. She couldn't even begin to contemplate how many it might be. One second was too long in her mind. But it was happening and she had the massive responsibility to deal with it. As the only remaining active Bird family member, it all fell on her shoulders to sort out the company, and she owed it to both Simon and Paul to get a grip and take charge.

On Wednesday morning, just two days before the funeral, the alarm went off at six a.m. Beth was already wide awake. She'd been telling herself over and over that if she could assure Simon that the company was in a good state and she had it all in hand, he'd feel a bit better about everything that was happening. He might not, but she needed to believe in something positive.

She got herself dressed before waking Scarlett, and they were both ready and waiting for Jim's arrival at eight o'clock. He could only help with childcare that morning before he was needed back at Malancy HQ, but it was something.

Ever since she'd picked Scarlett up from Jim's house, the morning after Simon had been arrested, Jim had been nothing but a huge support. Well needed support.

As kind as Jim was, though, Beth knew she couldn't rely on his help for long. It wasn't fair. She knew she'd have to find a nanny soon. Although she was incredibly fearful of making the wrong decision again. And how was she to make such a big decision about the welfare of their daughter without Simon's input? Why had Jane done this to them?

After Beth had thanked Jim, who seemed delighted to help, she left the house and took a moment in the driver's seat of her own Aston Martin, trying to soothe the constant rage that was burning her insides.

She glanced at Simon's shining Vantage waiting near the garage. Nobody was allowed to touch Simon's precious car, and she would certainly be honouring his wishes in that respect. But that would mean that beautiful car would remain lifeless for years. Beth couldn't help but compare the car to Simon. Two incredible entities being stuck doing nothing. What a waste. A horrendous waste.

She took a breath and began her lonely journey to the office; her heart pounding every inch of the way.

She parked in Simon's spot. Well, technically it had become their spot, even though it had Simon's name formally set on a post in front of it.

She stepped out of the car, a tremble to her legs, and she made her way through to the reception and up to the tenth floor, not making eye contact with anyone.

She sat at her desk and looked over at Simon's empty chair. It was to be a constant reminder of their horrible situation. Such torture.

She needed a cup of tea.

She turned her computer on and then made a beeline directly for the kitchen. She kept her head down and made a very swift cuppa before darting back to her desk.

She sat down again and looked out across the Executive Floor. All seven directors were there and they were now all reporting directly to her. Just the idea of it made her nauseous.

She took a few deep breaths, going over and over in her mind what she'd planned to do. Practising it hadn't been easy, and now it was seeming virtually impossible. She wanted to cry at the prospect of letting all of these people know that Simon wouldn't be joining them in the office again anytime soon. But she had no choice.

She slowly sipped at her tea, telling herself that she needed the caffeine before doing anything else. The perfect delaying tactic.

When she'd checked through her emails and she'd drunk every last drop from her mug, she exhaled slowly. She could delay no longer.

Mustering up all the strength she could find, she grabbed her laptop and strode out to the middle of the floor.

'I need to call an impromptu board meeting,' she announced, addressing all of her fellow directors. 'Could we all be in the board room for nine thirty?'

'What's this about?' Nathan, the Finance Director asked.

'I'll tell you all in the meeting.'

'Where's Simon?' he pushed. 'Is he going to be in the meeting too?'

'Just meet me downstairs at nine thirty,' she asserted.

Unable to bear the stares of the other directors, she quickly made her way down to the first floor where the boardroom could be found.

She flopped on a chair at the front and rested her head on the table. It all felt so very wrong.

About ten minutes later the directors started to appear one by one, most of them with mugs in their hands, all seeming very laid back compared to Beth's rigid pose.

When they were all seated, it went very quiet, before all seven pairs of eyes turned to Beth expectantly.

She cleared her throat.

'I have some news that is going to affect the business for the foreseeable future.'

'What's going on?' Oliver, the Sales director asked.

'I'm going to share with you the truth. The absolute truth. What we decide to share with other people is still yet to be decided, but I know Simon would want his fellow directors to know the truth.'

Beth could feel the tension rising. She paused as she dug deep for the strength she needed. 'A couple of weeks ago our daughter, Scarlett, was kidnapped.' Beth could see this stunned the room.

'She was kidnapped by Damien Rock, our former Sales Director. It's too complex to explain how or why, but you can believe that Scarlett was in grave danger.'

Beth paused again. That had been the easy bit.

'Obviously, we tried everything in our power to get her

back. But it has cost us all gravely. First of all, when we were battling to rescue Scarlett... Paul Bird... he got caught in the cross fire. I don't really know how to say this. He's... no longer with us.'

'What do you mean?' Nathan asked.

'He suffered a fatal wound.'

The shock that swept across the room was unbearable. Beth wanted to be anywhere but here. Why was she having to do this alone?

'Someone killed him?' Eric asked.

'It was an accident. It's a long story that I don't want to go into now.'

No one said anything for what seemed like hours, then finally Eric asked, 'Is Simon okay? I guess he's got a lot to deal with.'

'You could say that,' Beth replied. 'As you can imagine, this was an incredibly stressful time for all the family. Not to mention the fact that we also had to deal with a whole world of non-Malants being gifted with our power. I'm sure it will come as no surprise when I tell you that Simon was left with little choice than to take drastic action.'

The tension was almost suffocating as the room anticipated what she was about to say.

'Simon turned to dark magic.'

There were small gasps of shock and Beth quickly added, 'It was the only way to save Scarlett and sever the spell that gave non-Malants magical abilities.'

Beth waited for a second. She could see that everyone wanted to say something, but no words formed.

'You must know that Simon acted in the best interests of everyone,' she continued. 'There was a criminal attacking his family and the future of our community was at stake. However, dark magic is nevertheless illegal, and in using it - despite the fact that he stopped so much bad from happening - he is facing criminal charges.'

This time the gasps were far more audible, and the obvious bafflement only increased Beth's nausea.

'He's been arrested?' Nathan murmured.

'Yes. And I have nothing more to say about that. All you need to be aware of is that I will be acting CEO until Simon's release, which I hope will be very soon. He acted in the interests of the greater good. I'm hoping our government will see sense.'

'Aren't you effectively in charge of the government?' Eric asked.

'It seems not everyone is in the position to abuse their power,' Beth answered, before swiftly changing the subject. 'I'm sure Simon will still want to have input on major decisions. There's no reason we can't keep him in the loop on things. But clearly he won't have an active role in the company during his time away.'

'We've lost both Bird men?' Oliver noted sadly.

'No,' Beth stressed vehemently. 'Simon is on what I'm thinking of as a sabbatical. A Bird family member is still in charge and it will most definitely be business as usual.'

Beth knew there were a million more questions that were teetering on the lips of each of the directors, but they were wise enough to hold back on asking. She was sporting her best stern face, trying to mirror her husband's strength and control, and it seemed to be having the desired effect.

'As you can imagine, this is terribly personal and painful for me. Therefore, I want to minimise the people who know about this, at least for the time being. At least until Simon has been sentenced. Or cleared. Or whatever.'

'Whatever you think is best,' Eric said.

'Thank you. I'm going to finish off some paperwork and then I'll be working from home for a few days. I'm sure you can all understand. But please, I will be on the end of my phone and email any time of the day, should you need me. Treat me now exactly as you would have treated Simon.' Beth shook her head. 'I don't mean I'm replacing him. I know how much you all respect him. I could never fill his incredible shoes. I'm just saying, if you would have gone to him with something, please now come to me.'

'Thank you, Beth,' Nathan said. 'We're here to support you too.'

Beth held her head high, trying to push away the teary emotion that was grappling with her. 'Thank you. I appreciate that.'

She stood up, grabbed her things, and made her way back to her office.

THIRTY-ONE

By the time the day of the funeral finally arrived, Beth had never felt lower. Simon was meeting them at the Malant hall in Clapham, then he was being allowed to join them briefly at the wake at a local hotel, before he would be taken straight back to prison. Beth could barely believe it was happening.

Beth's parents had travelled down the night before to be with her, and they were a huge help with Scarlett. They'd left Beth's brother in charge of their coffee shop so they could be with Beth to support her. And she was grateful for any help she could get.

Jane hadn't involved Beth in any of the plans. All Beth had was an invite. Her dad drove them to Clapham, and they arrived a good half hour before it was due to start.

There were dozens of people there. Beth hardly recognised any of them. Paul was so popular. So loved.

She stood outside, desperately awaiting the arrival of Simon; her heart pounding, her stomach nauseous.

Eventually, with just ten minutes to go, a black car pulled up and she saw Simon in the back. At least Jane had given him the dignity of arriving anonymously. Not that Jane needed to fear him escaping. Not with that sadistic contract in place.

He stepped out and his eyes instantly met Beth's. She ran to him and threw her arms around him.

There were no words that seemed right. They had so much to speak about, but this day was about Paul. Everything else at that moment had to take second place. No matter how desperate the situation was.

'I've missed you,' Beth said, kissing Simon gently on the lips. 'I hope you've been okay. They wouldn't let me see you.'

'I know. They said it was an admin error that meant they couldn't process visitors. Whatever that means. Obviously Jane's behind it. I never knew she could be such a manipulative bitch. I'm glad Paul's away from her.'

Beth noticed red patches sting his eyes, but he didn't let the tears fall. He held tight, just as he always did.

'Shall we go in? Go and say goodbye to a terrific man?'

'Jane said I could make a speech. I don't think she was very happy about it, but I pointed out that it would look odd if I didn't. Anyone who knew Paul, knew of me. I have to say something.'

'Of course you do. I can't believe she wouldn't want that.'

'I can't believe anything about her anymore.'

'Let's not think of that today. Come on.'

All Simon could manage was a nod.

As with most Malant venues, unless you knew it was there, you'd never see it. Despite its grandeur on the inside, outside it looked barely like a door. It was how they kept non-Malants at bay. And for the non-Malant guests, they'd just been told it was a well-kept secret. A spot Paul had found and loved.

The gentle music faded out and they all sat down. When everyone was settled, the Celebrant started speaking. She firstly welcomed everyone, before sharing stories of Paul and bringing to life just what a wonderful, joyful man he was.

Simon was shuffling through the notes of his speech next to Beth. She rarely saw him so nervous. She linked her arm in his and held him closely.

It would be one of the last times she'd be able to do that.

She took a breath. Her tears should be for Paul, not for the mess of her life.

'And now Paul's nephew, Simon, is going to share a few words,' the voice of the female Celebrant said.

Simon glanced at Beth. There was a look in his eye that she hadn't seen before and it left her quite unnerved. He walked to the front and stood behind the lectern.

His eyes gazed over the two hundred people before him. There were so many people there. Some had even flown in from New York. Paul would have been touched.

'Paul Bird was the best man alive,' Simon began, an unexpected quiver to his normally solid and stable voice. 'Not just now, but of any time. He'd had many tough decisions to make through his life, but he stood firmly by them. He was a man of honour. He taught me that honour is more important than anything. Stand up for what you believe in and always be brave.'

Beth watched as Simon's face began shaking, as if it were trembling under the agony of his grief. It was rare that Simon ever looked anything but strong, yet the man before her was definitely crumbling. It was heart wrenching.

'When my parents died,' Simon continued, 'I didn't even know I had an Uncle Paul.' He paused for breath. 'I was a boy that everyone feared and I was thrust upon a man who had been enjoying the life of a bachelor. It could have been a disaster. Paul would have had every right to resent me. But he didn't.' Simon paused again and Beth could see him physically struggling to carry on. 'He took me into his home and loved me as his own. He made me the man I am today. I owe everything I am to him. He was the only person...' Tears began streaming down Simon's face.

He took a few seconds, shaking his head.

'He was the only pers...'

Simon stood back, physically trying to regain his composure. But it was too much. The recent pain, loss and incredible stress all finally got the better of him and, then and there, Simon broke. The strongest man Beth had ever met disintegrated in front of her eyes.

He leaned forward, his face a dripping mess. His lip was quaking as he tried to continue, but his voice was lost behind his sorrow.

'I miss him so much.' With that Simon fell to his knees. He sobbed in front of everyone and a desperately sad stiffness gripped the room.

Beth immediately shot to her feet. She dashed to the front and took Simon in her arms.

'What am I going to do without him?' he wept in her ear. 'I don't know how to function. He was everything to me. I don't know...'

'I know. I know,' Beth said.

'It's all going to go wrong without him.' Simon looked at Beth. His eyes were red. Agonisingly red. His face was pained and the tears were relentlessly pouring down his cheeks. Seeing him like this tore at her.

'Would he have wanted me to go to prison?' he whispered. The sheer despair in his question sent a chill through her. 'I want to ask him. I want him to tell me that Jane is wrong. I need to hear it from him. He always knew the right thing to do. I can't be on my own now. I need to ask him.'

Beth's own eyes started to sting. Nothing had ever hurt her more than seeing the man she loved so crippled with grief. It was as if Paul had been Simon's pillar. He'd helped to give Simon his insurmountable strength. With Paul gone it was inevitable that Simon would weaken. Paul was more than an uncle; a guardian. Paul had been Simon's rock when everything else in his life had been falling apart. No matter how much Beth knew Simon loved her, no one could ever replace his uncle.

'Paul would be furious with Jane,' she said. 'Her actions are despicable. We won't let her get away with it. We'll fight her. Together we'll fight her.'

'She was going to take Scarlett off us.'

'You mean the contract? I saw it.'

'No. Before that. She was going to call social services. Get Scarlett taken away. That's why I pleaded guilty. I had no choice.'

Beth had been feeling quite unstable, but hearing these words seemed to lock everything together. A bolt of anger – the sort she'd never experienced before – shot through her.

The dark magic had constantly been taunting her, but since she'd attacked Jane so violently, Beth had tried hard to keep it away. But suddenly, hearing just what depths Jane had been willing to sink to, Beth could hold it off no more. The swirls of darkness found their way in, exciting her need for vengeance.

'Trust me, Simon. She won't get away with this. She doesn't deserve the Bird name. Family was everything to Paul. She isn't family anymore. We're going to sort this.'

'Hang on, you've seen the contract?' Simon said, his face relaxing with what seemed like hope.

'Yes. Jane gave me a copy. She said it was so I could understand the terms, but I don't think she could wait to rub my face in it.'

'Can you carry on?' the Celebrant enquired.

'Sorry,' Beth said to her. She turned to Simon. 'Do you want to continue?' she asked.

'Can you get it to me?' Simon asked Beth.

'What?'

'The contract. You need to find a way to get it to me.'

'Don't you have a copy?'

'No. Part of the agreement was that I wouldn't be allowed to keep a copy. They know how good I am at breaking contracts. My lawyer has a copy, but I'm only allowed to see it during his short visits. I need time to study it if I'm going to find a way out of this.'

It suddenly clicked with Beth the very reason why Jane was keeping them apart. Control was part of it, of course. But Jane also needed to make sure that Simon never got the chance to find a loophole that would allow him to break free. Jane knew that Beth would do everything in her power to help him escape. This could mean that Beth would never be allowed to see Simon. That could not happen.

'I will. I don't know how yet, but I will get a copy to you.'

'I can finish it for you, if you like,' the Celebrant said.

'No. I'll finish it,' Simon said, his hands still trembling.

His eyes didn't leave Beth's face for a moment, and then he rose to his feet.

Beth looked out at the hundreds of eyes staring back, but she refused to move from Simon's side.

Jane would see just what a doting wife was like. Jane was going to pay for what she'd done. Jane was going to suffer and Simon was going to be free.

'Paul was the only person to believe in me when everyone else feared me,' Simon said, and it jolted Beth from her inner rage. She took a breath and listened to his words. 'When I was lost, he gave me a purpose. When I doubted myself, he gave me untold strength. When I wanted to hide, he gave me solace and a place to disappear to. And he never questioned it at all. When I told him that I'd met my soulmate, he made the world stop so that I could be with her.'

A flash of the first time Beth had met Paul dashed through her brain. His primary concern had always been for Simon. Everything else in the whole world came second. If only the same could be said for Jane.

'Paul was the most remarkable man,' Simon said, concentrating intently to control his tears. 'He was smart and witty, and could make anyone do anything. He had a smile that everyone fell for and a look of disapproval that would pull you into line in an instant. There was nothing you couldn't love about Paul. It is one of the saddest things imaginable that he was taken from us so early. He had so much life left in him. So much left to give. The world will be infinitely smaller without him, and such a darker place. He was the light in all our lives and there won't be a second that goes by when I won't miss him.' Simon paused to take a breath, his tears winning the battle. 'All I want to say is thank you for everything you've done for me, Uncle Paul. I couldn't be more grateful and I couldn't love you more.'

Simon placed the notes on the lectern before him. He looked out quickly across the room and then he turned to Beth. He wrapped his arms around her and she held him tightly. But as he sobbed on her shoulder, she wasn't thinking about him. She'd even stopped thinking about Paul. The only thing consuming her mind now was the need for revenge.

THIRTY-TWO

Simon's court case was scheduled for the following Tuesday. It had been a torturous weekend for Beth. All she'd been able to think about was what spells she could conjure up that would wipe the fake sense of morality off Jane's face once and for all.

Beth still wasn't allowed to visit Simon. There were still these non-existent admin errors. She'd got the contract ready to go in an envelope on the table, but she hadn't been able to fathom yet just how she was going to get it to him.

He was an expert at breaking contracts, just as he was an expert at writing them. She was sure if he could scour every word, he'd find the missing link that would set him free. But he was never going to be able to do that without the paperwork, and he was never going to get that if Jane wouldn't let Beth see him.

It's not like Beth could even magic a copy over to him, as that would break the terms of the contract. Yet again, Jane seemed to have everything tightly under control.

Beth's parents had stayed with her over the weekend, and when the day of the sentencing finally came around they were there to look after Scarlett. Beth was so pleased that all she had to concentrate on was whether Jane was going to get her way or not.

She arrived at Malancy HQ just minutes before the court was in session. Traffic had been awful. She parked up swiftly and scurried to the second floor court room.

The instant she reached the door, she was greeted by Jane.

'Hello, Beth. I wanted to catch you.'

'Just like you caught my husband?'

'It's my job to catch criminals. Simon used dark magic. It's illegal. I couldn't excuse it.'

'But you could excuse me using it?'

'We both know you didn't turn to dark magic. You were dragged into it due to your connection to Simon. It's very different.'

'So you'll accept that's different.'

'You need to know I'm not the bad person here. I've done my best by Simon.'

'Of course you have.'

'I've had a good conversation with the judge. I presented a very convincing case to minimise Simon's sentence. I am sure he'll be out of prison before we know it.'

'Oh, I'm sure of that too.'

Beth pushed passed Jane and entered the court.

It was a small and simple room, with just a few chairs for visitors, two tables for the defence and prosecution, and then a grander table at the front for the judge.

There were so few Malancy court cases, it really didn't warrant much more. There was a larger court with room for a jury just down the corridor, but with only around ten prosecutions each year in the Malancy world, what they had was more than enough.

She headed to the front where Jim was already seated.

'Hi,' she said to Jim. 'Thanks for being here.'

'I wouldn't be anywhere else. I'm sure it will be fine. Jane has put in a good word.'

'Isn't she a saint.'

Jim couldn't respond.

Jane followed in behind, but took her seat on the other side. Beth never thought she'd see the day they were on opposing sides like this.

Simon was brought into the court. His eyes searched for Beth immediately, and he smiled the second he saw her.

He looked weary, as if he hadn't slept in a week and a huge burden was weighing heavy on his shoulders.

Jane would pay for this.

'All rise,' an official said, and the few people in the room rose to their feet.

A middle aged judge entered the room, his face blank, giving nothing away as to what he was thinking.

Everyone sat back down and there was a moment of tense silence before the judge spoke.

'This is one of the simplest cases I've ever come across. Mr Bird, you turned to dark magic, and you've admitted freely to your guilt. Which is wise considering the insurmountable evidence against you. Mrs Bird – Jane Bird that is - and your lawyer have spent time with me, talking me through the case and explaining that you were in a dire situation as your daughter had just been kidnapped. They both painted a picture of a desperate man who made a mistake. A mistake he's bravely owning up to.'

Beth relaxed a little as she felt this was going in the right direction.

'However, I find it hard to be so forgiving,' the judge said, and Beth stiffened. 'You are in a position of great power. You have a huge responsibility for all of the Malant people. While I grant you that this responsibility was bestowed upon you and is not one of choice, you still eagerly accepted it and have been overseeing the Malancy government for some time. That responsibility must come with a sense of discipline. You can't have all that power and still find it acceptable to become a slave to your emotions. No matter how dire the circumstances, I find your actions to be completely reckless.'

The judge looked down at some notes before him, and Beth stopped breathing.

'The sentence for using dark magic is ten years.' Beth found herself shaking her head. 'But I believe that this sentence doesn't match the irresponsibility, nor does such a sentence send out a message to our people that we take our law very seriously. Therefore I am sentencing you, Mr Simon Bird, to fifteen years in prison.'

'No!' Beth shrieked, shooting to her feet. 'You can't do that!' She turned her head to Jane. It looked like genuine shock was slapped across Jane's face, but Beth had stopped believing anything.

'Mrs Bird, please sit down,' the judge ordered.

'He's not guilty of anything. This is utterly ridiculous! Do you know what he's done for you? What he's sacrificed to make sure you have a good life? To make sure you still have your powers?'

'If you do not desist, Mrs Bird, you will be arrested.'

'You can't arrest me. You have no power. You don't know what real power is.'

The fear on Jim's face said it all. Beth could feel her eyes had turned jet black with anger, and her skin was crawling with the liberation of dark magic.

'If you do anything, you will set into motion Simon's contract,' Jane warned. 'You can't use magic in any way to affect his sentence.'

'Please Beth,' Simon pleaded. 'There's another way. You know there's another way.'

Getting Simon the contract and having him find a potential loophole seemed like too much effort. It was far too longwinded. Every inch of Beth was crying out for action. She wanted to cause pain. She wanted to see everyone suffer, just as she was suffering.

A small smirk grabbed her lips. 'You're right, darling. I can't use magic to affect you in any way. We'll find another way to set you free. But I can use my magic to exact revenge on people. That's got nothing to do with you.'

Beth turned her gaze to Jane. She flicked out her hand and Jane was sent hurtling across the floor.

'Beth, no,' Jim warned. 'You can't do this.'

'I can do whatever I want. Literally no one can stop me. The only man in the entire world who could is unable to use his magic. Jane made sure of that. So here's a loophole for her. If she's shackled the only man who is equal to my strength, how is she going to prevent me from killing her?'

Beth took one step forward towards Jane when a spasm across her muscles halted her, and then fifty thousand volts of electricity jolted her to the floor.

Waves of pain every few seconds shot through her. She looked up to see a policeman to the side of her holding a taser in his hands, but there was nothing she could do. She'd lost control of her body.

'That's enough!' Jim shouted.

The pain ceased pretty quickly, but Beth was left stunned to the floor. She couldn't move.

'What have you done?' Simon shouted. 'Let me see her!' But his voice was trailing away as he was being escorted back to the prison.

'Get Mrs Bird out of here!' voices called, and Beth knew they meant Jane. Scuffles and urgency seemed to surround her, but all she saw was Jim's worried face above her.

'Shall I arrest her?' a voice said.

'No,' Jim snapped back. 'You leave her alone. She needs support to get over this, not punishment. We all know it's not her fault that she's tinged with dark magic.'

'That seemed more than a tinge, Mr Malant.'

'You leave her to me. Make sure Jane's okay and don't worry about Beth. I'll take care of her.'

After a few moments, Beth was able to rise to her feet. She took a few breaths, but she was generally fine.

'Who did that to me?' she asked.

'You were getting out of control, Beth,' Jim replied.

'You haven't seen out of control.'

'You can't keep doing this. I agree, Simon is not being treated fairly. But let's trust in the system we built. Let's appeal. See if we can get him freed early.'

'He'll have a criminal record for doing nothing!'

'He did turn to dark magic.'

'It's not as simple as that! I wish all of you other Malants could experience what having innate abilities is like. It's all so easy for you. Use a stone or a plant, and other than that it leaves you alone. But what if it was alive in you? It's suddenly not so easy to control then. You're all so closed minded and stupid.'

'I agree with you, Beth. I do. But fighting like this won't get you anywhere.'

'Let's just see about that.'

THIRTY-THREE

A few hours later and Simon was sitting in the noisy prison canteen eating his dinner. In reality, it had been the most overwhelming day, but something about the monotony of prison life was making it all seem like a dream. Had Beth really gone mad like that? Had she really been tasered?

Simon was terrified that she wouldn't be able to break away from the grasp of the dark magic and that she'd too end up in prison. What then? What would happen to Scarlett? If only Beth could get that contract to him. If he could escape these walls he could help her, but that document was literally the only chance he had of breaking free.

Simon took a breath. There was nothing he could do. He had to have faith that Beth's strong, good nature would win through in the end. He was literally trapped and helpless. The only thing he had left was faith.

Simon poked at the mash potato on his plate. He couldn't face another mouthful so he pushed his plate aside.

No one was sitting next to him. Everyone had been giving him a wide berth, and he'd been keeping his head down and his distance from everyone in return.

At present, no one was aware that Simon couldn't use his abilities, but he knew it was just a matter of time before the other prisoners got word of the contract. Questions would be asked and this couldn't be kept a secret. The whole point of the contract was for Jane to show she was in control. It would need to come out at some point. But Simon would enjoy the peace and quiet while it lasted.

The other men might have been keeping away from him, but it didn't stop the stares. The only person to actually speak to him had been Damien, who had appeared back in the prison just hours after Simon had arrived there. Damien hadn't hesitated in bestowing a desperate apology at Simon's feet. Not that Simon had wanted it, or accepted it. He'd just told Damien to get lost. And now Damien was joining in the staring too.

Dozens of eyes seemed to watch Simon wherever he went, as if they were waiting to see what he might do. As if anything could happen at any moment and everyone needed to be ready for it. Ready for whatever hell was heading their way.

If only they knew the truth.

However, there was one set of eyes more than anyone's that burned a hole right into Simon's head. It was George Malant. He had been watching Simon relentlessly.

His stare wasn't like the others, though. George was more contemplative, as if he were studying Simon. His irises had followed Simon everywhere, virtually magnetised to Simon's body. There was something lurking behind George's glare and Simon wasn't afraid to admit that it unnerved him.

He doubted George would try to hurt him, but he could sense that George was biding his time for a reason. George had once been the most powerful Malant alive – in a political sense. Now both of the most powerful men were equally constrained. George clearly wanted to say something; do something. Simon could only wait.

But he didn't have to wait for long. Simon stood up and headed back to his cell. His plan was to read his book and burn away the three remaining hours until lights out. Or at least attempt to read his book.

In reality, he had been struggling to concentrate on anything. But he knew he had to try. Allowing his emotions to take charge could lead to him accidentally using his magic. His power was so in tune with his emotions, he couldn't take the risk. He needed to find a way to stay calm and focused, as impossible as that seemed right at that moment. And his dull book about a fish that had started to show human features was the perfect antidote to excitement.

He sat on his bed and rested his head against the wall. He picked up his book and found were he'd got to. But before he could even finish the first sentence, George was standing in his doorway.

'Good evening,' George said. 'I will admit, you are the last person I ever expected to see in here. Jane certainly did a number on you.'

'Good evening,' Simon replied, focusing on his book and refusing to acknowledge anything else George had said. Simon couldn't ignore the trepidation he felt by George's presence, but he certainly wasn't going to show that.

'How has she managed it?' George asked. 'She couldn't have taken away your powers. No. No one could ever do that. I should know, I tried.'

Simon's eyes moved from the page of his book to George's face. 'I still have my magic, but I won't be using it in here.'

'She always was a clever one. The sort of woman you definitely want on your side.'

'If you don't mind, I'm getting to a good part in my book,' Simon said. 'Perhaps we can catch up another time.'

George moved into the cell and took a seat at the little desk in the corner.

'I hear it was a lovely funeral.'

Simon gave George his full attention. 'As lovely as funerals can possibly be. Is there something you want?'

George glared at Simon and Simon could swear there was a pinch of distress in his expression. George quickly rose to his feet and he pulled the cell door to, blocking out the world around them.

'There's something you need to know,' he said, coming back to the seat.

Simon placed his book down and sat upright. 'What?'

'I toyed with the idea of telling you that night, when you came to see me. It was there, on the tip of my tongue.'

'What?' Simon said, growing impatient.

'I don't know whether I regretted it or not that I never said. And then you walked in here and a little voice told me it wasn't a coincidence.'

'A coincidence?'

'I think the universe, the Malancy, whatever it might be... I think it wants me to tell you.'

'Tell me what?'

George hesitated. 'There's a spell,' he said.

When he didn't elaborate, Simon said, 'There are lots of spells.'

'There's a spell that you don't know about, but I think you should. It's up to you what you do with it, but I think you should know.'

Simon sat back, getting restless with George's unhurried way of delivering this information.

'I'm sure I'll find out if I need it,' he said, picking up his book again.

'I want another five years taken off my sentence and I'll tell you.'

'I'm sure you do, but I no longer have the power to make that a reality.'

'Yes you do.'

'No I don't.'

'Of course you do.'

'If you haven't noticed, I'm not really using my magic at the moment.'

'But I bet your wife still is.'

Simon placed his book aside. 'You want to serve just ten years now for treason, kidnapping, aiding and abetting. Need I go on?'

'I don't think this is about what sentence I serve. It's about what good I can do for the Malancy moving forward.'

'What could you possibly offer the Malancy?' Simon asked, growing more and more irritated with George's desperate attempts at freedom.

'Paul Bird,' he muttered.

This caught Simon's attention. 'What about Paul?'

'You could bring him back to life.'

Simon shook his head. 'Don't.'

'It's true.'

'No it's not. Don't mess with me like that.' Simon could feel the anger churning within him, making him feel sick.

'You remember the story of the original Malants? How they lost their children in the fire five hundred years ago, and that's ultimately what created the Malancy?'

'Every Malant knows that story.'

'But what you won't know is that, despite Samuel and Elizabeth having more children after that and starting a new family, they could never get over the death of their first two sons.'

'Obviously. Who could? It was a tragic loss.'

'So they spent all their time working on a spell to bring their sons back from the dead.'

Simon sat forward, his ears now fully engaged with George's words. 'They brought their sons back from the dead?'

'Eventually,' George said, hesitantly. 'It wasn't without its issues, though. By the time they even got close to perfecting the spell, too much time had passed. What returned to them was not really the two boys that had left them.'

'How much time had passed?'

'A few years.'

'Paul has only been gone for a couple of weeks,' Simon noted, his heart throbbing.

'As you know from when we last met, there is a whole world of documentation on the Malancy that you've never seen, that has been passed through my family directly from Samuel and Elizabeth. Others down the line who have had access to this documentation have used the original spell as a guideline. It took two hundred years to perfect, but eventually a successful spell was cast. A young woman was brought back from the dead. It was my great, great, great... I lose track of how many greats now... but a very distant grandmother.'

'She was resurrected?' Simon asked with fearful hope.

'And lived for another thirty years.'

'I couldn't,' Simon said, sitting back. 'Everyone knows that Paul has died.' He paused, the hope radiating through this body. 'What did people think when she came back from the dead?'

'They thought whatever they were told to think. You're a brilliant man, Simon. You can spin this whatever way you want. There are far more important things that you have to worry about. This spell will come with other consequences.'

'Spell?' Simon said as it dawned on him that using his magic was not going to be possible.

'I'll reveal no more until you give me your word that my sentence will be cut again.'

'I have no current power to do that.'

'But Beth has.'

'Jane won't let me see her.'

'Send her a letter. Phone her up. Do it through your lawyer. Use your imagination, Simon.'

'I suppose I could find a way.'

'Good. Then give me your word.'

'You trust my word?'

'More than any man I've ever met. Any man that willingly allows himself to be incarcerated for actions that saved his family - and the world for that matter - is a man I trust implicitly. I know if we shake on this, you'll honour it to the death.'

Simon knew he would too. He was nothing if not honourable. Paul had made sure of that. But cutting George's sentence wasn't the issue here. Could he really bring Paul back? What would the consequences be?

He supposed there was no harm in at least hearing about it. Then with the facts to hand he could make his decision.

But just getting the facts would mean he'd agree to cut George's sentence to practically nothing in relation to his crimes.

But it would mean Paul could come back.

Simon thrust out his hand, ready to shake on the agreement. He refused to think any more about it. Paul was all that mattered.

'You have a deal,' Simon said.

George smiled and shook Simon's hand in return.

'Very well. This is what you need to know. The spell takes immense power. As I'm sure you'd expect.'

'If other Malants can do it, I'm sure it will be a breeze for me.'

'It's a little bit more complicated than that,' George said.

'What do you mean?'

George took a breath. 'You can't perform this spell with good magic. It's just not possible. You have to turn to dark magic, and you have to be completely submerged.'

Simon held himself tight, determined not to show George just how much this shook him.

'Even then,' George continued, 'with the extra abilities that dark magic provides, another Malant would still need a thousand elements to do this. That's why there are only three successful cases on record. But I'm sure you'd only need to succumb to dark magic and that would be enough.'

'That's still quite a task.'

'Indeed. If you want this to work, you need to lose every grain of good magic within you. I mean it. The good magic will pull back the spell and render it powerless. I can't emphasise that enough.'

'Are you serious? Or do you just want me to turn to the darkness?'

George's face became grave. 'I've never been more serious. This is why I've been hesitant to share. Simon, you with only good magic are an unstoppable force. I dread to think what will happen to the world if you submit to the darkness completely. You would be limitless and without inhibition. It's a terrifying prospect.'

'Then why tell me at all?'

'Because it's all the bargaining power I have left. I want to be with my wife. I want my life back. Or a semblance of my life, anyway. I was rich and powerful and now I'm treated the same as any other inmate. Even you set free with darkness is less scary than fifteen more years of this.'

'You really are selfish, aren't you.'

'Am I?'

Simon didn't respond.

'We both know you have a good soul. One of the best. That's why you were chosen. I doubt there's anyone in this world where the darkness will have more of a battle to win over the good than in you. Even that wife of yours would surrender more easily.'

'Why do you say that?' Simon asked.

'She hasn't had to build up the resilience that you have. She's had a much easier time of things. Her naivety might seem like a good trait, but I believe it will be her undoing.'

'Don't talk about her like that,' Simon snapped.

'You must agree? No matter what she goes through,

she has this innocent optimism, where good will always triumph.'

'If only more people were like her.'

'It's not a practical way to look at the world. When things get really bad, she won't have the grit to truly survive. I can't imagine how she's coping at the moment.'

'She's the strongest, bravest woman I know.'

'Stronger than Jane?' George pushed.

'Jane wouldn't know what hit her if she came toe to toe with Beth.'

'In terms of magic, yes-'

'In terms of anything. Now leave Beth out of this.'

'Fine,' George shrugged. 'If you believe she's so strong then she'll be able to pull you back from the darkness if you decide to commit to this spell. But be warned, that will be one hell of a challenge.'

'You just said my innate goodness will put up a battle. Won't that help me get back?'

'It's a possibility. Truthfully, I'm curious to find out.'

'What is the spell then?' Simon asked. 'How do I cast it?'

George focused on Simon. 'Only once you have completely succumbed to dark magic can you cast it. It won't work otherwise.'

'You said.'

'Then you need to project a healing spell. But with ten times more power than any other healing spell you've ever cast before. You'll need something personal of Paul's to be able to do it.' George glanced across at a photo of Paul that Simon had stuck to his wall with Blu-Tack. 'That will do. Anything that relates directly to Paul. Focus on his picture, the last place you saw him, and a very intense healing spell.'

'That's it?'

George rolled his eyes. 'For any other Malant that's like climbing Mount Everest only to find Kilimanjaro has been placed on top of it. It would be a virtually impossible feat.

You make it sound like a walk in the park.'

Simon remained very still. Leaving out the fact that he'd have to give in to dark magic, this would be a spell he could easily cast. It was all seeming too attainable.

'Where would Paul reappear? In here, with me? He wouldn't be trapped in his coffin, would he?'

'No! Don't be so dramatic. You'll imagine him in the last place you saw him. He'll reappear there.'

'In the middle of a hotel room?' Simon asked. That could be quite shocking for whatever guest was in the room that night. Although that did seem like a very small detail in comparison.

'I'll leave you to ponder it, shall I?' George said standing up. 'I always liked Paul. It wouldn't be a terrible thing to have him back in the world. But darkness or not, I'm counting on you to keep your promise.'

'You know I will.'

George nodded. 'I'll bid you farewell, then. Happy thinking.'

George left the cell without turning back and he pushed the door to again behind him.

Simon sat up straight. Could he really do this?

THIRTY-FOUR

Beth had played along with Jim. She'd let him follow her home. She'd let him tell her parents what had happened and explain that she needed looking after. And then she'd taken herself to bed, claiming to be exhausted, assuring all her family that she was feeling much better and she'd managed to gain some perspective.

Well, she had. Jane had ruined her life. How were things ever going to be the same again? Beth had been happy. As happy as she was ever going to be with that stupid, moralising husband of hers. He was hardly the perfect man, but he was her man, and Jane had taken that away. And now Jane was going to suffer for it.

The second Beth had closed her bedroom door, she'd teleported straight to Jane's house.

She'd tried to, at least.

The second the flash of the teleportation spell worked, she was instantly bounced out of Jane's living room and forced onto the expansive driveway, shut out by the lame protection spell that had been cast across Jane's mansion.

That wasn't going to stop Beth, though. Beth was the most powerful Malant alive. Literally now, as Simon had been constrained and Beth was letting the darkness enhance her already incredible abilities.

Jane's pathetic little protection was going to stop her for long.

Beth edged to the side of the house and she pressed her hand against it, feeling the tingle of energy from the spell.

She knew instantly it was Ralph's doing. It had the stench of a scholar. It was all neat and tidy without any imagination behind it.

Beth had no idea where Ralph lived. She doubted he'd still be at Malancy HQ, but that was hardly an obstacle. She closed her eyes, did a short and snappy location spell, and then homed in on Ralph, who was sitting all relaxed in his study.

In a flash, she was standing behind him.

'Good evening, Ralph,' she said.

He jumped up, knocking his paperwork all over the floor of the small and untidy room. He was always studying something. Nerd.

'Mrs Bird? What are you doing here?' he gasped.

'I need you to take down the protection spell on Jane's house.'

'What?'

'You heard me.'

'But I've only just put it up, a few hours ago.'

'It's stopping me from getting in.'

'I think that's the point.'

A delightful smile tickled Beth's lips as an idea came to her.

'Never mind. Don't worry about it. You don't have to do anything. As Simon has shown me on more than one occasion, the power is all in my hand.'

'What does that mean? What are you going to do?' Ralph seemed terrified, and he had every reason to be.

'Hold still.'

Beth forced Ralph still and then she placed her hand across his chest – right across his heart.

'No, Mrs Bird! No!'

'Simon never kills anyone. I'm sure I won't.'

Ralph moaned with pain. 'But... my other spells... So many spells...'

Beth let go and took a step back. 'What spells?'

'I cast most of the spells for the government. So much good work would be undone. You can't take that risk.'

Beth considered this for a moment, and once again she smiled. 'I can't, or you can't?'

She placed her hand across his chest lightly. 'Your move,' she said. 'You either take down the protection spell on Jane, or I stop your heart – hopefully not killing you – and all the spells you have in play get broken. Over to you.'

'You can't do this!'

'Actually, I can. Simon makes it look really easy. And I'm dying to give it a go.'

'But what about Mrs Bird?'

'Her name is Jane Parker. She is no longer a member of my family.'

'What are you going to do?'

'Nothing she doesn't deserve.'

'I can't let you hurt her.'

'I don't think you're quite understanding this. You have a very simple choice. Either Jane loses the protection spell around her, or every spell you've cast that is currently active gets severed when I stop your heart. Those are your options. What will it be?'

Ralph's eyes showed the horror he felt, and tingles of joy sparked through Beth.

Not that far across London, Simon stood up from his bed. He took the picture of Paul in his hands and studied it.

He missed Paul so much. It ached inside of him. How could he turn down the opportunity to bring Paul back?

But it would mean losing himself to the darkness.

Simon quickly shook his head. With Paul back and Beth fighting for him, he couldn't believe that they'd let him become trapped behind the darkness forever. As George had said, even his own body wouldn't submit without a fight.

Simon sat back down as the biggest problem of all hit him.

He couldn't use his magic. If he did this then he'd never see his daughter again. He'd be saving Paul to lose Scarlett.

That was when logic snapped into life.

The whole of the contract was hinged upon Paul's death. If Paul was to come back to life then the contract would become null and void. It was the ultimate loophole. Doing this would not only bring Paul back, but it would set Simon free. And Jane's insistence on blaming Simon for Paul's death would finally backfire.

Simon felt another jab of fear. What if the spell didn't work? He wouldn't have Paul back and he'd still lose his daughter. That would be disastrous.

Simon shook his head again as he focused on reality. There hadn't been a contract in nearly twenty years of his working life that he hadn't been able to break. There had to be a loophole. There always was. And if he'd broken the rules of the contract anyway, he could magic up his own copy and not even wait for Beth. It would be simple. Too simple.

He stared at the photo of Paul. Could he really live his life without his uncle?

He knew in that instant that he'd never forgive himself if he didn't try. No matter what the consequences of doing this were, the consequences of not doing it – the torture of the regret – would be worse.

Without thinking any more about it, for fear that he'd talk himself out of it, Simon took the seat at his desk and he placed the photo before him.

Beth closed her eyes and teleported back to Jane's house; back to the driveway she'd left just minutes before. Although Ralph had made the obvious choice and had removed the protection spell, Beth was a little disappointed that he hadn't fought more. She would have liked to have tried stopping his heart. To see how easy it really was. To see just what it felt like to manipulate someone's organs with nothing but your fingertips.

Another smile popped onto her lips. Just because she couldn't do it to Ralph, it didn't mean all was lost. That's exactly what she could do to Jane! She had been struggling to come up with the perfect punishment for the woman who had ruined her life. Squashing her vital organs one by one would be such a poetic solution. She could start with her liver for practise, then move to her lungs to squeeze that hot air out of her, next to her brain to prevent her from plotting the demise of future families, and finally Beth would crush Jane's heart. Crush it entirely. Leaving it broken. Just as Beth's was.

Beth walked up to the front door. It swung open at her command.

'Mrs Parker!' she said. 'I have a surprise for you!'

Simon slowly closed his eyes. The time for thinking was gone. He had to do it, and do it now.

He let the darkness in, feeling it so easily slipping through his body.

Red flecks danced across his skin at first, as if they were joyful at how Simon was capitulating. Then they became fiercer. Thick crimson shards dashed across every inch of his flesh as he let himself sink deeper.

Oh, it felt so good. It was like scratching an itch that had been taunting him for years.

He relaxed into his seat as he welcomed in the tsunami of evil. It began thrashing away at anything worthy within him.

He knew Beth would be screaming at him right now.

Telling him off for doing this. Not understanding what his uncle meant to him and how this was the absolute right decision.

Beth was such a whiny woman. She was always telling him off and stamping down her righteous nonsense. Moaning about how they were being victimised. How could that be true? Victims were weak and Simon was not weak.

He felt the power surge inside of him as he acknowledged how right George had been. Beth was nothing more than a stupid, innocent girl who had no right playing in the big, bad world. She was such a simpleton who had no clue about reality.

The more the darkness devoured his body, the more irritated he became with her.

He began to realise how much she'd been holding him back. Imagine where he could be right now without her? How had he been so pathetic to believe he'd been in love?

He could see it now. The clarity that the darkness was giving him made the truth stand out like a beacon. He didn't love Beth. He never had. He'd been shrouded by a spell because they were the two chosen ones. To keep the Malancy alive they'd needed to get together and conceive a child. But the darkness was showing him the truth. The truth that he really couldn't stand her. She was nothing more than an aggravation that he couldn't wait to get rid of.

Maybe staying in prison would be a blessing to get away from her.

Back in Buckinghamshire, Beth was striding across Jane's huge house. There were guards inside, but Beth was easily able to knock them away. Her immense power rendered all of their efforts futile. She was even ready for more of their tasers, leaving everything in their arsenal useless and limp.

By the time she reached Jane's bedroom, she found the

heartless bitch quivering on the bed.

'You don't want to do this, Beth. It's the dark magic. You would never want to do this. Simon will never forgive you.'

'It's you he'll never forgive.'

Beth forced Jane down, flat against the perfectly made covers.

'What are you going to do? Beth, this isn't you. You're one of the nicest people I've ever met.'

'Isn't that funny. I used to think that about you. It must have been Paul that made you seem nice. Now without him your true colours are shining through. And I don't like them.'

'Please, Beth. Please! I was just doing my job.'

'You were punishing Simon for Paul's death. Admit it.'

'No! He used dark magic.'

'What do you think I'm doing now? The law is black and white you said. But it's grey when it comes to me.'

'I told Simon I'd protect you.'

'You should have protected him. He was your nephew.'

'His actions were illegal.'

'He saved the world. Again!'

'Paul died.'

'It's not his fault!'

'But it is. Can't you see? The second Simon turned to dark magic, Paul's fate was sealed. It is his fault.'

'And now you've had him locked up for fifteen years.'

'I didn't expect that. I truthfully didn't. I thought a couple of years would be enough. Enough to punish him for his reckless decision. That's all.'

'You bitch. You abused your power. You abused your position.'

'And what are you doing now?'

'I'm going to make you suffer for it.'

Beth pressed on Jane's stomach, feeling for her insides.

Jane let out a shriek, but this time it just bounced off Beth. The dark magic had so deeply consumed her, her true self was now far too deep. It had no hope of being set free.

A wonderful renewed sense of liberation opened up within Simon as he sank down the final depths to absolute darkness.

He was now free from all of the shackles that his so-called decent life had constrained him with. No more wife, family and responsibility. Simon was now going to do whatever he wanted. And the first thing he wanted was to get his drinking buddy back. He'd missed having fun. It had been a lifetime since he'd actually enjoyed himself.

He was a multi-millionaire who never spent money on frivolities. His luxury car collection was about as extravagant as he got. What an absolute waste.

Life was just beginning for Simon. He could feel it. Why had he not set himself free before? This was marvellous!

His eyelids flicked open as his new found freedom concreted itself within him; his eyes now jet black like shiny drops of oil.

The power magnified itself more and more until he finally hit the bottom depths, all of the goodness having been completely expunged.

At the very same second that Simon hit those depths, Beth seemed to snap back to reality. Jane's cries for help shuddered her and she jumped back off the bed, freeing Jane from her grasp.

Jane panted and wept and all Beth could do was watch. What had she done? How had it happened?

The blackness in Beth's eyes vanished, and any evidence of dark magic could no longer be found.

'I'm so sorry,' Beth said, trembling. 'Are you okay? Are you in pain?'

All Jane could do was sob. She couldn't speak.

Beth tried to clear her mind. What had she done? Had

she actually hurt Jane?

No, she didn't think so. It was close, but she hadn't actually got there. Thank God.

'I'm so sorry,' Beth said, fearful tears building up in her eyes. 'I'm so sorry.' And with that she ran away. She ran into the night. She ran until she could run no more. She knew she'd never forgive herself for what she'd done.

Simon took a moment to enjoy the brilliant sensation of freedom that expanded across his body. He shuddered and it instantly shook away all the red marks of his destruction. His chocolate eyes once again popped back into view, removing any evidence of his submission. The darkness was no longer infecting him. It now was him.

This was the new Simon Bird. He'd eradicated his past self completely. A grin broadened on his lips as he felt the euphoric buzz of his new life.

What a wonderful fresh start this was.

He took a breath, the air seeming more vigorous than ever before. He cleared his lungs and turned his attention to the picture before him. It was time to begin the most important spell he would ever cast.

He closed his eyes and did as George had instructed.

He brought the image of Paul to his mind, flashing in scenes of where Paul had been stabbed, whilst all the time sending out the powers of healing in Paul's direction.

He felt the spell intensify, and a deep, blood red pool ignited around him.

He focused more and more, building up the images in his mind whilst concentrating on the idea of healing.

The cell burned brighter and brighter, the walls now drenched in vivid rays.

The spell reached its peak and Simon felt the energy explode within him. Then the scarlet beams instantly vanished and Simon opened his eyes.

The spell was done, but had it worked?

Simon momentarily hesitated as he considered that he

might never see his daughter again. Then a smile curled up on his lips. He'd love to see Jane try to stop him. No contract in the world could stand against the new Simon Bird. The world was now his toy and he couldn't wait to start playing.

He stood up, ready to see his uncle again, and he closed his eyes.

Within a second he appeared in the hotel room where Paul had been stabbed just two weeks before.

He'd landed facing the door, but before he had a chance to turn around, a high pitched scream pierced through his ears.

He turned to find a shocked couple lying in the bed; the woman in hysterics. But that quickly seemed unimportant when he focused in on his rather befuddled looking uncle standing in the centre of the room.

'Paul!' Simon cheered, throwing his arms around him.

'What the fuck is going on, Si?' Paul asked, his face a mass of confusion. 'Where is everyone? Who are these people? Where's Jane?'

'It's a long story. A very long story.'

The relentless screaming was too much and a flare of anger shot through Simon. This selfish woman was ruining his high.

'Shut it!' he yelled pointing his finger and literally zipping her mouth shut. He then did the same to her partner before he could react.

'Simon!' Paul said. 'What are you doing?'

'I'm trying to enjoy this reunion with my uncle.'

Paul seemed to take a moment, looking between the couple and Simon over and over, as if trying to work out what was going on. 'But they're still staring at us,' he finally said. 'I don't like being watched.'

Simon smirked. He was more than happy to assist. He pointed his index finger towards the terrified pair and a red strip covered their eyes.

'What's that? A little red ribbon?' Paul chuckled. 'Are

you going soft on me?'

'What did you expect me to do? Blind them? I might have come to my senses, but I'm not a monster. I still believe people should be treated fairly.'

'No, you're right. You always make me proud. Now can you please tell me what the hell is going on. I feel very strange.'

'Good strange?'

'Like the best I've ever felt strange. There's something I don't know, isn't there?'

'Fancy a boys' night out? Suite on Park Lane? Showing the girls in the West End just what heartbreakers we can be?'

Paul studied Simon for a second, almost hesitantly. 'Like the old days?'

'The very old days. Before I got all boring and concerned about doing good by the world.'

'You did get a bit boring, mate. I didn't want to say anything. It's understandable. You went through a lot. But if those days are behind us, I'm not going to complain.'

'I can't thank you enough for all you've done for me, Paul. I mean it. Your patience with me all these years won't go unrewarded.' Simon hugged his uncle and he felt utterly complete. More so than he could ever remember.

'There's just one thing we need to consider,' Paul said as a seriousness cast itself across his face.

'What's that?'

'Are you paying or am I?'

Simon burst out laughing. 'I've just brought you back from the dead. This one's definitely on you.'

'What?' Paul asked with shock.

'Come on. Let's get to the hotel, get a beer in our hands and I'll tell you the whole sorry story.'

'Dead?' Paul turned pale, but Simon barely seemed to notice.

'All will be explained soon.'

Simon glanced at the pair trembling beneath the covers.

'Don't worry, you two. The spell will fade within the hour. As I said, I'm not a monster. Have a good night.'

'Have you got your car?' Paul asked. 'Have I?'

Simon grinned widely. 'We're not going to need a car ever again. Well, I'll still use my Aston Martin, of course. The girls love it. But for now, it's teleport all the way.'

'Teleport? Really?'

'Grab my hand, Paul. We're about to have the best night of our lives.'

THIRTY-FIVE

After aimlessly roaming the streets for about an hour, berating herself for her shocking actions, Beth teleported home, back to her bedroom. And she did it all using her regular power. She was shattered in so many ways when her head hit the pillow, too tired to even cry herself to sleep.

The next day she put a smile on and assured her parents that all was well, and they left as planned. They needed to get back to their coffee shop, and Beth couldn't bear seeing them. Seeing anyone made her feel guilty. Just the thought of Jane's name made her want to vomit with shame.

If she thought Jane had torn the family apart, what had Beth's actions done?

It was now Wednesday afternoon and Beth was in the play room with Scarlett, trying to keep her daughter occupied. There was no way Beth could work. Her mind was far too consumed with worry.

Her ears pricked up as she heard something. It sounded like someone had opened the front door. Her skin prickled at the thought of who it could be.

Would it be Jane? Was she here to arrest Beth as well?

Beth was in no state to argue with that. Her actions had been horrendous.

She grabbed Scarlett in her arms and she poked her head around the door. She couldn't see anything, so she edged out of the room and took a few steps closer to the reception area.

She nearly dropped Scarlett when she saw in front of her Simon. He was casually looking through the post left by the door as if he hadn't a care in the world.

'Simon?' she asked. She didn't know what to do. She wanted to run and throw her arms around him, and for him to take all of this pain away, but she couldn't be sure she wasn't hallucinating. In fact, maybe she was. Because it definitely looked like Simon, but he seemed so different. So empty.

'Hello,' he said, opening a letter and not even looking at her.

'What are you doing? How are you here?'

Beth stepped forwards. She placed Scarlett down and studied the man before her. She edged a little closer until she could feel his breath on her. It really was him!

She threw her arms around him, but he didn't put his arms around her in return.

'How are you here? Is everything all right?' she asked, pulling back to look at him.

'Everything's great.'

'What are you doing here?'

'I'm not in prison anymore.'

'I can see that. What happened?'

'Paul's alive.'

Beth stepped back. She didn't know what to say to that. That was the last thing she expected.

'Turns out you can cast a spell to bring someone back from the dead,' he said, with a satisfied smirk that was so unlike him. 'So I did.'

'He's alive? You brought him back? Oh my God! Is he okay? Where is he?'

'He's at a hotel on Park Lane. We went out last night. Hit the West End. God I needed that.'

Beth's mouth dried up. 'You went out? You were out of prison and you didn't tell me?'

'I didn't think you'd notice. I wouldn't have been here anyway.'

'But it's been awful here without you.'

'Don't be so dramatic.' Simon bent down to see Scarlett. 'How's my favourite girl?'

'Hang on, you can see her? Everything's okay?'

'Of course. The contract was hinged on the fact that Paul was dead. That's no longer the case. Thanks to me.'

'I can't take this in. This is too much. Does Jane know?'

Simon picked up Scarlett in his arms and hugged her, before he turned to Beth and shrugged.

'What does that mean?' Beth asked. 'Is Paul going to see her? Did he see her last night?' Beth's stomach churned as flashes of Jane crumpled up in bed, crying her eyes out, raced through her brain.

'He won't be seeing her anytime soon. He's fuming with her. I don't think he'll ever forgive her for locking me up. What a bitch.' Simon turned to Scarlett again. 'We'll never see Aunty Jane again, will we? No. She's dead to us, isn't she.'

Part of Beth was relieved to hear that Simon wouldn't be seeing Jane anytime soon, but his words also didn't sound like him. Jane might have put him through the mill, but Simon was naturally a kind man. His tone seemed quite different to the man she knew so well.

'Are you all right? Did something happen in prison?' Beth asked.

Simon thought through his answer. 'I got some peace and quiet. Oh, and I started a good book. Well, actually no, it was utter shit. But I do find I want to know what that fish is going to do. I'll have to make sure I take time to finish it.'

Beth tried to think of something to say, but this exchange was far too bizarre. The man before her certainly looked like her husband, but he was acting like a complete stranger. Her brain was desperately trying to compute everything that was going on, but it seemed Simon wasn't interested in waiting. He placed Scarlett back on the floor and pushed passed Beth to head up the stairs.

'Where are you going?' she asked.

'Upstairs. Is that a problem?'

This attitude totally threw Beth. 'No. Are you sure you're all right?'

'I'm fine. I'm better than ever. Everything is suddenly crystal clear. The only problem I have is that it's taken me so long to realise it.' Simon jogged up the stairs, not looking back.

Beth stood motionless in the middle of the reception, bewildered as to what was going on. Maybe the stress had finally got the better of her.

'Do you want a cuppa?' she shouted upstairs. She needed to do something.

'No. I won't be staying long.'

'Where are you going?'

'I'll explain when I'm down.'

Beth wanted to ask more, but she just couldn't find any more words. 'Okay,' was all she could mumble back.

She went into the kitchen to put the kettle on. Something she knew she could control.

As soon as the water was boiling, she placed Scarlett in her high chair and gave her a drink to keep her occupied. Thankfully Scarlett was behaving herself, but Beth could sense it wouldn't last for long. Scarlett crying really would be the final straw to collapse Beth's sanity once and for all.

She poured the hot water into her mug and swirled around a tea bag.

'I'm off then,' Simon said from the kitchen doorway.

'Where are you going?'

He took a breath. 'I'm going to stay with Paul for a few

days. In the hotel. Give you some time to get your things together. Find another place to live.'

Beth felt the world around her crack. 'What are you talking about?'

'It's not personal. Just being away has given me some time to assess things. I don't think it's working between us. You must agree.'

'What? You've only been gone for a couple of weeks. How could you change your mind about our whole relationship in two weeks?'

Simon just shrugged.

'What aren't you telling me?'

Simon rolled his eyes but still said nothing.

'What's the matter?' Beth pushed.

'You. Analysing everything. Can't a man change his mind without there being some secret underlying conspiracy? There's nothing else to tell. I'm just bored with you.'

The cracks around Beth got bigger. 'I can't believe you're saying this.'

'I don't love you anymore. It's as simple as that. But I want to be fair to you. You are the mother of my child. You can stay here... for what... what the hell, stay for two weeks. Until you find somewhere else to live. It's not all bad. I won't contest you in the divorce. You can have half of everything. As I said, fair's fair.'

'Fair's fair? Divorce? Where has this come from?'

Simon's face became grave. 'Were you not listening? I don't love you anymore. I'm trying to do the right thing by you still, though. You have to concede how good I'm being about all this. This is, after all, my house, yet I'm willing to stay in a hotel for two weeks to let you sort yourself out. Ungrateful bitch.'

The tears stung Beth's eyes as the cracks opened even wider.

Simon stepped over to Scarlett who was sitting quietly, chewing on her bottle of juice. 'I'll miss you, baby girl. I'll be back soon.' He turned to Beth. 'You can have half of everything I own. I don't care about that. But I'm getting custody of Scarlett.'

Terror zipped through Beth. 'What?'

'You're a very unfit mother. And we both know Scarlett loves me more than you.'

'What?'

'You hired a nanny who ultimately kidnapped her. Very, very poor mother.'

'We made that decision together.'

'I'm sure my lawyer will see it differently.' Simon moved closer to Beth to address her very directly, his eyes scorching into hers. 'I'm a very powerful man, Beth. I'm willing to be fair to you. That's only right. But try to push me and you'll regret it.'

'Who are you?' she asked.

'I'm Simon Bird. And for the first time in my life, I actually think I might be happy.'

Beth stood agape as Simon walked back over to the door. He bent down and she noticed the suitcase that he grabbed in his hand.

'You're really leaving?' she asked.

'My lawyer will be in touch.'

'Can't we talk about this?'

'I think you'll find we just did.'

He turned to Scarlett, his face softening. 'Bye, Letty. I love you. I'll see you really soon.' He then quickly glanced across at his wife. 'Bye Beth.'

Simon turned around and seconds later Beth heard the front door slam shut.

Instantly the cracks exploded and Beth felt her whole world crumble around her.

A sickening dread engorged her as she dropped to the floor and cried.

How could her marriage be over, just like that?

What on earth had just happened?

The only thing she knew for sure was that the man

she'd just seen was not her Simon. Something terrible had happened and she had to find out what.

To Be Continued....

Find Out How The Adventure Began

The Dark Nest is the fourth in The Bird Books Series. If you haven't already read how the adventure started, the first three books are:

- *Bird* – find out how Beth and Simon first met

- *The Birds* – life is turned upside down for Beth and Simon as they start to realise the truth about their destiny

- *Free as a Bird* - things are not right for Beth and Simon, but the biggest problem is they can't remember what's wrong. They don't even know who their enemies are as they battle on following the dramatic ending of book 2

The whole series is available from Amazon.

Book 5 in the series will be coming out soon.

To find out more about The Bird Books, visit www.lindsay-woodward.com

ABOUT THE AUTHOR

Lindsay is a British author who lives in Warwickshire with her husband and cat. She's had a lifelong passion for writing, starting off as a child when she used to write stories about the Fraggles of Fraggle Rock.

Knowing there was nothing else she'd rather study, she did her degree in writing and has now turned her favourite hobby into a career.

Lindsay is also the author of:
- *Emmett the Empathy Man*, a comic tale about a superhero who comes to life with disastrous results.

- *In the Blood*, a science fiction love story about two people who could never have possibly met yet know everything about each other.

- *Shape the Future*, a science fiction love story about a girl who is told that her boyfriend is cheating on, only to realise that the truth is far more shocking.

- *Invisible*, a hugely entertaining romantic comedy about a girl who is invisible. But then everything changes when three men coming into her life.

All of her books are available on Amazon.

To find out more about Lindsay and her books, visit www.lindsay-woodward.com

Printed in Great Britain
by Amazon